DROP-DEAD GORGEOUS

AN ENGAGING NOVEL

Topay

by Navy Topaz

Indie Publishing Navy Topaz

Copyright © 2016 by Navy Topaz

All rights reserved. No part of this publication may be reproduced, distributed or transmitted in any form or by any means, without prior written permission.
The copyrighted drawing, photos and covers are by Navy Topaz.

Publisher's Note: This is a work of fiction. Names, characters, places, and incidents are a product of the author's imagination. Locales and public names are sometimes used for atmospheric purposes. Any resemblance to actual people, living or dead, or to businesses, companies, events, institutions, or locales is completely coincidental.

Book Layout © 2015 BookDesignTemplates.com
www.navytopaz.com   Quebec, Canada
Drop-Dead Gorgeous/ Navy Topaz -- 1st ed.
ISBN 0-919719-11-8 Print   ISBN 0-919719-12-5 EBook

Beauty begins the moment you decide to be yourself.— *Coco Chanel*

CONTENTS

Defloration	1
Carpenter-Ants	7
Shattered Hope	18
Birth of a Star	23
Bye-Bye Boss	38
Networking	60
Rivalry	79
La-La Land	91
Primal Instincts	105
Illusions	117
Diadem	131
Home	140
The Flaw	148
Mystical Geometry	158
Dolphin	166
Amends	178
Oblivion	184
Flight	189
Harmony	196
Understanding	203
Temples of Love	207
Revelation	213
Reconciliation	218
Runaround	223
Public Appeal	228
Sanctuary	231
Influence	235
Cat Fight	240
Bondage	245
Hunted	253
Winner	255
Triumph	257
Book of Fairies	260

CHAPTER ONE

Defloration

THOUGH HER GIVEN name is Celeste, everyone called her "Les". She hadn't yet shed her baby fat, so she was chubby during her childhood; her awareness that she was pudgy bothered her. She had the impression that her father, Brent, and mother, Alice, were convinced that this ugly duckling of theirs would never amount to much; in response, she played in her make-believe world with a rag doll, that became her bosom friend. When her brother Michael was born sixteen months after her birth, she felt that her parents shifted their hopes on him. Les was a content but lonely child who quickly learned to cater to her brother's wishes and needs to obtain some parcel of her parents' favors. It appeared to her that everyone was satisfied by the order of things, where she remained subservient to her family; after all, it relieved the parents of some tasks, while her brother was the prince; as he grew up, Michael displayed his sloppiness with impunity, to her disgust. It seemed to Les that, throughout his life, Michael found this normal.

Things became different after she started school and kids started teasing her; she was the object of their taunts: "Mom there's a boy in school that calls me 'fatty'."

"Just ignore him he'll eventually get tired of it," Alice reassured her.

Celeste followed her mother's advice by not reacting to being insulted; the kids stopped harassing her, as her mother predicted.

In third grade, Les met Trish, who became her best friend for life; unfortunately, nature did not endow Trish with grace and beauty; Trish was very slim while Les was plump. The pair became easy target for bullies:"There goes the witch and her broom.", "Chubby and her toothpick."

By this time, the tormentors realized that the pair couldn't sustain looking indifferent; moreover their lack of spunk amplified their vulnerability. The pair was a permanent target for the mockers' contempt. Les sought comfort from her parents who had little sympathy and reminded her to feign indifference. At least, Celeste could share her misfortune with Trish, on the phone or during slumber parties. The pair's only recourse was to be as discreet as best they could and to exchange their concerns among themselves.

***

At the onset of puberty, Les was afflicted with pimples that worsened the bullying: "There's pizza face."

That led malicious classmates to call her "Jumbo pizza".

Her dread increased in frequency and intensity. She became reclusive, refusing to go out of her room, except when strictly necessary.

Then Leisha came around with her band of bullies, who made it a point to pester Les and Trish whenever they could, preferably in front of others. They felt good for intimidating the weak and helpless; it was their quest for domination. Nature had seemingly rejected the pair that did not deserve to survive, much less thrive. In school halls, Leisha liked to shove Celeste until she had her back to the wall. Celeste felt paralyzed, like an animal that had been snared in a trap.

Les cried, whenever she was alone. Her nights filled with tears and terror, so she became tired and discouraged at life.

Alice knocked on Celeste's room, "Sweetheart, I'd like to talk to you."

"What about?"

"Please let me in."

"Leave me alone."

"You seem unhappy dear."

"So what?"

"Your father and I would like you to have fun. You sulkiness isn't good for you. You could have hobbies and go out like other girls your age."

"I'm not like everyone else."

"Your father and I have agreed that you should talk to someone who can better understand you. "

"That won't solve anything."

"Talking to a professional would be good for you. He'll know what to do."

"I don't want to. I'm not crazy."

"Of course not dear, but it might help."

"Go away."

"Sleep over it dear. We'll discuss it later."

She did comply.

***

Alice went with Celeste to plead her case to the school principal who, with a sympathetic face apologized, "I understand Celeste, Ms. McCawley. You are not alone in your situation; however, we have limited resources. I wish we had teachers patrolling the corridors to watch for these incidents, unfortunately we don't. My feelings go with you. We will do what we can to avoid these incidents."

Then Alice and Celeste asked the psychologist for a diagnosis, "Your daughter is the victim of bullying. She's intimidated and terrorized to the degree that she has become fearful of appearing in public. We call it agoraphobia. Concurrently, she feels persecuted and I believe that it is a mild case of paranoia. These causes have made her depressed, so I prescribed some medicine. I strongly recommend that she follow her treatments to overcome these problems. Have you talked to the school authorities about this hazing?"

"Yes. They told me that they are doing all they can."

"With time perhaps things will subside!"

"Perhaps, in the meanwhile Les is hurting."

"Celeste, you must continue her treatments. They'll help."

Alice and Celeste sought the guidance of her pastor, "What are we to do? The poor child is in a crisis. I went to talk to the school principal, who will do what he can for her. I even have her followed by a psychologist, who prescribed some medication but that doesn't seem to help very much, except making her groggy and apathetic."

"God has inscrutable ways that will eventually resolve the problem. You must have faith, that the most important thing. She can take all kinds of pills, but they won't do any good if she wavers in her faith in God. I would recommend that you pray with her. I will also pray for the child and for her to remain steady in her faith."

Les attended school regularly and her life did not improve much. Eventually, nature took its course and her puberty progressed. Much like a flower that blooms from a tightly wrapped bud, she started to reveal her hidden beauty to the world. Her baby appearance mellowed, her body developed feminine curves, her voice became more authoritative, men scrutinized her breasts, glanced at her buttocks, her skin cleared and she lost her excess fat. Now she became sexually attractive and she unwittingly drove young men half-crazy. As young studs approached her, Leisha and her bullies sensed that a force much stronger than their own was opposing them.

Trish confided to Celeste that she wasn't much interested in boys, though one or two asked her out. She was more interested in sports, particularly gymnastics. She went out with one boy called Darryl, who never uttered a word, so Trish claimed.

Matt was a studious classmate. He approached Celeste but she rebuked him by responding that she was busy; in reality, she refused because nobody had been remotely interested in her previously and she was surprised at his advance. She talked about it to Trish who agreed that Celeste should play hard to get. Matt asked Les out again and, though she was tempted, she refused because she didn't want to known as an easy girl, as Trish had coaxed her to do. The third time she accepted; they went out on her first date, at the end of which he gave her a friendly kiss she could not avoid, despite his bad breadth. They went out a few times and gradually the kisses became longer and more intense. Then he started petting her. At first, she fended him off, but she reluctantly let him have his way. At school, she was regarded as Matt's girlfriend and conversely, he was her protector, so the bullies stopped their hazing. Les was thrilled at being accepted by her peers and at not being hassled anymore.

Gradually, her nightmares stopped and she quit taking her pills and going to the psychologist.

One day, Celeste and Matt went to a party where they mingled with the crowd and had fun. When they were alone in a room, he asked her to give him a blowjob. This was the first time for both of them. Celeste had watched many demonstrations on the Web, yet she was hesitant. After he insisted, she was somewhat willing, and so she did her best to satisfy him. He looked like he enjoyed it. After he drove her home, he gave her a lingering French kiss.

Even though Les told Matt many times she didn't want to go all the way, he claimed repeatedly that others teens in their school simply accepted it as a rite of passage. He seemed determined that this was going to be the night. He prodded her to hang out in his parents' basement; she followed him cautiously.

He put on some romantic music.

"Would you like some wine?" he offered to lower her inhibitions. They were underage but Matt's parents allowed them to have wine.

"Just a little."

She drank a sip.

"Would you like to dance?"

She got up and he gently took her in his arms. He led her to the slow rhythm of the music. He kissed her on the mouth and she responded; she shut her eyes. The kiss wandered onto her cheeks and her neck and she resisted, in token. He nibbled at her earlobe; she heard the sounds of his mouth. He pursued his peregrination and kissed her on the mouth, letting his tongue slide inside her mouth, as he liked. He groaned.

As he attempted to pet her left breast, she held it with her hand. His other hand slid across her waist onto her hips. Time vanished. He took her hand and placed it over his rigid penis inside his trousers, as he had done before as a signal that he wanted her to give him fellatio. She enjoyed it very much, now that she was accustomed to it. She went back and forth to the rhythm of the background music. His erection was becoming stiffer and she liked to feel the power she provoked. He did not want to come right away, so he stopped her. She looked at him.

He began taking off her blouse. She continued stroking him slowly. He tried to take off her bra, but he was floundering, so he pulled it down and she had to help him unclip it. He petted her naked breasts and her nipples reacted with firmness. She was pleased that he enjoyed her body; she felt vindicated from all the vile comments that had poisoned her past. He continued on his adventure and reached the mound of Venus, where he searched the way to arouse her. As he was exploring, her legs relaxed and exposed the way to victory; she was at his mercy. He pulled down her panties and he removed his clothes. They were both naked, as newborn children.

"You told me that you had your period four days ago, so there shouldn't be any danger of getting you pregnant."

She didn't respond.

Since they were both virgins, there was no danger of transmitting any disease.

He got on top of her and he attempted to push his manly organ inside her waiting shelter.

"Ouch," she warned, "Be gentle!"

He was glad that this door to bliss had never been pried open, but his key had difficulty in penetrating her keyhole. It finally found its place.

"Aw," she moaned.

She lost the innocence of youth. He rammed her a few times and he couldn't control the outburst. "Oh fuck. Oh fuck," he cried out in ecstasy, as he grabbed her in his powerful arms and squeezed her as tightly as he could.

His desire having been satisfied, his body collapsed on her limp body.

Her mind is indelibly imprinted by the memory of her defloration, along with the fear of being hurt by a male and the guilt of allowing it.

CHAPTER TWO

Carpenter-Ants

AS SHE BEGINS her womanhood, Celeste obtains that people call her by her given name, Celeste; she has had enough of the aggravating diminutive.

It's Thursday, another drab, dull and dreary day of the end of October when the leaves on the ground are soggy and people feel damp and cold. Oakville Ontario, as seen from space, is a small city on the west side of Lake Ontario, a suburb of Toronto. We zoom to the Falgarwood ward, Grosvenor St. near the mall, where her father bought a one and a half storey house, when he started working for the nearby car manufacturing company. An Internet search reveals little of Oakville, other than it has restaurants, motels, a provincial park and a garden. It's a nice a cozy town, where anyone would appreciate bringing up children and live a quiet life. The house's main floor consists of a living room, a kitchen with a counter allowing two persons to cook, a small dining room and an owner's bedroom. The second floor has two rooms with two dormers and a bathroom; the basement is made of cinder blocks and has an unfinished laundry room, a small bathroom and a recreation room; in the front lawn, there is a small perennial flower garden and in the back, a yard to play; the car is in a carport.

Celeste is a comely young woman from a middle class Canadian family. She expects that she will have an easy life with her boyfriend Matt, that they will have two kids and that they will enjoy each other with her family and friends. She hasn't yet shared her hopes with Matt.

She would like to have a stable career as a Web designer; she aspires to no more.

She's interested in the plastic arts, such as paintings, drawings, pottery and so forth, but mostly in computer arts that now encompasses other art forms. She goes to museums regularly and she joined a few cyberspace art groups.

She likes contemporary music and dancing, even if it means dancing with girls.

She loves eating sweets, particularly those glazed doughnuts and cupcakes, but she tries to avoid them. Her life will not improve with this kind of love.

She enjoys nature, especially flowers and birds. In fact, she actively fights to preserve and protect them, whenever she can. She is concerned about the environment and she expresses her concerns in this regard.

***

Celeste gets up lazily after the clock's second ring; she calls herself a 'second ringer'. She puts on her dressing gown and heads straight for the bathroom, glad that her brother Michael has not yet occupied it and filled it with his personal odors; she locks him out and disregards his complaints when he arrives. She brushes her teeth that also freshens her mouth and her mood. The shower is next, being careful to keep her thick hair dry. After she gets out and dries herself, she combs her long, plush, satiny, sepia mane that she restrains with a red ribbon, so much in fashion, ever since Princess Christina wore that to the royal wedding. She makes sure that her locks are contained, so that they don't fly away on their own whim and fancy; one such strand, aptly nicknamed "Mickey", takes pleasure in annoying Celeste by obstructing part of her face. Celeste keeps on thinking that her mother will not approve of her new hairstyle, because she always complains about Celeste's hair. Every morning when she untangles them, she rehashes her mother's dreaded comments. What will it be this morning? She wishes that she could do whatever she wanted, without having her mother on the lookout for any potential criticism. She promises herself not to reply at anything her mother will say.

Next, she puts her thin black rim glasses that give her a serious look, but her eyes are tired. She looks at herself in the mirror and she's displeased at the two laggard pimples, on which she again applies medicinal cream to make them go away. She never had her eyebrows trimmed or her eyes highlighted and she never enhanced her lips. She likes her natural look. She's tall, with a velvety skin complexion. She has a sweet appeasing voice and a smidgen of innocence. Her natural smiling face gives a friendly and sympathetic first impression.

Back in her room, she searches her drawers and closet to choose what she feels would be the best combination for the day, considering what she will do, depending on whom she'll meet and where will she be going? She feels good about herself, though conscious of her weight, but she uses shaping tights to make herself look slimmer. She has generous breasts secured in a shapewear bra, the kind that allows her to run without worrying that her full breasts will bounce. Then she adds a little something to attract attention; this morning, she chooses large circular earrings. She likes their elegant look. Now that she's ready, she climbs down to the eat-in kitchen.

As usual, Alice is watching and commenting the news on TV; not even the mutt, Gyp, listens to her chatter; Celeste sometimes refers to her mother as "our news anchor". Alice briefly glances at Celeste who slips into the kitchen. Celeste is sure that her mother scrutinized her in detail and was about to launch some unwelcomed remark about something or other.

"Did you sleep well honey?" was her mother's comment this morning.

She was probably holding back some observation, but did not want to discuss it right away. When will she release her review? If she had spilled it out right away Celeste would have been relieved of the pending comment, but no, she delays her delivery only to make it more brutal later on.

Her brother Michael has the look of a nerd with his mushroom top hair, black rimmed glasses, washed-out blue jeans and a T-shirt with a big interrogation point.

Celeste pours two cups of coffee her mother brewed and she prepares two breakfasts of eggs and toast for herself and a bigger portion for her brother who kisses her on the cheek as he arrives to eat, "Thanks sis!"

The words "You're special" are inscribed on her preferred coffee mug.

Her mother purchased most of the furniture when they bought the house and little has changed since. She feels "comfy" with her old things that have become part of the family. The old sofa sits where she nurtured her children and the kitchen table reminds her of the many happy days she had lunch with her family and friends. Every single object has a particular meaning and she holds on to each one of them.

Breakfast is over and so, Alice packs her things, puts on her overcoat and heads for the car.

Celeste looks at the kitchen clock that dominates the kitchen wall and she repeats her routine.

"Bye, Michael!" she says, as she leaves and nobody pays attention, except for the dog that raises its head for a second.

Michael will depart shortly to attend university.

Alice waits patiently in her car.

A few moments later, Celeste gets in the passenger seat.

"You changed your hairdo this morning!" Alice mentions. Finally, the anticipated comment has arrived.

Celeste explodes. "Yes, it's the new fashion, but of course you wouldn't know that. You've had the same hairdo for years, so you wouldn't appreciate mine. Why is it that you always have to tell me what to do? I can't change my look without you criticizing the way I do things. Yes, I want to look my age, is that so much to ask?"

"I'm sorry if I offended you!" Alice attempts to abate the discord.

"Every day you slip some quip into our conversation. I'm tired of that. I can't deal with that anymore."

A long silence follows.

Alice drives Celeste at the Oakville train station.

"Bye!" Celeste gets out.

"Bye dear!" Alice replies.

As Celeste waits for the commuter train that will take her to Toronto, she reflects on what had just happened. Her mother constantly reminds her of something, or assails her with some reproach. This is very annoying. She wants to live her life without worrying about her mother's constant supervision. She's not a child anymore and she doesn't want to be treated as one. If she had the chance, she would move out.

As she enters a commuter train wagon, she shows her travelling pass. She recognizes many familiar faces. Young people are busy talking on their phones or scrambling their nimble fingers on their laptops in virtual games, while others are reading some text. Some people, mostly middle age women, are talking endlessly to other people they know about every little event that constitute their life. Some are trying to complete their sleep by snoozing. Most people have blank faces thinking of some unresolved issue at home or at work, oblivious to others around them. Some young men are peering at women, who in turn try to appear indifferent. Some commuters read the overhead ads to distract themselves. There's always some young woman that has a piece of clothing, hair, make-up or apparel that she's trying to fix or adjust so that she might look as perfect as possible.

The GO train stops at Union Station, exactly thirty-eight minutes after its departure. The workers scramble out and head for the metropolis. She enters the procession that leads to downtown Toronto like a colony of carpenter ants marching to claim their piece of rotten wood. Some go directly to a particular shop to buy a coffee and perhaps some sweet roll. Some enter the city, like modern gladiators who are yearning to fight the great arena of the world. Some enjoy looking at the store displays that exhibit carefully presented products to solicit attention. Some are absorbed by their electronic device, while others are trying to continue their conversation, to win their game or finish reading their text. There might be an odd one who heads for the toilet or who attempts to fix a problem with their clothing, hair, make-up or apparel. Most are unaware of their surroundings and go to their destination in a well-rehearsed way. Celeste is proud of being part of the carpenter-ant parade; she likes belonging in a group.

Celeste arrives at the Robinson, Johnson & Assoc. office, smiles and wishes "Good morning" to everyone she meets, particularly to her boss, Mr. Sinclair, who is early to a fault and who pleasantly returns her greeting, without ado. Celeste hangs her purse and her coat and sits at her desk where she turns on the computer.

Mr. Sinclair is a workaholic; he boasts at arriving before the staff and leaving after their departure. He works longer hours than other staff. He has no family picture on his desk. His office walls display various diplomas and certificates. He is most proud of his Bachelor of commerce degree from McGill University. His conversations are limited to his work. Middle age and ambitious, he's a fair-looking man, pleasant to work with. He hired Celeste a little more than two years ago and she is waiting patiently to get a permanent post; she hasn't dared asked him about it. Celeste likes him, but he's a bit too straight; she refers to him as "The Ruler".

She goes to her cubicle and takes a second of relief to relish at the photos on her desk. There is the one of Matt holding her under his right arm; there is the family Christmas, shot during happier times five years ago, with her father, her mother and her brother.

She glances at the date on a calendar with images of tropical trees. She checks her email, quickly eliminating the sales promotions that don't interest her for the moment. She checks out her personal messages; Trish sent the latest news as well as a reminder for their daily lunch. Celeste replies and confirms that they will meet for lunch at Frescati. She refers to it as "Fresking".

Back to work. As a graphics designer, she builds the Web page she conceived for a budding engineering company headed by Chris Norgate, an enthusiastic entrepreneur. He met her to explain what he wanted; he's cool to work with; he likes to be called by his given name, rather than Mr. Norgate. She enjoys her work because it lets her use her imagination and her flair to create appealing artwork. Every so often, her co-worker Judy gets up and checks Celeste's progress. Though Judy isn't her supervisor, she has many years of experience being in her forties and all; she has some white hair and that calls for a minimum of respect.

Celeste's thoughts keep wandering. Celeste's boyfriend is about to move to Europe where he just got a promotion. He didn't ask Celeste to come with him and that bothers her. He makes her feel like a pet, soon to be abandoned. She tries to concentrate on her work and to forget him but he keeps popping up in her daydreams.

Her relationship with Matt lost some excitement after he went to McMaster University to obtain a Masters in Business Administration, yet they get together as often as they can. She suspects that he has another girlfriend, but she never confronted him. She trusts him, to a certain extent, as much as any man can be trusted.

Matt is a lank young man who enjoys partying and joking around. He particularly likes to make fun of people, like snapping his towel at colleagues in the gymnasium showers. He wants to have a good time, often at others' expense. When he got a job offer to work in London, he immediately grabbed at the opportunity without talking about it to Celeste; he revealed it to her only after the fact and that still annoys her. Celeste is certain that they will eventually get married. Now, she ponders on his debonair attitude and wonders why he hadn't already told her that he would bring her to London; she fears that he never will.

Had she been close to her dad, she might have talked to him about Matt. That didn't happen because two years ago he left and since then, he didn't visit his family anymore; Michael kept contact with him but Celeste didn't.

"How is it going?" Mr. Sinclair says annoyingly, catching her daydreaming.

"It's fine," she answers submissively, as she resumes work.

At noon exactly, along with everyone else Celeste gets up and heads for the exit, except for "The Ruler" who has lunch at his office. Celeste puts on her jacket and heads quickly for Frescati, before it becomes overcrowded.

There, she places a pack of utensils on a tray and pushes it on the railing.

"The usual?" the quick lunch cook asks.

"Yes please," she says with a smile, glad that he recognized her.

Her lunch is prepared in a hurry and she quickly pays the exact price, plus a tip that she puts in the glass container. She takes her tray to her favorite table where she sits down, while Trish's meal is being prepared. Trish is wearing what Celeste calls her "nobody look", gray dress with off-gray scarf. She has gold-rimmed glasses and dark brown short curly hair that makes her appear as much as an ordinary person as could be; nobody notices her and that's fine with her; at least, she doesn't hear any of the rude remarks that troubled her youth.

As Celeste is waiting for her meal to be prepared, she gets a call on her smart watch.

"Hi," Trish texts.

"Hi," Celeste recognizes her.

"Did U C the hunk sitting behind you? He's absolutely the top." Trish coyly remarks.

"No," Celeste answers.

"Well, take a picture of him with your smart watch," Trish asks.

Celeste complies discreetly.

She looks at the Instagram and sends it.

"nb," Celeste texts.

Trish smiles and brings her tray to the table, glancing at the hunk and smirking at Celeste.

"How was your morning?" Trish asks with her up-speak intonation.

"So, so. With all that is going on, I couldn't help but think about Matt. Perhaps he's going through a phase. I don't know how men think. The situation might overwhelm him, having just graduated and having the world open to him. Once he's settled in London, he'll probably come back to earth and ask me to follow him there."

"He's obviously seeing other girls. You're in total denial. You should realize that he isn't into you anymore."

"I won't give up on him so easily, after all, we've been together for all many years."

"You've been going out together forever, yet he hasn't yet proposed to you! Doesn't that mean anything to you?"

"He just found a dream job and that's all that's on his mind."

"Anyhow, we'll see how he reacts at his going-away party you're having this Saturday."

"I'm sure he'll come around."

"By the way, did you watch the news of Sean and Nicole?"

"You mean from the reality show, Real Romance?"

"Of course who else would I have been talking about?"

"No I didn't watch it, what's the latest news?"

"The show producers found out that Nicole is pregnant."

"You're joking! YOU ARE joking!" Celeste exclaimed, astonished.

"Sean was devastated, shattered, demolished. She led him to believe that she wanted to marry him because he was the only one in her life. She's an utter manipulator."

"I didn't see that show. Why did she hide that she was going to give birth?"

"She wanted to become famous. The media is bound to follow her every move. She's the rave of the waves."

"I wouldn't mind becoming famous, wouldn't you?"

"And be like her? I'd rather die!"

"Aren't you tired of always doing what other people tell you to do?"

"What's wrong with my life I ask you? I have no great ambition."

"I just wish that Matt would ask me to come with him. That's all I want."

"By the way is everything ready for Matt's going-away party tomorrow night?" Trish asks.

"Yes. You'll be there to help me out with your boyfriend won't you? I'm counting on you."

"Girl, I wouldn't miss it for anything."

"Michael will also be there to help us out."

The rest of the conversation is about the current events in the glam world. They finish their lunch and are on their way back to work.

***

Next evening, Trish rings the doorbell at Celeste's home.

Celeste is about to answer but Michael opens the door:"Hi Trish! It's nice of you to come and help! This is my girlfriend,

Mary."

"It's a pleasure to meet you Mary. Celeste told me so many sweet things about you! Here's my boyfriend Darryl."

"Hi Darryl!" Michael answers.

"I'm sure that every word she said about me is true."

"That's good to hear!" he replies with a smile.

"Come on in, let's go to the basement," Michael points the way.

They start hanging balloons, ribbons and the 'We won't forget you!' sign.

They prepare snacks and the punch.

The guests arrive gradually. Matt's entrance is chaotic as everyone tries to congratulate him at once. Matt rejoices at the attention he's getting. He greets everyone coming in. He gives Celeste a quick kiss as she approaches him. "Thanks for this going-away party."

The music invites people to dance, but few do.

Matt loves to talk about himself and his plans for the future that involve much travelling in Europe and the Far East. He boasts that he might learn some foreign language. He's on the up-and-up.

Celeste tries to hide her feelings and goes on, as if nothing happened. She's as gracious and cordial to her guests as she can fake it.

At the end of the evening, Matt tells Celeste:"That was a great party Celeste!" as he kisses her amicably.

Everyone goes on his way, except for Celeste, Trish, Darryl and of course Michael who cleans the place. After a few minutes, Celeste sobs.

Michael asks her:"What's wrong?"

She's dismayed and she runs to her room and locks herself in.

Michael asks Trish:"It was a good party, what is she crying about?"

"It's Matt."

"What about Matt?"

"She thought he would bring her to London with him."

"Oh!" he reacts, still clueless.

CHAPTER THREE

Shattered Hope

IT IS A RAINY Saturday morning and the McCawley household is late and lazy. Celeste is reading a magazine in the living room while Alice is knitting some woolen socks. Michael takes Gyp for a walk and they come back all wet. Gyp is rolling on its back from one side to the other, to dry its fawn colored hair. Celeste rescued the forlorn mutt from the local pound.

Alice warns, "Don't forget to dry his feet. You always forget and he dirties the whole house. When will you learn to be careful?"

"Yes mother," Michael answers submissively.

Gyp rubs itself on the furniture and the walls and then against Alicia's leg, as if it purposely wanted to irritate her.

"Gyp is still wet and now he's drying himself against my dressing gown. You just don't listen to me. You don't care what I say. You're past being a teenager that provokes his parents. You're a man and now and you should act like one.

You aren't the one who has to clean the clothes and the house."

"I'm the one who takes him for a walk," he deflects her comments, as are most remarks his mother throws at him.

As usual, Alice watches the news and keeps commenting them and nobody listens.

Michael goes to his room and then to the bathroom.

When he comes out, he tells his sister, "Time to make me breakfast, sis!"

"Leave me alone!"

"I'm hungry."

"Go away."

"It's your PMS, I suppose!" Michael replies as he descends the stairs.

He asks, "Mom, could you make my breakfast?"

"Ask Celeste, I'm watching the news."

"Celeste won't stop reading that stupid magazine, she has PMS."

"All right. Do you want some pancakes?" Alice answers as she gets up and heads for the kitchen.

"No thanks."

"Didn't she have her period ten days ago?" she adds.

"I don't know. She's in a lousy mood, so it must be PMS."

Alice prepares Michael's breakfast and pours some more coffee for herself. She asks Celeste, "Are you all right sweetheart?"

"I just want to be left alone."

"If you need anything I'll be glad to help you."

"No thanks, I'm fine."

***

As a present for her sweet sixteen a few years back, Celeste's parents let her decorate her bedroom to her tastes. The walls are green, a particular green, a Pantone™ Paradise green she applied along with a large wall sticker of various jungle animals. An eco friendly duvet set bedding adorned with giant orchids covers her panel storage bed. One bed table matches her bed board. She has a small table where she has a laptop and a monitor displaying a panda motif; her mouse pad has a toucan image. She has a large closet and a table dresser. The furniture is painted Pantone™ Star White. She has pictures of Macaw parrots hanging on her wall. Since her family name is McCawley, when she was young, she associated her family name with that of the Macaw parrot. There are two cushions on her bed one has written "Love is happiness" on it and the other "Happiness is Love".

***

The gentle morning goes by quietly and Celeste retreats to her room.

Alice goes to Celeste's room and knocks.

"Celeste, I'd like to talk to you, honey," she says softly.

"I want to be alone," Celeste answers rather abruptly, sore that her mother is again meddling in her affairs.

"Sweetheart Michael told me about that you expected Matt to invite you over to London, where he got a dream job. Please let me in. Let's talk about it."

"Come on in," she concedes to get it over.

Celeste is lying on her bed. The wastebasket if filled with tissue. Her eyes are red and she's crying.

"Did Matt hurt you?" she says as she caressed Celeste's cheek as she had done so many times when Celeste was sick.

"Matt is going to London alone. He didn't tell me that I'd go with him."

"Did he say that?"

"No, but he would have told everybody at the party if he would have wanted to bring me with him."

"Maybe he's waiting for something. Maybe he'll ask you later?" Alice said in a sympathetic voice.

"I organized that party for him; it was the perfect occasion to tell everybody that he was going to bring me with him."

"Give him a chance. Perhaps he thinks that it it's a foregone conclusion and that it's obvious. I'm sure that he'll eventually get around to it."

"I know him. He would have done so already," Celeste responds harshly.

"You've been together for six years. He can't go away without saying something."

"That's what he does. He didn't even talk to me, whether he should accept this job; he told me, after he got it."

"Well there you go, he told you. He'll eventually tell you that he's bringing you with him."

"We've never seriously talked about marriage or even of staying together."

"These things take time. Be patient; he'll come around."

"I'm tired," Celeste says to stop the torture.

"You should eat something. Do you want me to bring you a grilled-cheese sandwich?"

"No, I'm not hungry."

***

Celeste gets dressed, comes downstairs and helps her mother

prepare dinner. Michael is sitting at his place in the eat-in kitchen. He's playing a game on his laptop.

"Michael, give us a hand won't you? You could set the table." Alice suggests.

"Don't you see I'm busy?"

"You're playing a game while we work. Come on and help us for once." Celeste reprimands him.

"I've got to finish this game."

"Men like to play games. They think that life is just one big game." Alice says.

"And we're their toys!" Celeste adds.

"Have you been played?" Michael says, while playing on his laptop.

"Yes, I've been played. Matt used me to have fun during all of those years and now he's throwing me away to find another toy."

"You're exaggerating dear" Alice reproaches to her, "he might get around to asking you. Be nice with him. You we should invite him and have a talk with him."

"I'm telling you, he dumped me. You just don't get it mom. It was like dad, you were in denial until the end. You didn't believe that he was cheating on you and you were completely taken off guard when he left." Celeste cries out.

"Leave your father out of this!" Alice replies on the defensive, after receiving verbal slap.

"Dad wasn't faithful to you and now Matt isn't faithful to me. That's the way men are."

"Hey I'm here!" Michael intervenes.

"Mom, why exactly did dad leave?" Celeste asks.

"I told you he left because we weren't getting along." Alice replies.

"You told me that he must have found a younger woman?" Celeste asks.

"He must have had." Alice replies.

"Michael, does dad have a new girlfriend?" Celeste asks.

"I don't know if he does or not. He hasn't told me and I haven't seen one."

"Mother, why did you tell me he had a new girlfriend?"

"I'm sure he has one, he's hiding the fact."

"Mother!" Celeste exclaims.

"Why don't you ask dad?" Michael suggests.

An ominous silence begins. Celeste had never contacted her dad since he left, Alice didn't want to talk about it anymore and Michael continues with his game.

CHAPTER FOUR

Birth of a Star

IT'S MONDAY, AFTER that awful weekend. Celeste is on automatic; she turns off her overloaded senses; she sees the world as a bokeh, an out-of-focus photo, and the sounds mingle into a single white noise, a constant mashup of sounds. She keeps on pondering: "How can Matt do this to me?

Why didn't he talk things over?

Is there a chance that he'll bring me to London?

Perhaps mom is right.

What did I do to deserve this? I did everything he wanted so how can he set me aside this way?" she ponders.

When she gets at the office, she tries her best to greet her coworkers. She feels a bit ashamed, as if everybody knows what happened.

"Good morning Mr. Sinclair!" she manages to say with a forced smile.

She takes off her coat and starts working as quickly as she can, absorbed in her work and her self-questioning.

She gets the email confirming lunch at Frescati. No doubt, Matt will be the subject of conversation at lunch. She's apprehensive of that encounter.

***

As she leaves for midday break, she's self-conscious and jittery.

When she gets there, Trish is already munching.

She joins her.

"Hi," Celeste greets her best friend with a mild voice.

"Hi, how are you?" Trish says in a consoling tone.

"Good, considering."

"I understand. Any news?"

"No."

Trish is wearing a purple suit with a pink taffeta shawl meant to lighten the atmosphere.

She tied her hair in a single braid dangling in the back of her head.

"What Matt is doing to you, is wrong."

"Yeah, tell me about it."

"He's so selfish. He only thinks of himself."

"He cares more about his career, than he cares about me!" Celeste says, as she holds her tear.

"Now dear, don't cry for him, he isn't worth it."

"I can't help it."

"Did he ever tell you that he loves you? You never confided it to me."

"No."

"He obviously loves himself, but I wonder if he's capable of loving someone else?"

"I figured that he never loved me. I was his play thing, someone to pass the time by."

"Why don't you let him go? Forget him."

"I still have a sliver of hope. Maybe mom is right?"

"I just don't trust him, I never did."

"You never told me that."

"Well I'm telling you now."

"He enjoyed having sex with me but he never said that he loved me," she repeats.

"You should have stopped having sex, until he declared that he loves you."

"You think so?"

"Yes, why should he enjoy sex with you, if he doesn't love you?"

"I thought he did."

"Next time, make sure he tells you."

"There won't be a next time, I'm through with men."

"You will find someone to love you I'm sure, a smart girl like you."

"How about you? Have you found your prince charming?"

"It might be Darryl for all I know."

"I wonder what my fate will be?"

"By the way, I've got a surprise for you."

"What is it?"

"Or, I should say for us."

"Tell me what it is." Celeste shakes her head, as she does when she gets irritated and wants to part her hair at the sides of her face.

"I've got two tickets for Saturday in two weeks."

"Is it a reality show?"

"Noooo."

"Is it a talk show?"

"Yes."

"Well don't keep me guessing, tell me!"

"It's the Dyann Winter show."

"Are you kidding, the Dyann Winter show?"

"Yes. Can you go, it starts at 9 o'clock?" Trish asks with a glorious smile, as she hands Celeste her ticket.

"I wouldn't miss it for anything!" Celeste answers and reads the ticket and kisses it.

"After the show we could eat in a good restaurant."

"Absolutely." Celeste answers as she puts the ticket carefully in her purse.

***

The ticket does the trick and lifts Celeste's outlook on life for the next two weeks.

***

On the last Friday before the show, the pair has lunch.

"The show is tomorrow morning," Trish remarks.

"I know, I know."

"I have a secret to tell you."

"Well what is it?"

"Promise me that you won't be upset."

"This sounds bad."

"Promise me."

"Ok."

"When I applied for the tickets by email, I told the producers that you just broke off with your boyfriend."

"You didn't?"

"Yes."

"That's intimate. You shouldn't have."

Celeste purses her lips, upset.

"There's more. They answered by asking for your picture and they wanted some details about you and your life."

"What details?"

Celeste is offended at the coming indiscretions.

"Like what size clothing do you wear, how old you are, what kind of work you do."

"You didn't. I'll never forgive you for this. Now my life will become public. How can you do this to me?" Celeste asks in an angry tone.

"The show is fun."

"At my expense."

"You might even win a trip for two to some exotic place!"

"I certainly wouldn't bring you along!"

"Oh come on, be a sport."

"If you put it that way," Celeste finally concedes.

"Great."

They part as friends.

***

It's Saturday, time to go to the show. The bubbly pair is wearing casual clothes, slacks and sweaters. They have the usual make-up, or the lack of it. As she does on weekends, Celeste wrapped her hair in a bun, held by a tie at the back, while Trish again has her braided tail.

They go to the metropolis by train and now most people are relaxed and enjoy the ride.

Trish asks Celeste "Did Matt talk to you these last two weeks?"

"No, he didn't."

"He's a coward."

Next, after a pause, Trish asks, "You did bring your ticket?"

"Yes."

"Did you notice that it has a star on it?"

"No, I didn't. Why?" Celeste says, while searching for the ticket.

"Yes dear, you are going to be a star of the show."

"What did you do?" Celeste is baffled.

"You'll see!"

"I wish I never came. You are embarrassing me more and more."

"Just come along."

"If you weren't my best friend, I'd leave right now."

"Be cool."

The bubbly pair gives their tickets to the attendant and they go to their assigned seat. Celeste is a bit surprised that they aren't sitting together and that she is in the front row. The audience if formed mostly of women in their twenties and thirties.

Soon, an audience coordinator presents himself and makes a few jokes. There is an APPLAUSE sign above and the audience coordinator invites the audience to clap their hands when the sign lights up. He practices it a few times and he encourages a competition between the left and the right side of the audience, until he's satisfied of the audience's participation.

Then a familiar voice shouts:"Here's Dyannnnnn!" announcing the queen of the media.

Dyann Winter walks quickly among the cheering crowd unto the stage. She has a Hollywood smile, as she waives to the prepped-up audience.

"Good afternoon. What a wonderful audience!" she says, as the applause sign lights up and people cheer and applaud.

"Today we have a special show. We take three members from the audience and we will give them a makeover of their appearance. Will you please stand up and join me on the stage."

Dyann points to the first row where Celeste and two other young women are sitting. This is the first time that Celeste is under the limelight and applauded my hundreds of strangers. The young women walk up to the stage and are greeted "What's your first name?"

"I'm Susan."

"Welcome Susan.

And you are?"

"I'm Mary."

"Welcome Mary. How about you?"

"I'm Celeste," she says nervously.

"Welcome Celeste."

"We are about to change your lives. You are three young women who came here in your casual clothes. My staff is going to change that and show how beautiful you are. Are you ready?"

"Yes," the three women answer in unison.

Some staff members guide each of them to their respective room. Celeste's name is written on her door with a gold star above it. She is excited and her heart beats quickly.

The door opens to a torrent of light that gushes out of a small white room, as if she entered the porch to heaven. One middle age man with Indian features and three superb women are waiting with a smile. He has the slick hair of a panther, that will entrance your dreams, the dark blue eyes of a Siberian Husky that can pry into your soul, the lips of a lover and the wrinkles of a man having witnessed a rich and mysterious life. Three luscious women, dressed in white angel like robes, flank him. He tends a hand and says in a voice that can seduce any woman to do whatever he wants: "My name is Akarsh of Impact Fashion. These are my assistants, Oksana the hairdo goddess, Romina, the beauty wizard and Klara the style whisperer. Be so kind as to come in to my universe."

Amazed isn't the word to describe the overwhelming sensation that makes Celeste's body shiver. She enters the room, as if she enters a magical palace. Celeste shakes each person's hands. Akarsh sits down near the entrance. He is wearing a wonderful baby blue shirt with a narrow collar, a striped dark blue bow tie, white slacks and sport shoes.

The three assistants deploy a screen to separate the women from Akarsh who explains "Celeste we will transform you to become the woman you were meant to be. The first step is to undress you completely and leave your past behind."

Celeste complies with a slight hesitation, intimidated by Akarsh, as if he were a Greek god.

Klara proposes: "Please transfer the things you keep in your old tote into this new clutch."

The clutch is of the finest pyramid embossed gold calfskin, so Celeste is more than enthralled at this invitation.

Romina invites Celeste: "Would you like to make yourself comfortable," as she shows the reclining chair. Celeste lays down on it.

With a magnificent tenor voice Akarsh hums an enchanting song in a foreign language.

"This is unreal," she thinks.

To add to the atmosphere, the room fills with a sweet smelling fog.

Oksana starts by removing unwanted hair, wherever she finds it. Romina colors the nails of Celeste's hands and feet with a golden glow. Klara massages Celeste's skin with rose scented oil, making it shine.

Once they are finished, Klara presents Celeste with a black bustier and satin slip.

The women fold the screen.

Akarsh unashamedly scrutinizes Celeste from head to toes and tells her: "This is a good start! Now I will transform you from great, to astonishing.

Let me have the pleasure to see your hair down."

Celeste removes the hairpins that release her hair, which falls on her chest and back.

"From now on, you will let them down. You will show that you are free and that you are proud to display this feminine attribute. You are not beautiful, you are beyond that and you will stun the world!"

"Oh!" Celeste instinctively agrees, while taken aback. She willingly falls under his spell.

"And I have some contact lenses to replace your glasses." She puts them on, secretly glad that Trish helped this process.

Oksana brushes Celeste's hair and uses her talent to amplify them and make them twist and curl into a tantalizing wonder.

Akarsh opens a portfolio of beauty products and tells Celeste:"I began as a fashion designer. Now I create living masterpieces," as he applies foundation, blush, gold eye shadow, crimson mascara, eyeliners, lip-gloss and lip liner with the precision and taste of Albrecht Dürer.

Akarsh tells her:"I will dress you in an elegant city style that will be the envy of all."

He offers her a red satin dress with a black muslin top, a red wool coat and a black stiletto shoes with red soles. All the buttons and accessories, such as the 'Utmost Secret' pendant, earrings, bracelet and rings, are golden.

"May you now vanquish the world? This is not my request, it is your destiny," he declares with a devilish smile that makes Celeste shudder.

After receiving the signal, Celeste walks out of the room and onto the stage as if she is reborn.

"Be sexy!" Klara whispers.

She walks slowly with the rhythm of a jungle cat and walks onto the stage.

Upon seeing her transformation, the audience is transfixed and dumbfounded; they cheer in waves, as if they just witnessed the reincarnation of Nefertiti. Celeste slowly takes over the show;

she seems to have a predator's vision, her eyes fixed on her prey. She stands there absorbing the admiration and adulation with complicity.

After what seems an endless time, she starts to cry uncontrollably; her quality makeup doesn't smear, thanks to Akarsh. The audience is touched and expresses itself in a delirium. She moves with feline grace.

Celeste is experiencing a stellar moment some fortuitous people experience, such as a patient surviving a certain death or a blind person suddenly seeing. Celeste, who had been an ordinary person in an indifferent crowd, was now the center of attention of countless admirers. Previously her self-doubts humbled her and the snide and demeaning remarks haunted every second of her life. Now, she is convinced that these lingering doubts were from frustrated beings that discharged their venom on others, because they couldn't properly deal with their own feelings. She gains an absolute confidence that will metamorphose her outlook and belief in herself. Before, she was perceived as a victim, now she is becoming a stunning beauty, as the world has never encountered. Nature is claiming its rights. She cries, overwhelmed by the sudden adulation.

Trish can't help herself but to join Celeste on the stage and hug her. A mass movement is set in motion where everyone wants to have the same transformation; a crowd convenes around Celeste. Since Dyann feels that this collective expression of affection is getting precarious, she attempts to calm the atmosphere: "Would you please regain your seats!" "Please go back to your seats." "We have some gifts for you when you sit down."

***

The producer in the booth at the back of the studio says:" She's a ten."

His assistant says:"No, she's a DDG."

"What's that?"

"Drop-Dead Gorgeous."

***

After calm is reestablished on the stage, Dyann says:"This is the end of our show. I hope you enjoyed it. Come back tomorrow, I invited some celebrities who will tell all."

She then turns to Celeste and kisses her on the cheek:"Thank you very much for coming."

The audience slowly leaves, except for the few who are accompanying the stars, including Trish, who accompanies Celeste to her room.

Akarsh welcomes Celeste back:"You were stellar, astonishing."

"Thank you."

"I have a very special proposition to make," Akarsh entices.

"What is it?"

"I'd like you to become "it", the figurehead for the products you wore today. We would sign a renewable contract that will provide you free beauty portfolios, free hairdressing and free clothes, for every occasion. The main condition is that you must always use them. Every time you make a change in what you wear, text me so that I can approve or make slight modifications."

"I'll have to think about it."

Trish readily intervenes:"Celeste, you can't miss this opportunity. Take it."

Celeste adds, "I'd need some spending money to show your products."

Akarsh smiles:"Of course, this goes without saying."

"Then I agree," Celeste smiles back.

Klara says:"Keep on what we gave you. I suppose that I can dispose of your old clothes."

Celeste turns to Klara:"I suppose."

"We will bring you a new wardrobe tomorrow," Klara adds.

"Meanwhile I'm giving you a full portfolio of our beauty products along with detailed instructions," Romina completes the agreement.

Akarsh continues:"We will regularly come and help you out to make sure that you're happy and confident. You should contact Jim Farber; take his card. He's a promoter I recommend. I'll tell him you're coming. Over there, my photographer Derek will follow your every movement and take photos."

Celeste glances at Derek, also of Hindu appearance.

Trish is transported:"How lucky you are!"

Akarsh vents some of innermost longings:"Celeste, you're my Pygmalion. I fashioned you with my craft like Phidias, a Greek sculptor of antiquity, and I materialized a vision I've had since childhood. You'll be the apex of my life's dedication to beauty."

Celeste is touched and remains speechless; she accepts Akarsh's wondrous admission.

After a few minutes in silence, the producer and his assistant join the group in the already crowded room.

"I have some great news to tell you," the producer is proud to say.

Everybody waits in anticipation.

"We've received a deluge of twits and comments, so much that we can hardly keep up. This is sensational. The excerpt of the show with Celeste has gone viral. I can't tell you how much we're pleased. You can come back as often as you wish, to tell us how you are doing. Our ratings will soar. Congratulations," the producer kisses Celeste, Trish and the assistants on the cheek and shakes hand with Akarsh.

The assistant producer informs them:"There's a crowd forming outside and this will make it difficult for Celeste to leave. I've ordered some security men to accompany her to a limo that will drive her home with her friend."

Celeste follows the security guards who whisk her and Trish out of the studio, past the cheering crowd and into the stretched limousine.

"This is unbelievable," Celeste admits.

"This is fabulous. Who could have predicted that we would be coming back in a limo and treated like a goddess? I guess you're ready to find your prince charming!" Trish quips.

"I've got enough for today."

The ride home is quiet, as they listen to new age music to absorb all that happened.

***

The limousine stops, Celeste kisses Trish and goes home.

She opens the door and goes in.

Alice looks at Celeste and is flabbergasted. "Oh dear!"

"Hi mom."

"What happened?"

"Trish and I went to the Dyann Winter show and I had a makeover done."

"You sure did! I saw it. You should have told me before."

"Do you like it?"

"Of course, I didn't realize that you could have that look!"

"What do you mean 'that look'?"

"You're so glamorous!"

"Why thank you."

"Michael, come and see this." Alice shouts.

"In a minute."

"Wow, you're a new person," Alice is proud to boast.

"No mother, I'm still your daughter," Celeste replies, not quite realizing what just happened.

Michael comes down and, in turn, is flabbergasted:"Sis, you're a beauty."

"The sponsors want me to show off their high fashion clothes and beauty products, wherever I go. They'll provide me everything."

"You're kidding!" Michael exclaims.

"You're blessed my dear!"

"Tomorrow, I'll receive my wardrobe. They'll even give me some spending money."

"Super. I've got to tell all my friends," Michael says.

"You can watch the show on the Internet," Celeste replies.

"Let's do it," Michael says as he opens the TV and fiddles on his portable.

They sit down in the living room and Michael finds the show and fast-forwards.

"I'm the last candidate," Celeste helps.

When he gets to Celeste's entrance she says, "This is it."

"That's what Akarsh said. He says I was 'it'."

"What does that mean?" asks Michael.

"I don't quite know," Celeste answers.

They're astounded at the awesome impact Celeste made when she came on the stage. They watch the show up to the end, when the cheering crowd surrounds her.

"This is going to have a considerable impact on your life my dear," her mother says with a little apprehension.

"All the guys will want to go out with you," Michael adds with a smile.

"You think so?"

Michael switches channel nervously and he says:"No doubt. I wonder what Matt will do?"

Alice replies:"He'd better be awfully nice!"

"I'll find out what he'll do," Celeste says somewhat sarcastically.

"I'll bet," Michael is quick to add.

As he flips the channels, Alice stops on the news:"Here."

The TV anchor states:"Today Dyann Winter had a makeover show that attracted attention on all media. A young woman, by the name of Celeste, was transformed into one of the most beautiful women we have ever seen. She is the buzz on the Internet and the social media and many thousands of twits and messages about her continue to fill the social networks every hour. This is sensational. We've never seen such frenzy on that show."

"It's all about you sis!"

"This isn't happening! It's all a dream." Celeste exclaims in disbelief, while closing her eyes with her hands.

"Well, I sure wouldn't wake up, if I were you!" Alice replies.

"Sis, I didn't realize you were so cute!"

"Oh shut up!" Celeste replies.

"You don't even have big boobs," Michael teases.

"They're just right. I'm sure Matt likes them." Alice defends Celeste.

"Don't talk to me about Matt," Celeste replies a little crossed.

"What will you do?" Michael asks.

"I don't know.

Anyhow, I'm exhausted, I'm going to bed."

Celeste leaves, while Alice and Michael look again at excerpts of the show.

CHAPTER FIVE

Bye-Bye Boss

THE NEXT MORNING they all get up as they had always done on Sundays with Celeste having no makeup, wearing glasses and her old familiar clothes; Alice is comfy in her dressing gown and Michael in his shabby garbs. As usual, Celeste prepares breakfast to help her mother.

"Thanks sis. Well I'm glad you came back to the real you."

"This may be the last time you see me this way."

"What do you mean?"

"Soon I'll always have to be dressed and made-up as a high fashion model. I made a deal with Akarsh."

"You're kidding. You'll have to do that all the time?"

"Yep."

"I just lost my sister. That other artificial doll isn't really you."

"Well big boy, you'll just have to get accustomed to it."

"Even at home?"

"Yep. That's the price I have to pay just in case somebody shows up."

"I like to look relaxed."

"Is that what you call it?"

Michael gets up and runs to his room, he picks up his camera and runs back to the eat-in kitchen and says:"I have to take pictures of my real sister before she turns into some fashion doll."

"Promise you'll never send them to your friends or post them on the Internet."

"I don't know."

"Promise or I won't let you do it."

"Ok, I promise."

"Mother, did you hear?"

"Yes sweetheart."

"Fine then."

Celeste is flattered and smiles as she complies with Michael's request of assuming coy poses.

***

Later that morning, she accompanies her mother to the Saint Simon's Anglican Church service. Her friends recognize her and salute her in a special way, but she makes no fuss. Celeste can tell that some acquaintances discreetly talk about her. She has the feeling that their behavior will shortly change after she is dolled-up.

After the service, they go home and the women prepare lunch. Michael goes to see his girlfriend, Mary. He's eager to tell her about the goings-on.

In the early afternoon, the doorbell rings and Celeste answers; there's a shiny black luxury car and a delivery truck stop in front of the house.

"Good afternoon Akarsh," she says nervously.

"Isn't it a wonderful day to be reborn!" he proclaims with open arms.

"Come in," she answers without responding to his welcoming arms.

"My crew will bring in your wardrobe and beauty products if you don't mind?"

"This is my mother, she'll show them the way."

"How fortunate you are to have such a charming daughter!" Akarsh emphasizes.

Alice guides the two assistants to Celeste's bedroom where they unload and unpack clothes, shoes, hats, contact lenses, exquisite beauty products, precious perfumes and sparkling jewelry. Celeste and Akarsh follow. He leaves an envelope on her desk.

"As we agreed from now on you are our figurehead who will, at all time, flaunt your beauty to the world. Be bold, be brash!"

Akarsh and his crew leave as quickly as they came.

Celeste is taken by the moment. She gazes at the horizon. After taking a deep breath she climbs the stairs to her room, discarding her glasses, her gown and letting her hair down. She closes the door.

She was apprehensive that Akarsh wanted more that he announced and she's relieved that he had not become intimate.

She emerges a hour later as her glamorous self, as magnificent as she was on the show.

"Mother, I'm going for a walk with Gyp."

That was an unusual occurrence, but Alice understood.

***

She trots to the Valleybrook Park where some people take notice of her; she acts as if nothing is different.

"Aren't you the girl on the Dyann Winter show?"

"Yes, have a good afternoon."

More and more people identify her, yet she jogs, as if nothing happened.

She's being gawked at more and more, stared at and pointed at, but she acts unperturbed.

She returns home, as if her stroll in the park was commonplace, but she's aware that she's become the center of attention. She isn't certain that this behavior would last; perhaps in a week everyone will have something else on his mind. Perhaps this is a fad. Still she feels safe returning home.

She spends the rest of the day with her mom, putting away most of her worn clothes and old beauty products to be given to a charitable organization.

***

Monday morning, she gets up with energy and quickly goes to the bathroom and locks the door. Michael is late again and he makes his presence known. She gets out and goes in her room to her dressing table. It takes her quite a bit of time, more than the usual, especially since the beauty products are new to her.

When she goes down to the eat-in kitchen, Michael is already there, and can't help but scan her from top to bottom with his inquisitive eyes.

"You're all dolled-up this morning!" he can't help saying.

She merely smiles.

Alice looks at the news, while the dog sleeps.

"Does this mean that you won't prepare breakfast for me anymore?" Michael inquires.

"Sure I'll prepare breakfast; it's going to take a little more time that's all."

"I can't wait to tell my friends that I had my breakfast served by Celeste. Can I invite my friends over for breakfast?"

She looks at him with a "you simpleton" expression.

***

Celeste leaves in all her glory and accompanies her mother to the GO train station. She is apprehensive since this is the public initiation of her smashing new look. She enters the train station and waits the usual five minutes. Again, people start noticing her. Some men flirt with her with a smile that she doesn't return; she had seen them previously and they totally ignored her then.

She leaves Union Station, heads for the Robinson, Johnson & Assoc. office and as she walks in, she customarily greets everyone she meets. Some hesitate for an instant, completely failing to recognize her.

Mr. Sinclair is shocked at her appearance as he greets her, "Good morning."

She begins to work as if nothing happened, but that day, she's the etalk of the office.

She gradually gets accustomed to her new status, as the person to chat about. At lunch, she tells all to Trish who takes pleasure at becoming the focus of attention, as Celeste's friend.

Celeste's return home experience is similar to what she lived this morning.

On the commuter train, she checks her network of friends on her smart watch and there are now thousands of followers seeking information and asking to chat. She answers that she is flattered.

At supper, she explains her day to her mom and brother.

In the evening, she gets a call from Matt, but she doesn't answer it.

Later that evening Matt sends her an email that he'd like to see her. She also doesn't answer it.

***

Tuesday morning starts much like Monday, but this time Michael waits patiently for Celeste to make him breakfast. He quips:"I guess your coffee cup is right."

"What do you mean?"

"Your coffee cup; it says 'You're special.'"

Celeste laugh: "I always knew it!"

They eat and are soon on their way.

There are more people in the GO station and Celeste is beginning to feel uneasy at being the center of attraction. She remains calm and goes about her business. A young man, about her age, nicely asks her:"Aren't you the girl from the Dyann Winter show?"

"Yes." She answers with a smile and walks away.

At the office, she greets everyone. As she goes to her desk she comes across a partner of the firm, Mr. Robinson, who unexpectedly extends:"Good morning," that is echoed by Celeste.

He turns and tries to be suave:"Mr. Sinclair, you didn't tell me we had such a lovely employee."

On the defensive Mr. Sinclair answers:"She's been with us two years."

"Is that so?"

At lunch, Celeste relates what happened to Trish who mocks, "After two years he noticed you. I wonder why."

During the afternoon, Celeste receives a phone call from Mr. Sinclair:"Would you come to my office?"

"Right away."

Mr. Sinclair has a file in front of him that he glances at:"We've been reviewing your file. You've been with us for more than two years and we're happy with your progress; you've been doing good work. I'm glad to inform you that you'll be assigned a permanent post in our firm. You'll receive the confirmation shortly. Congratulations Celeste."

"Thank you sir.

Is that all?"

"Yes."

She walks away with a sense of victory. Yes, it feels good to be vindicated.

She finishes work and returns home.

Tuesday and Thursday are jogging days, but now she wears the most striking flashing clothing on the market. She has the thrill of jogging to the Iroquois Ridge High School and going around the racetrack. Some teenagers admire her and whistle at her going by. As she reaches the north side of the track, she notices that Matt is running towards her and then alongside her.

"Hi Celeste, I was certain that I could find you here. It's good to see you. I phoned and texted you, but I couldn't reach you."

"I've been busy lately."

"I heard about the show and I looked it up. That transformation is wonderful. You look absolutely fabulous."

"Thanks."

"Truthfully, you didn't care much about your appearance before."

"Well I do now and it's changed more than my look."

"What do you mean?"

"It's also changing my outlook on life."

"How is that different?"

"Well you, for example. Would you have come here to talk to me if I hadn't changed my look?"

"Of course Celeste. I care about you."

"Then why din't you ask me to go with you to London?"

"I thought you understood that! Of course I want you to come with me," he says, with as much gall as he can muster.

"We never talked about it."

"I'm sorry, I should have done so. Please forgive me."

"We never talked about staying together either."

"My bad. I should have done so. Please understand me, I was overwhelmed and I simply didn't get around to it."

"It's quite something to forget!"

"I beg you to believe me, let the past be and come and stay with me in London."

"I'll think about it," she answers with the pleasure of toying with a lie, as she had so often been the victim of.

"We've been together since high school; don't let this little mishap destroy our relationship."

"We'll see," knowing well that it was her turn to wield power over him.

"I've got to go," he says and kisses her on the cheek as he parts from her and heads home.

She's troubled. She did like him and he was part of her dreams and hopes, but she's putting it behind her now.

***

That evening Michael answers the phone. "Call for Celeste."

She's surprised. "Hello."

"Hi, this is Jim Farber. We haven't met. I got your name from the Akarsh and the producers of the Dyann Winter show."

"Hi."

"I'm a Hollywood talent manager. You can look me up in the Hollywood Talent Directory. I've been in this business for twenty five years and I represent the most successful entertainment actors in the industry."

"Go on."

"I'd like to meet you here at my office to discuss your career. On top of being exceptionally beautiful, I feel that you have a great potential to develop an international career."

"You caught me off guard, I'll have to think about it."

"I'll reimburse all your travel cost, so don't worry about that. I'd like to see you next week at your convenience. Can I count on you?"

"I'll give you my answer later this week."

"Keep me posted."

Right away, she checks on the Internet that he really is a legitimate talent manager; it appears to be true. He's an African American with a brawny demeanor with remarkable credentials. He started out when his pro-football career ended and he built a strong and reputable firm.

Since this offer was sudden, she isn't sure whether she'd like to go to California far from her family. It is a life changing decision that warrants some soul searching.

***

It's Wednesday, and finally the sun comes out. Outside, the brisk wind blows the autumn leaves.

It's a quiet morning. At home, Celeste shares her concerns

with her family:"Yesterday, Matt met me when I was jogging and he assured me that he wanted to bring me with him to London. I wonder if I should believe him."

Her mother quickly points out:"Sweetheart, I told you that he wanted you to come with him. So, he finally came around and asked you?"

"I don't know what to think."

Michael intervenes:"Maybe you should talk to dad about this?"

Alice's tone of voice becomes stronger and more aggressive:"Leave you father out of this. He hasn't helped you a bit since he left."

Michael doesn't want to be brushed aside:"I'm sure dad can help out, given the chance.

You haven't had contact with him for two years. You should try it. He's not as bad as mother portrays him."

"He didn't try to contact me either," Celeste replies.

"Yes he did but you weren't listening. Try it."

"There's another thing going on."

"The phone call you got?" Michael hints.

"Yes. A Hollywood talent manager invited me to Hollywood next week to discuss my career."

"That's fake," Michael cautions.

"No, I checked him out and he's a well known and successful talent manager. He'll reimburse my expenses."

"You'll have to clear up your relationship with Matt beforehand," Alice warns.

"I suppose."

"Go talk to dad," Michael is adamant.

She's confused, so she decides that she'll talk it over with Trish.

After arriving home that afternoon, she borrows the car to go to the nearby shopping center. She's a little jittery, because she needs to deal with an internal struggle that's been crushing her self-assurance and self-worth. She heads for the cosmetic counter at the local drug store where she wants to confront her high school nemesis, Leisha, who's a salesperson there. Indeed Celeste recognizes her from afar and hesitates at approaching her.

Celeste shakes her head to part her hair from her face. After a moment or two, Celeste meanders to the cosmetic counter. Leisha is there and she greets the potential customer: "Good afternoon! Are you looking for something particular?"

"Perfumes."

"We have a wide array here, if you'd like to Nickple some. Would you like to try this one?"

"Why not!"

Leisha sprays a test strip and hands it to Celeste.

"Aren't you the girl from the Dyann Winter show?"

"Yes. You recognized me?"

"Well you're all over the news lately. So, are you a local girl?"

Celeste is relieved that Leisha hadn't quite figured out that they had mingled previously.

"Why yes!" Celeste answers, dryly, remembering those humbling times she had suffered because of her.

"Maybe we've met before?"

"This is a small town. We must have!"

"I don't recall having met you before. We're about the Nicke age so there's a good chance that we've met before."

"We did, I remember it well."

"We did?"

"I'm Celeste McCauley."

"Yes I know."

"You and your fan club used to bully me."

"Bully you? I would never do that!"

"Oh, but you did! And you took pleasure in it."

"You're mistaken. You must be taking me for someone else!"

"Oh no, there's no mistake about it. Remember 'pizza face'?"

"It can't be!"

"So now, you're selling cosmetics. May be you should ask your clients what they'd like on their pizza face?"

Leisha walks away and hides in the back office.

Celeste has gained her dignity and her peace of mind. Never again will someone will put her down.

***

Thursday is less windy and a bit colder, it's a sign that winter is approaching. Akarsh has shipped the appropriate late autumn clothes she will wear.

On her way to the office, more and more people are waiting purposely to admire her. She always wished to get more attention for the right reason, so she doesn't shy away from it. Derek, the photographer, shoots some urban poses from the other side of the tracks.

She arrives at the office and quietly goes to work.

Later that morning, Mr. Sinclair walks by her cubicle: "Mr. Robinson would like to talk to you."

"Yes."

He retreats to his space while she heads for the corner office.

The mature secretary smiles:"Go on in, Mr. Robinson is waiting," as Celeste responds to the smile.

She goes in.

"Please sit down," Mr. Robinson says, as he casually peruses her personnel file.

"You've done well since your began with us and I believe that it is time for a promotion. I need a personal assistant to help me."

"I'm flattered, truly. To be frank with you, I'm presently considering another offer," she quickly answers, knowing well that this turn of event is a direct consequence of her new appearance. She has the sense that she acquired power over people and she intends to make the most of it.

"Naturally your new salary will be competitive."

"Actually, I'll need a few days off next week to weigh the pros and cons."

"Of course, that's no problem."

"Well thank you very much sir, I'll consider you proposal very seriously."

As she walks away, she feels his stare burning her buttocks.
***

Back at her desk, she calls Trish.

"Trish, I'm inviting you to lunch at The Loose Moose™."

"You're crazy."

"Akarsh prodded me to provoke folks to admire me, so I'll do it. We'll go to this swanky restaurant for people to watch me."

"It's going to take two hours."
"I don't care. I have a lot to discuss."
"I'll ask for permission."
"Great."
Celeste has no intention of doing the Nicke.
"Does that mean that we'll never go back to our haunts? No more Fresking?"
"No more Fresking for me, that's for sure."
"I can't afford that."
"I'll pick up the tab. More precisely, Akarsh will."
"You wouldn't dare!"
"He sure will."
***

They settle down on a cushioned bench at a corner table. Derek sneaks in, winks at her and takes pictures only to disappear.

"Yesterday evening, I went to the drugstore and guess who I saw?" Celeste confides to Trish.

"I don't know."

"Take a wild guess."

"I haven't the slightest idea."

"I saw Leisha."

"No!" Trish answers with childish delight.

"Actually, I heard that she worked as a clerk in the cosmetics section, so I wanted to confront my tormentor to ridicule her."

"You didn't. What happened?"

"She didn't recognize me at first, so she tried her best to sell me some products. I let her linger as long as I could. Finally, I asked her if she recognized me. She said that she didn't but she had the apprehension that she knew me. She asked if I had been on TV or the Internet. I confessed that I was on both."

"You didn't?"

"I told her who I am; still, she couldn't get a grip on it. Then I told her that, when we were young, she bullied me as 'pizza face'. She was stunned. Then I made fun of her. She walked away in shame. Then I left."

"Good for you."

"I got rid of this load on my shoulders. It freed me from many days of doubt and pain."

Celeste then detailed all that happened with Matt, Jim Farber and Robinson as well as Michael's suggestion that she get in touch with her dad.

Trish picked up that. "Your father will always be your father. He wants your happiness. Why not break the barrier between you two?"

"We were never very close."

"He might very well give you the advice you need."

"If he's so smart, why did he break up our family?"

"You could ask him. This is a good opportunity to clear things up."

"You think so?"

"Give it a try."

"Perhaps you're right."

Celeste pays the bill and keeps the receipt.
***

As she arrives late, back at the office, Mr. Sinclair is visibly angry but he doesn't utter a peep. She relishes at the power she has gained over him.
***

When she leaves for home, she gets the attention of a growing number of onlookers. She acts a little haughty, for the fun of it.
***

As usual, her mother picks her up at the train station.

Celeste vents her fears. "Travelling through the crowds is getting difficult because I'm being eyeballed."

"What can we do? We can't stop it, dear."

"Perhaps I could drive your car to work and drop you off?"

"I'll agree to that, if it will make you feel safer."

"Thanks mom."
***

Celeste relaxes in her room. She might as well meet Jim Farber to find out exactly what he proposes; anyhow, a trip to California will do her good. She decides to go alone, since Trish and Alice will be working. She calls a local travel agent to arrange a trip to Hollywood next week. She sends an email to Jim Farber to inform him of the exact time, date and place she will be there.

Just before supper time, she calls her dad:"Dad, it's Celeste."

"It's good to hear from you Cinderella," he retorts.

"I gather you heard what happened."

"Yes. My former coworkers hassle me about it."

"It's been a while since we've seen each other."

"A couple years."

"I need to talk to you about some decisions I'm about to make."

"Man trouble?"

"You could say that."

"Sure, come on over, whenever you'd like."

"After supper, if that's OK?"

"I'll see you then."

***

Celeste puts on another set of jogging clothes and she is on her way. She expects Matt to show up like last time, but she is undaunted.

Some teen kids are waiting next to Iroquois Ridge High School to express their budding masculinity by whistling and jeering.

She passes by, as if they aren't there, because she doesn't want to excite them anymore than they already are.

As suspected, Matt joins her on the north side of the track."So how's it going Celeste?"

"Everything is going fast."

"It's raining in London. I keep tabs on the weather there."

"Is that so?"

"Anything new with your career?"

"Why yes. Next week, I'm going to Hollywood."

"To Hollywood?"

"Yes."

"Are you going to visit someone?"

"Kind of, I'm meeting a manager."

"What sort of a manager?"

"A talent manager."

"Is that so?"

"What about me? What about London?"

"Well, I have to think of my career also?"

"But you're not an actress?"

"Not now, no."

"You've never acted before," Matt replies a bit wounded.

"Well, he wants to see me and he's funding all expenses. He must find me appealing!"

"He called you?"

"Yes, is that so surprising?"

"Well, no."

"Listen Celeste, I'd like to see you this weekend. We could talk about this."

"Maybe."

"I'll call you. I've got to go." He jogs away.

***

During supper, Michael is curious. "I heard you on the phone talking to dad."

"You snooped at my door?" Celeste is upset.

"I overheard, but I didn't do it on purpose."

"I bet."

"Well did you talk to him?"

"I'm going to see him after supper. Mom can I borrow your car?"

"Sure, sweetheart."

Michael inserts a comment:"I'd like to make a video of you and post it on the Internet."

"Why?"

"It might give me some visibility also."

"I'll be here for you," she replies; she accepts because she feels that it will be kind of a rehearsal for future serious interviews.

"You're a sweetheart."

"Keep that in mind!"

***

That evening, she drives to her father's apartment on Lakeshore Road West, close to shops near the factory where he worked. As she goes up the third floor, she smells the odors of the tenants' supper; somebody likes curry. She rings the doorbell and her father answers without inquiring who's there. He kisses her on the cheek, as he had always done. He's wearing some ironing-free beige slacks and a matching plaid shirt. He displays spanking new brown shoes. She believes that he has fewer, but greyer hair than he used to have. He still has his old pair of glasses with thick brown rims. He has many family photos on the walls and small souvenirs on the credenza.

"You've got a nice apartment, dad."

"It's comfortable and convenient. I have a couple of friends nearby with whom I play cards and go bowling."

"That's great."

"Let's sit in the living room. Would you like something: some wine, a beer, a soft drink?"

"No thanks, I just had lunch."

"What's this Cinderella story?"

"Trish coaxed me into appearing in a TV show where I got a makeover. Akarsh, the promoter, and his staff transformed me into this new glamour girl and the audience flipped over me. Akarsh then offered me to show off his products in my daily life, so I accepted. Basically that's it."

"So, with a few paintbrushes he altered you from a plain girl to an artificial beauty?"

"I could always count on you to encourage me!" She reminds herself of the disparaging comments he has the habit of making, and her reason for not coming here.

"So why did you come to me?"

"Before I make permanent changes in my life I need your advice."

"Go ahead, what's bothering you?"

"Well, there's Matt. As you know, we've been together since high school. He recently got a job offer that involves a transfer to London, England, and so he rented an apartment there. Before my makeover, he never talked marriage or that I would go with him. Now that I look like a princess, he hounds me to go with him to Britain. It sure looks as if he changed his point of view since the TV show. How can I be sure that he genuinely loves me?"

"Did he ever declare that he loves you, other than when he's having sex?"

"No, not even when having sex."

Brent takes a few minutes to reflect on this dilemma. "I suggest that you ask him to describe the apartment he rented."

"What?"

"Do it, that's all."

"Why?"

"Trust me."

That word initiated a chain of thoughts in Celeste's mind.

"There's another thing that's bothering me."

"You come to me only when you want something. You're like your mother."

"Well, I want to hear your version of why you left us?"

"Your mother never stops bitching, complaining and nagging. Whenever I was home, there was always something wrong that she didn't like or that I didn't do. I couldn't live with that constant bickering. I was fed up. At least now, I have some quiet and peace. I just couldn't live with her anymore."

"What about Michael and I, you abandoned us?"

"I didn't abandon you. You were with your mother a few blocks from here. Anyhow, I waited until you were out of high school before moving out. You weren't kids anymore. I was tired of always towing the line."

"What do you mean, you were toeing the line?"

"I was doing everything and she was bitching me constantly. She could have done more."

"She took care of us kids and the house!"

"That's about it, that's all."

"Before the separation, you stayed with your friends to watch sports. You didn't really care about us."

"I didn't want to go home to fight with your mother because that would have been even worse."

"When you left, you could have stayed in contact with us."

"Michael came and visited me. Nothing stopped you from coming. You were mad at me, so I didn't want to start a fight with you. You can come anytime you want."

"Sure, so you can make fun of me. You always did. I was never good enough for you. I couldn't meet your expectations. I must be your life's greatest disappointment."

"I didn't ridicule you. And no, you didn't disappoint me."

"You demeaned me when you said that I was plain. That is humiliating."

"I didn't mean to humiliate you."

"Well you did and I didn't need this." Celeste walks out without a goodbye.

***

At home, she heads straight for her room, but it takes forever to sleep. She's relieves that she told him.

***

All day Friday, Celeste is upset because of her meeting with her dad. She tries to shake it off, without much success.

Just before supper Matt texts her "Hey, what's up?"

"NTN."

"We should hang this wknd. We need to talk."

"SYT 10."

"C ya."

"buhbye."

At supper, Michael makes sure that Celeste will be there this evening. "Are you ready to become famous?"

"I am. Are you ready?"

"Everyone will know me. I'll be the envy of the town."

"You might very well become the talk of the town," Celeste replies.

***

Michael rearranges the furniture, then he brings a camera, lights and some microphones that he installs in the recreation room in front of the sofa; as a backdrop, there's a small triangular flag of the I.R.H.S. field hockey team.

He tests the equipment.

"I'm ready," he says to himself.

Michael leaves and comes back with his sister.

"Are you ready for the interview?"

"Yes."

"This will be the first time that I'm interviewed."

"It's also the first time I do this."

"Sit down on the sofa while I'll close the lights."

Celeste makes herself comfortable.

"Let's start. My name is Michael McCauley from Oakville. Celeste, how does it feel to be the Dyann Winter's makeover phenom?"

"It's been absolutely phenomenal!" she responds with an enchanting smile.

"Where did you go to college?"

"I went to Brock University where I specialized in Digital Media and Production; that provided me the opportunity to work as a graphics designer."

"That's enough of the serious stuff. Did your brother ever put on some of your lipstick?"

Though she's surprised, she smiles and goes with the flow. "Yes, he did a few years ago. He even dressed up as a woman. He was kind of cute."

Michael looks amused.

"Now that's interesting. Tell me is there anything you don't like about him."

"In fact, yes. He keeps pieces of old sandwiches in his desk drawer in case he gets hungry. Often he forgets them and they grow moldy."

"That gross!

Is there something else?"

"Now that you ask, there's something else. When he finishes chewing a gum, he sticks it under the nearest furniture. All the tables and chairs have some dried Michael gum under it."

"Oh no, that is grooooss!

Let's talk about you. What kind of binge do you do?"

"Sometimes, when I'm with friend, Trish and I watch romantic flicks all day long."

"And what do you eat? No lies!"

"We eat popcorn," she admits, ashamed.

"Is Trish your Best Friend Forever?"

"Yes."

"Do you tell her everything?"

"Yes."

"E-v-e-r-y-t-h-i-n-g?" he inquires.

"Nearly everything," she admits, a bit embarrassed.

"What's your favorite emoji?"

"A sunflower," she reveals while shaping a circle in the air with both hands.

"And what is your spirit animal?"

"It's a bird actually, the Macaw; it's so colorful, friendly and smart."

"How long have you been dating your crush?"

"Six years."

"What do you love most about him?"

"His ambition."

"What do you dislike most about him?"

"His selfishness."

"What does he do, that annoys you?"

"He grabs his crotch in public," she lies and she enjoys it. She couldn't believe that she said that. She rarely lied, yet it seemed liberating in some way.

"Yuck. Well thanks for your time Celeste."

Celeste gets up and smiles. "That was amusing."

"You were great. Tomorrow, I'll edit it and I'll upload it on the Internet."

"What will you cut out?" Celeste asks.

"Very little, certainly not the Matt revelation! Maybe the gum part." Michael smirks.

***

Saturday morning at ten o'clock, Matt rings the doorbell; Celeste answers and they head for the recreation room. He's wearing slacks with a chic sweater.

"You look ravishing." Matt hazards to say.

"It's in my contract."

"You moved the furniture?" Matt remarks.

"It was Michael, yesterday evening. He shot an interview with me."

"Oh yeah?"

"It'll be posted on YouTube™ tomorrow."

"I can't wait to see it."

"Tell me about London."

"Sure. I'll be working at the Soaring Tower, dubbed the Gherkin because the building is shaped like a pickle."

"Really! That's impressive." Matt has an inkling that she is mocking him.

"Anyhow I found an apartment they call a flat in Chelsea close to the Tube."

"How many rooms does it have?"

"London is very expensive so I rented a studio."

"So how big is it?"

"Well there a common room, a kitchen, and the loo."

"If I understand, there's no separate bedroom?"

"That's correct."

"So it's a bachelor?"

"It's a studio."

"Is it near the Kew garden? I love flowers."

"It must be."

"And is it near the zoo?"

"I guess."

"You didn't really think that I would go and live with you there, did you?"

"It would be just for a while. We would get a flat, once I was settled."

"That'll never happen. You only wanted me to move in with you after the TV show. You're selfish. Get out."

"Celeste, please give me another chance."

She calms down as she gets an epiphany.

"OK. I'll go and take a look at your flat."

"That sounds good."

"Well, buy me a ticket and reserve me a good hotel for next weekend."

"Sure, sure," Matt complies and scoots out while he had the chance.

She doesn't have any intention of continuing their relationship, but she wanted him to pay and suffer. It would be a solo trip for Matt.

The claws are out.

***

Sunday morning, Celeste and her mother go to church. They meet Mrs. Buxton, a long-standing church acquaintance. "What a lovely day."

"Isn't it," Alice agrees.

"My dear, is there some festivity you are going to, after the service?" looking at Celeste.

"No, why do you ask?"

"The way you are dressed, I was convinced that there must be some other more festive function you would be attending."

"From now on, I will be dressed in a festive way. I find it very elegant."

"I think that dressing more soberly would be appropriate in a place of worship, don't you?"

"I'm sorry if the way I dress offends you."

"Have a good day, my dear."

"You too."

***

Later that morning, Matt phones Celeste.

"I saw the video on the Internet. You accused me of grabbing my crotch in public. I never do that."

"I never mentioned your name."

"Everyone knows that I'm your boyfriend."

"You mean that you WERE my boyfriend."

"Whatever."

"They won't know if you don't tell them. I wouldn't boast about it if I were you."

"You bitch." He shuts off the phone.

That's the end of that. No London, no Matt.

***

The final break with Matt made her feel lousy. Perhaps a new beginning would give her some energy. She starts thinking of Hollywood. Since she'll be alone, she's wary of being lured into an unwanted outcome. She'll be careful, very careful. At least, the agreement with Akarsh is working out fine and that gives her some hope.

CHAPTER SIX

Networking

MONDAY MORNING is the beginning of a day, of a week and perhaps of a new life. Celeste packs her belongings in her brand new fashionable luggage that will undoubtedly attract everyone's curiosity with its distinctive futuristic look. Before she leaves, Michael wishes her good luck and kisses her on the cheek. Her mother comes by and, as mothers do, warns her to be careful and gives her a few recommendations that Celeste has come to abhor; she kisses Celeste on the cheek. "I love you dear," and she is on her way to work.

Her father sent her an email, also wishing her a good trip. She appreciates it.

She checks everything, the reservations, the tickets, the passport, the money. She's all set. It's her first time travelling alone. She is moving out of her comfort zone, a move that is necessary for progress and evolution. She is truly entering the adventure of life, where she will let destiny offer her unforeseen opportunities. The future is a mystery that she will participate in with enthusiasm. She is privileged and she intends to make the most of it.

When the hour has come, she calls a taxi; when it arrives, she puts on her overcoat, asks the taxi operator to help her with her baggage and she enters the taxi that heads for Pearson airport. She gives an appropriate tip to the taxi operator who loads the trunks onto a cart. She pushes a cart into the airport and, quickly enough, she gets offers to help her out. As she stands in line waiting to check in, the surrounding travelers check her out; she's used to it by now.

She clears airport security and sits down in the business class lounge.

Shortly thereafter, a tall young man, with a high and tight hairstyle, dressed in a smart tailored suit, sits next to her. He's wearing a conspicuous Rolex Oyster™ White gold watch. He's a little taller than she is. He has green eyes, very pleasant facial features and well cut curly brown hair. He's well built chiseled by regular exercise. "Celeste McCawley is it?"

Celeste is surprised. "Have we met before?"

"No. I just read you ID tag on your carryon bag."

"Yes."

"I saw you somewhere, I can't recall exactly where."

"I was on the Dyann Winter show."

"Oh, yes. You're much lovelier in person than on TV."

"Is that so."

"You're magnificent."

"Thank you."

"My name is Andy Czerny."

"Hi," Celeste is a bit uncomfortable, but she doesn't want to appear aloof.

"I'm returning to L.A. after having sold five helicopters to the Ontario government."

"Good for you."

"I work for THC, the Torrance Helicopter Company. Choppers are my life."

"I've never flown in one actually."

"Would you like to take a chopper ride once we reach L.A.? I could fly you around the city."

"I'm afraid of heights."

"Did you ever travel by air?"

"Yes, but that's different."

"Well, a chopper is just another kind of plane."

"It seems to me that I would cramp up or panic."

"Until you try i,t you won't know."

"Promise me that if I'm too afraid, you'll land right away."

"I promise."

"I'm relying on you."

"Where will you be staying?"

"At the Triz."

"How long will you be there?"

"I'm scheduled to return home next Sunday."

"I'm sure I can find a slot when we can do this. I'll leave you a message at your hotel.

Are you coming to L.A. for a visit?"

"I have an appointment with a talent manager. He might find me work."

"Well you've certainly have the looks.

I, myself, come from the Midwest, Lincoln Nebraska to be precise. It's a great place to fly. Charles Lindberg flew here. During World War II, the place was an aviation training center. That's where I learned to fly. My father is a farmer. I used to spray the surrounding farms with pesticides. There's nothing wrong with farming but I wanted something more. I went to college..... I was a decorated Army pilot... My parents moved to L.A. when I was a teenager..."

He talks about himself for the rest of the wait, but Celeste is vaguely interested, to put it politely.

***

Celeste checks in at the gate. She has a seat next to a woman. Once people are settled, the small talk begins, but soon enough, it gets interesting to Celeste who is passionate for animals and plants.

The woman is a biologist from Madagascar. "I just gave a talk on humble plants. Human survival may be dependent on neglected forms of life. I'm sorry, plants are my life's work, but I don't want to bore you."

"On the contrary, I adore plants and animals, particularly birds. Please go on."

The biologist focused on the baobab, a tree found in western Africa and Madagascar. There is one species in Africa and there are six species in Madagascar. In Africa, it's the tree of life for good reason. Some trees sprouted in the Middle Ages; some are even older than human civilization. They are part of the largest and oldest trees on earth, so much so that in Australia there is one that was used as a prison. The leaves are edible and are used as medicine against infectious diseases. The seeds can produce stable oil, used in the cosmetic industry. Its monkey apple super-fruits contain many nutrients, such vitamin C, fibers and antioxidant; their pulpy interiors have more protein than human milk. The tree itself is an excellent water reservoir, particularly appreciated in Africa. The branches provide nesting grounds for birds. Fire-resistant rope is made from its bark. Sometimes bats use their hollow trunks to make it their home, but their accumulated feces make it dangerous to take shelter in there.

Scientists refer to the tree of life, as the first life forms in the three domains of life, but that's another story.

That inspirational description fascinates Celeste.

As the plane lands, she praises the biologist.

They part ways.

Celeste taps her phone app to summon the limousine, as instructed by Mr. Farber.

***

As they enter the lounge, Andy approaches Celeste.

"Can I give you a lift? I have a brand new BMW."

"No thanks, there's someone waiting for me."

"I can't match that. Have a nice stay."

"Thanks."

A driver waiving a sign with her name fetches her and takes her to a superb shiny black sedan limousine waiting to take her to the Triz. As she gets in, the impeccably dressed driver hands her a credit card. "Compliments of Mr. Farber."

"Thank you, or rather thank him."

"Please hand me you smart watch, I'll add an app that will access the limo and hotel services." In a cinch, the app is operational. She thanks him with a smile.

As soon as she gets out of the limousine, a bellhop places her luggage on a trolley. The concierge, who prides himself in judging each of the guests recognizes that she's a DDG guest, yet she seems unaccustomed to drop-dead luxury; he makes her feel comfortable: "Welcome to the Triz. If there's anything you want, it will be a pleasure to serve you."

"I'd like to have orchids in every room."

"You will be delighted."

She has a junior suite on the 25th floor that has a breathtaking panoramic view over the city, one of the Santa Monica

Mountains and one of the Pacific Ocean.

She feels free. She dances around the suite while smiling at her incredible destiny, as if she is on top of the world beyond human problems. She twirls and twists to an internal music. She caresses the curtains, the bedding, the fine leather, the marble and the stainless steel. She thanks God for having given her this serendipity. She basks in the setting sun, taking in deep breadths. She soaks this total happiness into her soul. Her mind is producing her own drug of dopamine that's enhancing her pleasures. She surrenders to forces beyond her own, an ecstatic realm close to trance. She would never have done that at home and she would certainly not admit doing it.

The door rings and orchids are brought in.

She lies on the bed and falls asleep for an undetermined amount of time. Her present wellbeing is her only concern.

She wants to revel in sensuality, so once her luggage is unpacked, she taps the smart watch app and goes to the spa where she just ordered a massage.

The attendant named Jen is a lovely young woman with Asiatic traits who speaks in a muted and solicitous voice: "Welcome, will you have a glass of Champagne?"

"It would be my pleasure."

Celeste lies on the massage table with her face looking sideways. Jen lights some incense sticks that quickly permeates the warm air. A soothing music chills-out in the background.

Jen places some warm towels on Celeste's legs and lower back.

"Let yourself melt down on the mattress.
Close your eyes and take deep breadths.
Please refrain from talking and let me guide you.
Be attentive and focus on what I'm saying.
Be receptive to my touch.
Surrender to me and don't try to help me."

Jen oils her hands and starts feathering the neck and the shoulders to enhance the sensual touching.

"Relax your whole body.
Close your eyes and think that you're in a hammock in a

tropical forest near the seashore.

You can hear the birds.

You can hear the waves regularly dying on the shore.

Start by relaxing your jaw and your mouth.

Let your shoulders drop.

Let your arms fall.

Let your feet go."

Jen is rubbing the shoulders and the arms.

"Do not let your thoughts drift away.

You are in my hands and you're feeling terrific."

Jen applies long strokes along the back, aware to any sign of discomfort.

"You are now falling in a peaceful sleep, while listening to me.

Sleep.

Focus on my voice.

You are in a great place.

You love being here."

She caresses her legs.

"Let your mind go.

Listen to my voice.

Relax.

Now you will slowly turn around."

Celeste makes herself comfortable on her back.

"Relax your head."

Jen massages her temples and her cheeks.

"Let yourself enjoy the moment.

Dream of the tropical forest and of regular sea waves washing on a beach.

You have no care in the world.

Enjoy life.

Your hands are soft.

Your fingers are waiting to be caressed.

Sleep.

You've never felt better in your life."

Jen slowly travels down to her neck, shoulders, her arms and hands.

When she reaches her solar plexus, she is a bit perplexed.

"I'm at the center of your body, the hara. It reveals that your Ki is not quite centered. You are in disequilibrium. It is not serious for the moment, but you should take care to reposition your soul. It is a bad energy that is troubling you."

Jen resumes her passage and applies kneading pressure on her hips.

Jen rubs the thighs and the calves.

"Your body is floating on a cloud."

Jen massages the feet with tenderness, using its pressure points to appease any stress.

She leaves Celeste alone and lowers the lights.

Celeste sleeps, as if carried to Nirvana.

Eventually she awakes. Jen is waiting in a corner to help Celeste.

They do not need to talk. They are in communion.

***

Back in her room, Celeste ponders about the Ki equilibrium. She settled her internal struggles with Leisha and with Matt. She cannot grasp what else would perturb her serenity.

***

Tuesday morning, she has breakfast at the L.A. Market restaurant. Just for fun, she phones home. "Hi Michael, how are you?"

......

"You miss me already? I suppose you missed my breakfast!"

.....

"Say hi to mom."

.....

"I love her too."

....

"Ok.
Hi Gyp, this is Celeste.
Hi pooch."

.....

"Everything is great. Take care."

.....

Next, stop Wilshire Blvd at Jim Farber's office on the 7th

floor, where the receptionist greets her. "Mr. Farber is expecting you. Please take a seat."

She doesn't wait long before she's ushered in. It's not the grand office she expected, but a modest one, like an office that one might have in a small town.

Both parties recognize each other, from the media pictures.

"I'm Jim Farber. Please sit. Would you like a coffee? I always drink coffee; pure Arabica; now it's the only drug I take."

"No thanks."

"So are you enjoying your stay?"

"It couldn't be better."

"I'm glad to hear that."

"I saw you on the Dyann Winter show and the ratings soared because of your appearance. You have something that people adore, call it charm, call it femininity, anyhow it's got people reeling."

"Thank you."

"Akarsh has signed you up for his brands, has he?"

"Yes and I'm very proud of it. I follow his instructions to the dot."

"So I see. Hollywood needs someone like you, but you require some improvements. If you want to get ahead and achieve all your dreams, I'll have to straighten your imperfections."

"You know my imperfections!"

"That's right and that will take a lot of effort. You don't want to be a meteor that glows in the sky for a few minutes and fades away, never to glow again. You want to be a star that everyone yearns to watch and dream, day and night."

"What do you mean?"

"It starts with training in speech, by perfecting your pronunciations, your intonations, your acceptable vocabulary and your ability to read a teleprompter. Then you will get a guide for appropriate replies that will be very useful to answer aggressive reporters; you will be able to tell them to go to hell in an elegant and dignified way. You will follow courses in acting, dancing and in personality improvement. I will provide you the names of lawyers and accountants to help manage your finances and contracts, because you will be offered other sponsorships.

In return, I will receive a twenty percent commission on all your earnings for a period of ten years. It begins with a photo shoot and a video of your life. A web site about you will stimulate an Internet buzz. You will be introduced to producers, directors and influential people in many media. I will suggest a talent agent who will take ten or fifteen percent more of your take, but he or she will find you gigs."

"I have a lot to consider."

"Please give me your answer by the end of the week before you go back home."

"Aren't you a talent agent? Why do I have to pay for a talent agent?"

"As I told you, I'm a talent manager who will hone your qualities so that your image can be sold to as wide an audience as possible. A talent agent will find gigs for you. He'll find you some jobs. It's completely different."

"All right then."

***

Celeste returns to the Triz. The concierge recognizes her and hands her a message with his coordinates:

"Call me for the chopper ride around the city. Andy"

She arrives in her impeccable room where the maid placed everything in their allotted location, added orchids in a crystal vase and shaped the towels as a swan on the bed. Celeste drops Andy's message in the desk drawer.

She calls the concierge using the app. "Hi Charles, this is Celeste, this afternoon I'd like to be part of an audience in a TV show."

"That should not be a problem. I'll call you, as soon as I confirm it."

"Thanks."

In an instant, he confirms her departure time.

Since she has some free time, she does some exercises in the fitness room and then she goes to the pool area to take some sun.

Not long after, she goes back to her room, taps the app and dons a new dress and goes to eat at the Triz Club Lounge.

When it's time, she goes out to the limousine that drives her to Warner Brothers Studios™ in Burbank, gate 3, to the Hide & Seek cooking show where members of the audience rate dishes and try to identify the ingredients.

As she enters the studio, the showrunner talks to her, while a small camera scans her face.

"How are you?" the showrunner tests her mood and allure.

"Wonderful."

She walks away. The showrunner seeks her out. "We would love to have you on our stage to participate in the show."

Though she's surprised, she's thrilled. "All right."

She's fully aware that this is a show meant to entertain and she intends to do her best to do that.

"Just sit in the front row."

The pre-show starts by prepping the audience. Then the host, chef Sigmund Donnerblitz, walks onto the stage kitchen and proclaims with his signature accent and tone. "Good day ladies and gentlemen. Today we have the privilege of having Celeste, newly discovered by Dyann Winter."

All smiles and waiving to the cameras, Celeste has gained confidence in herself. The applause is warm and intense.

"Celeste in front of you there is a glass with a dark red liquid. It may have been modified. It may simply be colored water. It could also be grape juice or plum juice. Please taste it and tell us what you think it is."

She drinks a sip.

"It isn't wine."

"Correct, you are a connoisseur!"

"That taste is familiar to me, but I can't put my finger on it."

"Oh, you can put your finger on it!"

A mild laughter resounds.

"In fact, you can put all your fingers in it if you'd like!"

His slight German accent makes it funnier.

"Do you like putting fingers in your food?"

There's another wave of chuckles.

"Maybe you like to lick your fingers?"

"It's orange juice."

"Not quite, you should have licked your finger."

"Grapefruit juice."

"Applaud the lady, she is correct. Actually, the juice is from blood orange grapefruits. They're more dramatic."

After the applause he continues. "Yes today we are going to cook with grapefruits. We are going to make a fresh salad, a tasty sea bass with grapefruit juice and a wonderful grapefruit cheesecake. "

Celeste helps him make the dishes and the cameras delight themselves by showing her every graceful move.

When they're finished, Celeste adds an impromptu comment:"Do you want me to do the dishes."

"Your offer is so kind. This is the first time a guest has offered to wash the dishes."

This sincere offer sparked affection from all the spectators.

As she leaves the studio, many audience members propose jokingly that she help them with their dishes.

***

Back at her suite, a blinking light indicates that she received a message. She relaxes and ponders. Who could help her make the best decision? Perhaps she could even wait for some other opportunity. Perhaps there could be a better offer from another manager? Trish is a good friend, but she is out of her league to counsel her for this type of offer. The same holds true for her mother and Michael. She doesn't trust her father that much. Akarsh isn't close enough to her, so she decides to trust her instincts.

She texts Jim Farber to ask him for a list of six persons who are his clients and who she can talk to. Half an hour later, she receives such a list. She tries to contact four of them to get their opinion; two of them respond with very favorable opinions. It seems that the percentage of commission asked is a bit high, but within the standards of the industry. One has a nine years contract.

She wants more time before making a decision.

She inquires who sent her a message. It's Andy. She phones him. "I'll go for the helicopter ride tomorrow at ten, but promise me that we'll land if I'm too afraid."

"I promise.
You'll have to wear closed-toes shoes and slacks or jeans."
"No problem."
"See you tomorrow then."
"Bye"

She goes to a nearby quick-lunch place where she has a light supper.

Later that evening, she puts on a fabulous three quarter length white satin cocktail code dress with black stripes accentuating her feminine shape. Hmmm. She calls the limousine that drops her at the For Us cocktail bar.

Her looks are her reservation. "Table or bar?"

"Bar," she replies with audacity.

The handsome male bartender asks:"What will it be?"

"A Shirley Temple," she requests to keep her wits during the evening.

It's a little early and customers wander in gradually; there are scantily dressed girls coming out of a gilded cage to titillate the clients; some customers are curious to seek out the cable car in the back yard. A mirrored sphere spreads a starry sky above. A piano player plays Benny Goodman's melodies.

A salt and pepper man with a tan complexion is sitting on the bench next to Celeste. He's half shaven and has a Caesar haircut. He wears a pair of black rimmed glasses that accentuate his dark eyes. He's wearing a single-breasted tuxedo with slacks, black silk cummerbund the Japanese would envy, a black oxford, a white shirt with pleated front and a turn down spread collar and a black bowtie; he has the sort of clothes you'd expect in a publicity of a Scotch liquor advertisement.

"My, you're lovely! I wish I were ten years younger."

His deep voice and his subtle perfume seduced her immediately; she shudders.

"My name is Nick Dash."

"I'm Celeste."

"You are indeed!"

He checks her out, without any inhibition.

"You aren't from here. You must be from heaven."

She may not be speechless, but she doesn't respond.

"Forgive me for being so bold, I couldn't help it."

She looks down, somewhat shaken.

He snaps his finger to call a flower girl. He buys a lovely carnation and offers it to Celeste.

"Please accept this small gift in token of my apology."

Celeste's can't help but shine.

"Thank you."

He offers to shake hands and she accepts. "Let me start over again. I'm Nick Dash. I'm waiting for a friend. I find you charming. Where are you from?"

Since he didn't recognize her, it seems that he hadn't watched the Internet or TV recently and that was a relief.

"I'm from Oakville Ontario."

"What brings you to Hollywood?"

"I'm meeting a talent manager to discuss a possible career in show business."

"If I understand it correctly you aren't sure what you want to do in show business?"

"Honestly, it's being served to me on a silver platter."

"Then you won't make it."

Celeste is intrigued and somewhat troubled. "Why not?"

"Forgive me for being so blunt, you don't have the desire and the passion. You have to beg, pray and cry to succeed and from what you said, you wouldn't do that!"

"Did you beg, pray and cry?"

"I didn't cry."

"I gather that you think that crying is for women."

"Women cry when they lose control, while men are more likely to get angry when they do."

"So you got angry?"

"Yes."

"And what is your work?"

"Photography."

"You're a photographer then?"

"Yes, in a way; I'm in cinema. Right now I'm designing software for camera chips, more particularly Eulerian Video Magnification, but I won't bore you with the details."

"That's kind of you. So you like photography?"

"No, that's my point. Photography is my life; I think, I dream, I love photography and that's why I'm successful."

"So you're recommending me that I do that?"

"Yes I do. Please excuse me my friend just arrived. Let's share how we can be reached so that we can develop this further later."

Celeste obliges and they swap their coordinates.

"Celeste McCawley is it?"

"Yes."

Nick's friend approaches. "Ah you charmer, I see that you're with a beautiful young woman."

"Frank, this is Celeste McCawley."

"It's been a pleasure to meet you."

"I'll keep in touch," Nick says as he whisks him away to a reserved seating table.

She's absorbed with what Nick said. She watches him with the corner of her eyes throughout the evening. He touched her sensibility. It was as if, so far, her life had been on automatic and she found someone who inspired her to take control of her life. She needs to discuss it further.

Two other men hit upon her and she manages to avoid them.
***

It's a sunny, windless and clear morning, ideal for flying.

Celeste's limousine drops her at the Torrance Helicopter Company. She's wearing a camouflage style blouse and pants, designer aviator type sunglasses, genuine hiking shoes and a 'U.S. Paratrooper' cap for good measure. Andy comes out to allow her to pass the security. "You're dressed for battle," he quips.

"I'm nervous, hopping in a helicopter."

"Just relax. I'll stop anytime you want."

Andy notices Derek following Celeste: "Hey you scram!"

"He's my personal photographer who takes all glam shots he can," she intercedes.

Andy waves that it's OK.

Derek places small cameras in different locations inside and outside the helicopter.

In the factory, he leads her to the test flight sector. "Try this flight suit, to put you in the mood."

She dons the suit that fits her like a glove.

He also puts one on. "Now we're all set."

He gives some safety instructions, including the location of a life vest and an inflatable dinghy.

The two places helicopter is waiting on the tarmac. He checks the maintenance records. He removes the covers and tiedowns. He verifies the instruments and the metal fretting. He makes sure that the torque stripes are not missing or broken and that the cowl door is latched. He checks the fuel and oil pressure and that all gauges and lights are working correctly. He puts on the earphones and he makes certain that the radio and avionics work correctly. He starts the engine.

"Make sure your seat belt is secure."

Celeste is more than happy to follow orders.

The helicopter goes up and he practices autorotation. "I'm testing everything."

She's nervous but overcomes it.

"Are you all right?"

"I guess."

"I'll just go once around to find if you're comfortable."

"That would be kind."

Andy does his best to fly smoothly and not to jerk the helicopter.

"Do you want me to land?"

"No, I trust you."

"Los Angeles and its surroundings are vast. Today we're going to the Santa Cruz Island that is part of the Channel Islands. Few tourists go there and even fewer still, go by chopper."

"Is it near Santa Catalina Island?"

"No, that is much further to the south. The Channel Islands are a wildlife National Park that harbors a few indigenous species of flowers and animals such as a gigantic sunflower and the grey fox."

"That's one of my favorite flowers!"

They head for the Pacific Ocean. Celeste absorbs to her memory the grandiose beauty of nature.

They don't talk much; Andy merely points out certain details. She takes some photos of the rugged terrain. She's awestruck by the spectacular beauty and the spectacular setting.

"I can't land there because it's a restricted area," he mentions.

"Look there, it's the Painted Cave. It's one of the biggest sea caves in the world," he points out.

"There are two more islands but I'm famished, so I'm going back to civilization," he says as he turns north towards the Santa Barbara airport. Celeste wasn't that hungry, but she didn't make any fuss.

They land at the airport and he secures the helicopter.

They take off their flight suit. that they stash inside the helicopter. He takes a selfie with her at his side and the helicopter in the background. He transfers the photo to her smart watch. She's quite happy about everything. So far, it's a dream date.

They go to the airport restaurant where he orders a steak and she has a salad.

"Tell me about you," Andy asks.

"I'm twenty two. I'm from a small town in Ontario where I was working as a graphic designer. My best friend in the world is Trish. She insisted that I go to the Dyann Winter show where I was selected to have a makeover done. That's not my thing, because I'm a natural girl at heart, but the TV show called for it, so I went along. Well, the audience was crazy about me. They were in awe of what I had suddenly become. It was a wonderful feeling to have everyone like me and that sensation turned my life around. Before the show, I was a simple girl living an ordinary life and after that splash, I was idolized. Even at the office where I'm working, my bosses noticed me and gave me a permanent job; the firm's main partner not only offered to make me his assistant, he allowed me to take some time-off. It's amazing and wonderful. More and more people are recognizing me and want to talk with me. As you found out, I even have a personal photographer that follows me around. It's thrilling what I'm going through. It seems that I can ask for the moon and people will do anything to give it to me. What girl would refuse that?"

"I wasn't aware of your notoriety, truly, but I can vouch for your beauty. I think that the makeup and the clothes accentuated what you've always been, an exceptionally lovely woman. It seems that people around you have underestimated you."

"You're right Andy. My father regards me as an ordinary plain girl, in fact he told me so recently. After six years together, my ex-boyfriend wanted to abandon me to pursue his career in London. I ditched him, when I learned what kind of guy he was."

"So now, you've come to Hollywood to make the most of your newly found fame."

"I love being loved and appreciated. Yes, I came here in the hope that I'll be able to get into show business. I'm meeting a talent manager who will help me to achieve that. Isn't that exciting!"

"It sure is. That's great."

"So where are we going now?"

"We're going to fly over the Los Padres National Forest mountain range where we'll head east to the Bob Hope airfield where I'll drop you off. I trust you can have your limo pick you up there?"

"Yes I do."

"There are very few roads through the forest, so you'll see a very pristine natural habitat. We'll go around the Sespe Condor Sanctuary; if we're lucky, we might see one or two condor. They're an endangered species so we won't go close to the sanctuary."

"Wow.

This is a wonderful trip I would never have had a few weeks ago!"

"Enjoy it!"

As they approached the condor sanctuary, Andy notes that:"In the Andes, the condor is a sacred bird that represents the Inca and their descendents. There is a legend passed from one generation to the next about dying condors. Rather than hiding themselves on a ledge to die, they climb as high as it can and then they fold theirs wings and crash into the ground."

"That's terrible."

"They prefer suicide to a pitiful agony."

Silence follows.

They land at the airport late in the afternoon.

"It's been an unforgettable day," she says.

He stretches over and kisses her gently on the mouth.

"Keep your flight suit, you'll need it another day."

"Why thanks," she gets out of the helicopter. She waives him goodbye, as he takes off.

It was the best day of my life, she says to herself. She takes off her suit and folds it. She walks to the limousine that takes her back to her hotel.

She leaves a message to Jim Farber that she'll be there tomorrow morning.

She sleeps like a baby without a care in the world.

***

Next morning, her limousine drops her off at Jim Farber's office.

The receptionist has her wait a few minutes.

"You can go in now."

Unbeknownst to Celeste, the phone app, that the limousine driver downloaded, allows Jim to monitor everything she does, so he traced her helicopter tour and other activities; he reasons that if he's to pay a considerable amount of money to build her persona, he deems himself justified in monitoring his investment by following her every move.

"Hi, how is it going?"

"I'm enjoying every second of my stay."

"That's what I want to hear. I gather you've considered my proposition?"

"Yes, I have and I believe that it's fair. However, I'd like to discuss one aspect."

"Which is?" he replies uncomfortably.

"Ten years is a very long time, I would agree to five years, at the most."

"My proposition is very generous, but I need a ten years contract to recuperate my costs."

"It is a generous proposition. I would settle for seven years," she concedes after reflection.

"Nine years. Nobody else would offer you such a deal."

"Eight years," she negotiates.

"Agreed. Here is the contract. Please read it carefully. There are no small characters or legalese sentences."

He changes the duration of the contract and initializes it. She takes her time and understands all the meanings. There is a clause forbidding her to do anything that might be construed as being immoral. She initializes the modification and signs both copies. She keeps one. She will enjoy this level of luxury for eight years, as long as she abides by her training, her proper behavior and her performance obligations. On top of that, she will make bankable money and residuals for future performances.

"Welcome to our family Celeste. You will be living with our group for a month, and then we'll give you the opportunity to show the world what you have become, another you that will conquer everyone's hearts. Anyhow, I'll monitor your every move, so if you need any help we'll be there."

"I can't wait to begin."

He touches a button "Send Sybil in."

A middle age woman with black irises, a mystic face and long brown wavy hair comes in; she's wearing sexy slacks and a loose blouse; Celeste can't tell whether she's of Indonesian, Indian or even of Thai origin.

"Sybil, this is Celeste, our new super star I told you about."

"She's as glamorous as you said."

"It's a pleasure to meet you," Celeste extends her hand.

"My name is Sybil Shan but do call me Sybil."

"Sybil is now your tutor and mentor. She has all kinds of insights to help you. She holds much wisdom. OK you two it's time to get to work. Go on!"

They're on their way to the training studio near Santa Monica Boulevard called the Aquarium.

CHAPTER SEVEN

Rivalry

THE AQUARIUM is a nondescript business occupying the third floor of a Burbank building. Sybil leads Celeste to the end of the corridor, where various direct and indirect lighting brightens her corner office. The corridor is made of electronic privacy glass to allow light to get in and to increase security while maintaining privacy, when desired. The functions of each room, such as the Dance room, the Speech room, the Common room and so forth are identified on the door. Students are practicing in most rooms. There are security cameras covering the entire floor.

"Celeste let me give you an overview of your coaching. As agreed in your contract, this training is confidential. Should you fail to perform according to our standards, your contract will end. We don't intend to make you into an actress, a producer or a playwright. Our aim is to form you to perform presentations, such as advertising a product or introducing a person. It involves a great deal of work, much of it on your own. We'll provide the tools you will need, such as a sound studio or a video studio. You will be constantly judged and corrected; some comments may sound harsh. I will meet you every so often, to review your progress and to discuss your evolution. The contract allows us to pry in all the aspects of your life that will be reviewed, recorded and examined. There are three cameras in this room for example.

Since you will probably not be acting as someone else's character, you'll develop your own persona. I studied closely your performances on the Dyann Winter show and on the Hide & Seek show. You may think that you stood out because you are exceptionally beautiful, which you are, but in fact, another facet of your personality that touched people. You have childish mannerisms and it's in everyone's fundamental nature to love children. You have retained the reactions you had when you were a youth, including sensitivity to emotions, a touch of innocence, a fresh spontaneity and a natural inclination to be playful. Together, these are exceptional qualities. I'd like you to be acutely aware of these aspects, to preserve them and strengthen them. There will always be some folks that will criticize you for behaving like a child for example, but remind yourself that this is what makes you exceptionally attractive."

"It's a revelation to me!"

"Tomorrow put on your high heels and a jumpsuit."

"That's strange, but I'll do it."

"Another day you will receive exercises that incite you to act out your emotions. For example, there are actors who can make funny faces. You will be shown to use your body to represent and to provoke different emotions."

"I didn't expect that!"

"In addition, you must be able to speak standard American. For example, you can't say 'Eh', that Canadians have a tendency to use it to mean 'Isn't it?' we use 'Hey!' in a different context as alternate to 'Hi!' There are differences in written English, but that doesn't concern you for now. To improve your speech, you will register with the Open Learning Initiative from the Carnegie Mellon University and on your own you will follow the American English course."

"Ok."

"A very important ability is to convey emotions that are honest and just. Every day you will go to a special studio that will make videos of you predicting the weather locally and nationally. You and your coach will criticize your video and repeat it as long as necessary. We do not intend to make you a weather girl, though this will be an option. After all, who isn't interested in the weather?"

"Absolutely."

"Composure has made and has broken public figures. You learn to have the best reply to hostile questions. For example, you'll need to reply with confidence if, for example, someone accuses you of having a childish demeanor, which is true.

On occasion, you'll have to lie and feel good about it.

I'll subject you to mock interviews designed to provoke you. If your reply is remarkable, you might even be quoted."

"I wish I could do that!"

"You will learn some notions of etiquette. For example, that involves not being continually in touch with your smart watch. Also don't take any selfies, after all you have a professional photographer following you. Finally, you'll learn to manage your life, such as choosing good accountants and lawyers. You'll learn to plan what you will be doing and how to manage your time and the people you meet; there are some individuals you should strive to get to know, while there are some that you should avoid and some you just can't avoid, like the paparazzi.

The limo driver is watching you. You might be wondering if Andy Czerny is someone for you. Well, we've had him vetted out."

"You're intruding in my private life?"

"We're not intruding we're protecting you. Should anything happen to you it would put the contract in peril. Consider it a kind of insurance."

"I suppose."

"Well that's about all I have to say for now."

"And what should I answer?"

"Answer to what?"

"If someone asks me 'Are you behaving like a child?'"

"Oh, you can just turn it around and ask him if he likes children."

"That's clever."

"You could say 'I love children don't you?'"

"I'll remember that."

"When you might be embarrassed, just smile. It's devastating, believe me."

"Like so?"

"With some practice you'll become an expert, I'm sure! Only the Mona Lisa has achieved that to perfection!"

***

Celeste goes back to the hotel to sort out the adjustments

that are about to shake her life.

She has another massage at the spa.

Jen's comment on Celeste's Ki intrigue her, but she doesn't enquire any further, because she feels good.

She phones home. "Hi mom, how's it going?"

"Celeste it's so good to hear from you. I hope everything is all right."

"Actually, it's going much better than expected. I'm staying at the Triz in West Hollywood. I signed an eight years contract with Jim Farber, the talent manager. I won't be returning home soon, I have to study and to follow some training."

"We're already missing you. I was hoping to see you. Michael is very proud of you. He always talks about you and he follows you on the Web. The video he made of you went viral and Michael got some attention. Here, there's not much happening, except your uncle Jeremy has an awful cold, he had to be taken to the hospital."

"Give him my best regards. I'm sorry but I haven't been present on the social networks. I'll try and inform Michael of what is going on and he'll relay it to you."

"That would be nice, dear."

"I miss home."

"Take care. I love you."

"Love you mom."

This conversation relieves some stress.

She then calls Trish for a couple of hours, relating every detail of what happened. When she gets to talk about the date with Andy, Trish asks, "What kind of shoes did her wear?"

"When he was in the lounge, he had comfortable tan suede shoes with a white rim sole.

They were well adapted for wearing them a long time, without necessarily walking. When we were in the helicopter, he had some shiny black low boots that were easy to remove; they also had a white rim sole."

"He wears the appropriate shoes. At least he didn't wear the same shoes both times! I guess the word would be comfortable. Now that's a good omen."

....
***

Next morning, Celeste phones the Robinson, Johnson & Assoc. office. Mr. Sinclair receives her call. "Good morning this is Celeste."

"Good morning."

"Mr. Sinclair I won't be returning to work."

"You can't do that, you have to give us a delay."

"I'm not a permanent employee. I haven't yet received the status of a permanent employee."

"It's just a matter of paperwork. You will cause us severe damages if you quit without giving us a reasonable delay."

"I waited two years to get a permanent post and officially I haven't gotten it yet."

"You'll hear from our lawyers."

"You can tell your lawyers that my new address is the Triz in Hollywood California."

"Goodbye."

After supper, she logs in her computer and registers, to follow the online speech course that she starts to follow, until she is too tired to continue.

Robinson, Johnson & Assoc. never bothered her again.
***

The Posture room has three walls with mirrors and there's a large frosted window to let in the sunshine. Sybil is dressed in her black jumpsuit and wears high-heel shoes. A young tan skinned beauty with a black ponytail and wearing a jumpsuit is practicing style walking. Sybil introduces her. "Celeste this is Dolores Martinez, another student."

"Hi!"

" Call me Marty."

"Hi Marty!"

Sybil steps in. "Celeste today you'll learn how to walk the catwalk. For many centuries, Western culture has demanded of us women to be modest about our sexuality; in Africa and certain Latin countries, this notion has had a lesser impact. We occidental women walk mostly in a sexless way, supposedly not to provoke men. As for me, that's men's problem not ours!

Now, don't be shy. Put down your arms at your side, rotate your hands by forty-five degrees, away from your body and curl your fingers into your palms when you walk. Your arms will swing naturally and not hit your hips. We naturally tend to hold our arms above the waistline, so you should be comfortable doing this. When you rest your hands on your hips, turn your fingers inward, while your thumb faces forward. Your elbow will stay near your waist, while your forearm will clear your hips. Draw your shoulders back to swing your arms freely. This has the additional effect of thrusting your breasts forward; again don't be ashamed of that natural posture and gait. It's the same with your hips, let them sway and roll. You should walk by placing one foot in front of the other, as if you are taking an alcohol test; this will rotate your hips in a natural manner. Don't look down, be confident and look forward, but don't look straight at people, glance at them. Practice in front of the mirror and free your outer beauty.

Whether you're standing or sitting, stretch your head up, as if it is hanging by a thread. A long neck is very elegant, so keep your head high. It will also help you talk and sing more clearly.

Let's go."

Sybil smiles and leaves the room.

Celeste never paid attention to the way she walked. Sybil's teachings resound in her mind. Celeste gained pride in her femininity and now she would flaunt it with bravado. She practices for hours during that morning, gaining assurance of her posture and gait. She needs more practice to be carefree.

Marty continues the conversation. "I'm going to be the next Miss World."

"Wow!"

"I'm from Puerto Rico. I'm here mainly to practice my English because I have a Spanish accent."

"Your English is very good!"

"It has to be excellent; everything I do has to be excellent. Isn't it why we're here?"

"I suppose."

"I play the classical guitar. I play a perfect Malagueña; you probably heard it sometime."

"I wish I had your talent."

"What talent do you have?"

"None. I'm a graphic designer."

"Can you sing?"

"Not very well."

"Where are you from?"

"I'm from Ontario, Canada."

"What are you training for?"

"Nothing in particular."

"Maybe you will become Miss Canada?"

"I have no such ambition."

"What drives you to be here?"

"Destiny I guess."

"Is that so! Well good luck!"

"Thanks."

"Tell me about Sybil."

"An old employee told me that Sybil was a gifted dancer. She was a first rate performer at the Juilliard Academy in New York where she excelled in contemporary dancing. Apparently, one autumn day while taking a walk in a park, her leg fell in a hole hidden by leaves and the fall caused a Lisfranc fracture-dislocation of the left midfoot. Doctors used pins and wires to reconstruct the bones. She followed the prescribed treatments, including wearing a plaster cast and after a rigid arch support and a walking brace. After much physiotherapy, she was able to walk but she never regained the perfection needed to remain a top performer. A good eye can tell that she walks like a ballerina with her feet slightly angled outwards.

With determination and perseverance, she received her License in Fine Arts. She accepted her tragic fate and began teaching. Only those who were aware of her history could notice her ever so slight limp that will forever remind her of her misfortune.

It seems that she's of a Hindu descent. Nobody ever heard her complain of any pain, because her father was a mentalist and hypnotist who gave her the ability to overcome pain. He could make anyone forget any unbearable pain. He passed his secrets to Sybil who used them judiciously."

"That's enlightening."

***

At noon, Sybil comes in. "How are you doing?"

"Very well. I'm enjoying being a woman. It's kind of liberating to act as a woman and not be prude about it."

Marty is surprised at that comment, because she was always sure of herself.

"That's what I want to hear. Let's go to the Common room," Sybil retorts.

They stroll their way to the Common room, where there is a table with six chairs, a refrigerator, a microwave oven and a counter with cupboards and a sink.

"You can pick up any selection of the healthy foods in the fridge if you'd like.

Celeste I'd like to have a talk when I come back."

Sybil leaves to eat lunch outside.

Celeste takes a container and a drink and goes to a table to eat. Marty and a slender young Asian American man join her.

"Celeste, this is my Sidney."

"Pleasure."

"Would you like to play a game?" Marty enquires.

"Why not!"

"I'll ask a question and you give your best answer. You'll have a minute to cook it up."

"Shoot."

"What would you change in your physical appearance if you could?"

Celeste answers immediately. "I'd lose some weight."

Marty turns to Sidney in a disapproving way. "I wouldn't say that. I'd say that God has made me as I am and I'm thankful of being that way. This is a much more positive idea of my body, don't you think?"

"I should have said that?"

"Let's try another question. If there were one thing you could change in the world, what would it be? As for me, I would get rid of pollution. The world should be a clean place for our children."

After thinking about it for a second, Celeste has an answer, "I would get rid of poverty. Nobody should go hungry and should be homeless."

Sensing that her answer might not be as good as Celeste's reply, Marty changes the subject. "Anyhow we've got to be prepared for all kinds of tests."

Marty switches her attention to Sidney and Celeste has a quiet lunch.

***

Sybil meets Celeste after lunch. "I'm so pleased to be your tutor and mentor. I'd also like to be your confidant because if I'm going to reach your soul, so you need to let me access it. It might seem unprofessional, but we are at a level that's beyond strictly business. Great artists let their guts and heart hang out for everyone to share. You will have to expose your innermost persona and that implies that you have cleaned out all your sensitive facets. You will become vulnerable, but you can deal with it. Is that OK with you?"

"If that's what I need to improve myself, I'll do it."

"Well Celeste, tell me about your feelings."

"Well my pet peeve concerns my ex-boyfriend, Matt. We met when we were in high school and we stayed together until a few months ago. I was certain that we would get married and live the North American dream of the husband, the home, the kids and the predictable suburban life. Everything came crashing to a halt when Matt got a job in London, England and he didn't ask me to accompany him. He dumped me without openly admitting it. This tore me apart. I confronted him with his intentions and he tried to avoid it.

After I appeared on the Dyann Winter show, I became famous and he tried to paddle back and woo me to go with him. I broke up with him, unlike him who didn't have the guts to do it. His betrayal hurt my feelings. I began to distrust people and question their honesty. It also made me angry with men, in general.

This brings me to my father. He had a small job in a car factory and the promotions just passed him by. He became bitter and he carried these frustrations at home. My mother didn't support him and she just complained at everything. She's dissatisfied, at life in general and with my father in particular. I can't stand her anymore. I'm somewhat estranged with my father, because he throws his frustrations on me, whenever he can.

Then there is my brother, Michael. He was always the favorite sibling and I treated him as such, so there's no animosity between us. We get along most of the time, though he's a... Never mind.

I love our dog, Gyp. He's an ordinary stray dog, but I love him."

"I fully appreciate your being honest; it's very revealing of you. I have one remark for the moment; now, you're in the spotlight and you're becoming famous for your beautiful body and demeanor, you should consider another form of beauty; it is to build a beautiful life and let the world enjoy it. This is much more difficult to achieve than physical beauty. I would like you to dwell on that."

"Fine, I will."

***

That afternoon, Sybil gathers Marty, Celeste and two other candidates and leads them to the pronunciation room where they receive instructions and exercises on intonation, accentuation and volume range.

After the session, Sybil gives Celeste tomorrow's address and gives her a recommendation. "Try to have fun with the kids."

"Is that all?"

"Yes. That's all there is to it."

"I'll do my best."

Celeste had never been around children that much, and so this is a novel activity for her.

Once the pronunciation class is finished, Celeste takes the elevator to the main floor where she meets Marty and Sidney. Celeste is very satisfied. "This was a good day. I learned a lot of new things," she tells Marty and Sidney.

"Ditto," Sidney agrees.

Celeste takes her phone and calls for her limousine.

"Calling your boyfriend?" Marty asks.

"No, I'm calling my limo."

"Oh sure, and your butler?" Marty replies, sarcastically.

"Don't you have a limo?" Celeste asks candidly.

"A limo? No. Sidney gives me a lift to my apartment. Don't you have a boyfriend?" Marty snidely responds, a bit vexed.

Marty stays around to see if the claim about the limo is a joke. Celeste realizes that Marty is getting jealous and Celeste becomes uncomfortable. Jealousy fuels Marty and envy forces her to become better.

The limousine does come and Celeste gets in.

Marty is flush with envy. "Why does she have a limo and I have to get a ride? That's unfair."

Sidney tries to support her. "You should ask for equal treatment."

"I will. This is silly, I'm training for Miss World and she has no particular talent and she's the one riding in a limo!"

In the background, Celeste notices the paparazzi, which become aware of this rift and they take telephoto shots that can become smut. Celeste sees one, who's feels lucky to have caught Marty giving the finger to Celeste's departing limousine; who knows, one day it might be worth a small fortune?

***

"This is Andy. How is it going?"

"Great. I'm surprised at the quantity of work involved!"

"Is that so?"

"There's posture, pronunciation, body language..."

"You must be kidding?"

"Really."

"Anyhow, I got some company tickets in the premier seating of the Lakers basketball game Saturday afternoon. Would you accompany me?"

"With pleasure."

She'd never been in a premier seating; it was a fantasy come true.

"I'll pick you up at three."

"Ok."

Celeste could have made Andy wait, to spur his eagerness,

but, after all, she had nothing planned for Saturday and this will surely please her. She feels confident that she will be able to handle him.

She finishes the evening by practicing her American English.

CHAPTER EIGHT

La-La Land

IT'S A BIT STRANGE to see her coming out of a limousine to work at a daycare, but after all this is Hollywood. The personnel was advised that she wouldn't be a regular employee, but that seemed obvious from the onset. Yet Celeste tries to fit in as much as possible, in her designer clothes and perfect makeup. Derek, the photographer, follows her every move and takes a gazillion photos of her with the children.

At first, she emulates the other workers but, understandably, they wanted to teach skills to the kids, whereas Celeste plays with them and is carefree. She doesn't realize it, but the interaction with children relaxes her and heightens her sensitivity to various primal instincts. She simply bathes herself in childish playfulness and serenity.

***

Friday morning, she goes back to the Aquarium. Marty and Sidney avoid her, but she isn't fazed and she goes about her business. This day is devoted to personal affairs. The candidates learn personal finance, tax practices, retirement planning, investments, legal considerations and the like. Sure, it's boring and tedious; Celeste appreciates every second of it. Marty couldn't care less, because she already had a financial advisor for these nerdy things.

When Celeste leaves at the end of the afternoon, some other candidates watch her get into her limousine.

True to her assigned schedule, Celeste spends the evening studying American English.

Saturday afternoon, Akarsh gives his approval to the black slacks with a crimson printed motif, a black sweater with a scarlet mohair scarf and a slick burgundy lipstick to match. Andy arrives in the latest BMW™, kisses Celeste and opens the door for her.

"You look marvelous. With that outfit there's no chance of losing you in the crowd!"

They get in and drive to the Lakers stadium; Andy is proud to show off his sports car, accompanied by his latest conquest. Celeste enjoys being paraded as a trophy girlfriend.

As soon as they get out of the car, Derek, Akarsh's photographer, follows them and starts his work. The atmosphere and the mood would enhance the photos, especially since this opportunity enthralls Celeste. "The Lakers are playing against the Toronto Raptors. So, who are you rooting for?"

"Haven't you noticed that I'm wearing a black and red outfit? I root for the Raptors. I DO come from Ontario!"

They walk in amidst the excitement.

Andy recognizes one of his friends "Celeste I'd like you to meet Dave. And this is Cynthia."

"Hi."

"Hey!"

"Call me Cyn."

"Sin. Dave is lucky!" Celeste jokes.

They heard that joke umpteen times before, but they still laugh.

There is the famous yellow and purple court with the Lakers dance squad, exhibiting their long loose hair and scanty outfits.

Cynthia turns to Celeste. "I was a Lakers girl a few years back."

"Back then, I went to see her dance more than to watch the game." Dave admits.

"You do have that look and that 'It's good to be alive' smile."

The four laugh, root and cheer all game long. Andy drinks beer and Celeste lemonade.

The Raptors win, so the three Lakers fans hound Celeste. "Oh, you were just lucky. We have the best team."

"Luck follows me." Celeste concedes.

At the end of the game, they kiss and the groups part their way.

Andy is as proud as he can be. It's a feeling Celeste never had before, while she was going out with Michael.

They get in the car and Andy drives her to the Triz. He gets out of the car to open her door.

"Thanks Andy I had a wonderful date."

He kisses her on the mouth amorously. His powerful arms squeeze her and envelope her; she feels safe and protected. It is a lasting moment, before he lets go. He looks into her eyes and she looks down, bashfully.

She lets go her arm and walks to the hotel entrance. With a geisha-like move she learned at the Aquarium, she stops and looks back at him with a subtle smile. His heart nearly stops, as he is taken by her sweetness. She enters the hotel and goes to her room, where she takes a shower and goes to bed.

***

Sunday morning at ten, she goes to the service at St. Jude church in Burbank.

She returns to the Triz in her limousine.

That afternoon, she calls home to talk to her mother and to Michael. Her relatives have been following her on the social network that Jim Farber, who makes sure her every move is candied and commented, took over.

Then, she calls Trish to whom she details the events of every second of her week. Then, it gets to Andy, the juicy part Trish has been waiting to hear. "What is he like?"

"He's a jock, no doubt about it."

"That isn't your style."

"I'm aware of that, but there's something about him."

"What?"

"I don't know. There's this animalistic characteristic about him."

"You're attracted in the animal in him?"

"Maybe I am?"

"You're crazy."

"Maybe I am!"

"He isn't for you. I can tell that from here."

"I feel safe when I'm with him."

"You need a bodyguard. That's what you need."

"I can't help it; I'm attracted to him. He's proud of me when I walk next to him. It's quite different than with Matt."

"He treats you like a trophy then?"

"Well yes, I guess. We went out to a basketball game and he introduced me to his friend, Dave and his wife, Cynthia. She was a superb former Lakers cheerleader and she was visibly satisfied as her role of a trophy wife."

"Celeste, you're much better than that. Get a hold of yourself. This is the first guy you met there. You'll go out with loads of guys. Don't fall for the first hunk."

"He IS a hunk. I can smell his sweat."

"What is wrong with you?"

"He desires me. He's the hunter and I'm his prey. Next time we go out, he's going to move in on me, I'm sure."

"You're the artsy sensitive type, and he probably has never been in a museum. He's the kind of guy that would muscle you."

"I wouldn't mind that, in fact I was fantasizing about it."

"Have you gone crazy?"

"We're like the opposites of a magnet, we attract each other. He's completely different but hey, he's a guy."

"He'll contradict you and you'll fight all the time."

"Won't that be exciting? Aren't you tired of your predictable and safe life where nothing much happens? Don't you want to experience the unpredictable? I'm living it and I wouldn't miss it for the world. I like a man that's a challenge. I want a man who likes taking risks and who loves adventure."

"That man will eventually cheat on you. You don't want that."

"I'd rather risk that, than a guy who's always afraid."

"What's gotten into you? You're not the graphic designer who left here."

"I can't agree with you more. I'm a new person with a vision of my future. Before I was a walking carpet and everyone walked over me without a care. Now I can assert myself."

"It seems to me that your Andy will walk over you."

"It's not the same thing."

"Take care sweetie."

"You too."

***

Monday morning, Celeste meets Sybil for a review. "Celeste, how is your stay in La-La Land?"

"Wonderful and exciting."

"That's what we want to hear. We're very satisfied with your progress. You have shown determination and steady work. You are building your persona well."

"It is a lot of work, but I enjoy it. I admit that I couldn't get this kind of training elsewhere."

"And how was your time with the children?"

""I was surprised that it was so natural."

"An observer reported that you immersed with the youngsters very well. We'd like to you to adopt a similar approach, wherever you are. Adults are grown-up children after all. From now on, we'd like you to play with mature adults, as you would do with those children. Life is a game and you will be a cheerleader. People need to be encouraged and to have their pending decision reinforced."

"My brother, Michael, is always having fun with his apps. I'm sure he'd agree with you."

"So far, you've been Akarsh's halo girl. We want you to continue doing this for other products. A halo is a kind of golden circle that was drawn over the head of saints and gods, much like an "it" girl. This brings up the halo concept, where everything the haloed person does becomes a model to imitate. You must lead an exemplary life, in the sense that everyone will dream of living your life and owning what you will own. Nothing you will do, can be wrong. You must strive to be an ideal, women will want to become like you and men will want to become your friend. You have done this spectacularly well with Akarsh's fashion line, and we want to enlarge this. Now a fabulous jeweler wants you to flaunt his precious stones. Here is a small necklace you might need for casual wear."

"Really!" Celeste is enthralled as she delicately clips on the necklace.

"It's a fauna and flora design, we were sure you would like."

"That's very thoughtful of you."

"We believe in you. At first, you will be an online host for this jewelry. It'll be a little tedious at the beginning, but we're sure you'll learn quickly.

You'll have to find an apartment. It should be spacious enough to entertain people. We'd appreciate it if, every week, you would mingle with influential and powerful people who take notice of what you wear and the luxurious life you have."

"I'll do my best."

"Now do you have any question or complaint?"

"Well there is one thing bothering me." Celeste says after gaining her composure.

"What is it?"

"Well it seems that I'm the only one who has a limo with a chauffeur. I can see that the other candidates are peeved off about this."

"You'll just have to deal with that. It's part of your training."

"How should I deal with it? Please help me."

"It depends on you, hon. A certain number of people remain aloof, some express disdain. Some want to remain friendly. Some have a mixed reaction. There's no perfect solution. You'll have to find your way and that will become part of your persona. Who do you want to be perceived as?"

"I guess I'm the friendly type."

"If you do that, you will inevitably hurt the pride of those who aren't favored. Those who are will expect more. That might end in a worse outcome."

"It'll go against my nature."

"You should recognize that your whole life is being fashioned by your new circumstances and we encourage you to adapt. You've had the chance of being an exceptional beauty. Use that advantage. Some people are born rich and they use their wealth. Some men are charismatic and they convey a sense of trust they use to promote their career.

If I may use a comparison, nature allows certain trees to bear particular fruits that can be gathered and eaten. Your beauty is a gift, and it is your privilege to profit from it and to have others enjoy it. Don't waste it. And, for heaven's sake, don't be ashamed of it!"

"Won't that be manipulative?"

"We are being manipulated by those who have money and power, so what is wrong to manipulate by beauty and sex?"

"Do I have to answer that right now?"

"Remind yourself that you have already taken the steps that will improve your life. Now you will acquire the mindset to accomplish your full potential."

"I feel like a butterfly that's coming out of its cocoon."

"Fly and stun the world!"

Accustomed to a safe lifestyle, Celeste is trust into a competitive and power-driven world.

***

Celeste acts in her usual friendly and smiling self towards the other candidates. Most of them have retained a sympathetic attitude towards her, some have the "What makes you so special?" look and a few including Marty have the "So you're better than us" attitude. Celeste doesn't want to show that their conduct doesn't affect her own behavior. She's certain that a good part of these negative reactions is the result of Marty's scornful comments.

When Celeste sees Sidney in the corridor, she stares at him for a moment and smiles; at first, he's confused. This is an exercise in power for Celeste and it works.

Another time she crosses him in the corridor and again she stares at him and smiles, as if to say "Hi handsome". He feels uneasy and he returns the stare and smile.

She catches him sitting alone in the Common room. "May I sit here?" she asks, pointing to a seat in front of him.

"Go ahead," he responds, visibly agitated.

She sits down. "How was your morning?"

"It went well," he answers thinking 'She's not as bad as Marty claims!'

"Marty didn't tell me what you're goal is."

"I'm going to be an online host."

"An online host!"

"I'll advertise products on TV shopping networks. I'll have to convince people to buy anything, from hair removers to all-purpose glue. I have an exceptional voice that conveys a sense of trust and authority so this is a natural outlet for me. I could be a sportscaster or a direct-response TV salesman for example."

"What would you like to sell me?"

Sidney is embarrassed. "I don't know!"

Marty approaches the two. "What is going on?"

"We're just having small talk," Sydney answers defensively.

"Why don't you mingle with your own kind?"

"Sidney is my kind of a guy," Celeste replies, "he's friendly!" Sidney is touched but doesn't let it show.

"Shove off, I have serious stuff to talk."

Celeste concedes and moves to another table. "See you later Sidney."

"Why were you talking to that pretentious little bitch?" Celeste overhears.

"She was nice to me."

"Nice my eye. She's just trying to piss me off."

***

Back in her hotel, Celeste reflects on her day. She isn't interested in Sidney, it's just a way to get back at Marty. True she acted against her character, but she felt good about it. Why should she remain as a passive victim-like being, that everyone around her plays with? She didn't want to harm anyone, but then, responding in kind, was gratifying. Would she become a bitch, she asks herself? She could certainly act as a bitch, but that didn't mean that she was one. She learned to play one role of real life.

***

She calls Trish. "Hi!"

"How is it going dear?"

"It's a whole new world I'm trying to get accustomed to. Frankly, I'm getting homesick. My brother isn't here to tease me, my mother isn't here to criticize what I do, and the dog has probably forgotten me. It's strange how little things take on a great importance with distance and time. I love the smell of home breakfast in the morning. I miss jogging peacefully with the wind gently stoking my face. Small things, like the floor cracking when I walk on a certain spot in the living room, caressing the dog while he licks me, the sound of Michael slamming the doors, mother stroking her hair as she listens to the TV."

"Are you done? Honey, you're in paradise!"

"So they tell me."

You'll come and visit us soon?"

"Not right now, but as soon as I can."

"At least you have me. I constantly follow what you are doing and I envy every second. I wish I were in your shoes, with all that glitter and glam. And to say this would never happened, if I hadn't prodded you to go to the Dyann Winter show!"

"Actually, I have some news. I'm going to be a halo girl. Though I agreed to do it, I don't feel prepared at all at being with a person or a product onlookers will associate with, as glamour and luxury."

"They believe in you, so they must have a reason, especially after investing all that money on you!"

"I suppose, but I don't have much confidence. I'm still a graphic designer, not a glam girl. This is going too fast for me, I don't think I can handle it for long."

"Cool down; you can do it if you want. Sure at first you'll have to adapt, but I'm sure you can overcome your fears."

"I'll be shaking all the time."

"You've been in front of an audience before, and you did great. This is similar."

"That was different. I was more of a spectator than a performer."

"They'll show you how. Give it a chance."

"It'll take all of my energy."

"Love you dear."

"You too."

***

During the week, she learns the rudiments of her job. One of the aspects is to promote products as an online host, like Sydney. She has to understand the product and its context, so that she has to be able to relate testimonials and short histories of past clients and their family members who are happy with the product. She'll have to keep attention on the subject by moving it, to keep the audience looking at the product. She will praise its qualities and characteristics for hours without losing the excitement and enthusiasm, so she should sincerely fall in love with the product. She has to be very expressive by smiling, clapping hands to attract attention and even screaming with joy and thrill. She has to express an urgency to buy the product.

Callers are filtered but she has to be personal with them by befriending them and complimenting them. She has to reassure the listeners that the choice is wise and popular.

She has to master these practices in a week and she feels overwhelmed.

***

Though she still flirts with Sydney during the week, she doesn't overdo it. Everyone keeps his distance, except for Sydney who is hesitating.

***

At the end of the week, Nick Dash phones her. "Celeste, this is Nick. How's life?"

"Great."

"I enjoyed our conversation and I'd like to see you again. I'd like to invite you to a private tour of Hollywood next Saturday. It includes an all star showbiz visit and all of the amazing spots of LA. It would be a great way to get you better acquainted with this place."

"Thanks a lot Nick, but I'll pass; since we met, I've been pondering on something you said. You told me I lacked passion. I'd like to talk about it."

"It would be my pleasure. How about Friday at 8 at the For Us cocktail bar?"

"OK."

"I'll see you there. Bye."

"Bye."

***

Celeste arrives a little late, as ladies must do. He's dressed in a smoking, as gentlemen must wear. They both smile. Soft music is playing in the background.

"You look astonishing."

"Thank you."

"I took the liberty of ordering you a Shirley Temple. If you don't mind, tell me about yourself, your life at home, your aspirations, your fears."

"Actually, I had a rather ordinary life, up until the Dyann Winter show. I have one sibling, my brother, Michael. He's two years younger and he's studying. I live in a comfortable house in the suburbs. I go to church regularly with my mother, Alice. My father, Brent divorced my mother a few years ago because they didn't get along anymore. He isn't very nice; he's rude. I admit that I dislike my father. He belittles me as often as he can. He actually takes pleasure in ridiculing me in front of others and my mother just didn't bother stopping my father's harassment. I hated both of my parents, my father for doing it and my mother for being indifferent to it. Maybe my father feels better by humiliating me, I don't know. He doesn't care that he constantly hurts my feelings. I never got used to it. Sometimes he makes me cry and he isn't even sorry that he did it. He treats me like a child that can't control itself. I told him that he hurts me, but he doesn't give a damn. He's a bad father.

My mother criticizes everything. There's nothing good around her and she feels helpless. She even excuses my father, as if she has no influence on him.

I have a dog, Gyp that I rescued from the pound.

In high school, I met Matt. He later studied finance and when he got a job in London and he didn't want me to accompany him there. To make a story short, I dumped him.

I'm a graphics designer and I worked in Toronto in a part time job. My best friend is Trish and we met every weekday at a restaurant where we had lunch together. I tell her everything; even now.

Trish tricked me to go on a show, where I had a makeover that transformed my life. Somehow, everyone was convinced that I was drop-dead gorgeous. They provided clothing, money and everything a girl could ask for. I don't have any ambition other than live a happy family life, but the events pushed me to this extraordinary adventure.

I met a jock in Hollywood, named Andy. Even though I'm terrified of heights, he convinced me to go along with him in a helicopter ride. I managed to control my fear...."

"Good for you!"

"I signed a contract with a talent manager, Mr. Farber, who sent me to a training center. I learned quite a few things, but the other students they call 'candidates' are envious of me because I have better conditions than they have. My mentor, Sybil, told me that my manager wants me to get accustomed to this kind of reaction. Anyhow, he found me a job as a host on an online network. I've tried, but I just don't have any passion selling skirts and appliances. You told me that I lacked passion and you're right, especially for that kind of work. I do love being a graphics designer but not to the point that I would put my family life in jeopardy. This is why I called you. What should I do?"

"You agreed to be where you are, so you do have a motivation; perhaps it was a secret desire of yours?"

"Every girl dreams of being popular."

"There you go! Perhaps you have a fear of the unknown that paralyses you. Perhaps your manager has a confidence in you, that you lack in yourself?"

"Maybe you're right."

"You need to believe in yourself."

"Yes. During your childhood you believed that you were just an ordinary girl but the world has proven that you are gorgeous. You are capable of wonderful things, but you must believe in yourself. Your passion will emerge, once you believe that what you're going through is real. Believe that you are doing is what you were meant to do! You are here for a greater purpose in life and you should embrace it!"

Celeste is thrown aback. "How can I believe in myself, after being crushed over and over again by my father? My father pounded on me that I was good for nothing."

"You're angry with him. That's all right because young adults have to sever their dependence of their parents, but use it to prove that you can succeed. Channel that emotion in a positive way. This is where you'll get the strength of your passion."

"Are you sure?"

"Yes. Many people that are born dirt poor and they use that realization to motivate themselves. They have the choice of letting poverty put them down, or of trying with their might to overcome it and to prosper. They don't use poverty as an excuse, but as a motivator."

"I'll have to think about that."

"I'll tell you more about myself. My family was poor. My father left my mother when I was five so I didn't know him. He never came back in our lives and he never helped my mother. I have two sisters, Tess and Vivian. Mom worked tirelessly to pay the bills. Most of all she kept motivating us to study and to succeed. We kept an intensity of purpose because of her persistent encouragement. Tess became a violin player and she plays in the Philadelphia Philharmonic. Vivian became a psychologist. Mom still works. She monitors all of us; she's our driving force; she keeps us focused. She constantly instills the passion in me and I'm deeply indebted to her.

Show them that you can surmount their negativity and become a winner."

Celeste doesn't answer.

She notices the distinctive flowery scent of his cologne that provides a frame of reference to this conversation.

She keeps remembering the times her father made nasty comments about her, that made her cry and even despair. Yet, she pulled through. She had the strength of character to do that. Now she will show him who she is, compared to what he is, an unhappy soul.

Nick recognizes that he jolted her, so he changes the subject because he doesn't want to stir up any more emotion.

"So now you feel at ease travelling by helicopter."

"It feels unreal, hovering over the city and the countryside. After a while, when I relaxed, I enjoyed it tremendously. It was liberating. I was like a swallow gliding through the air."

"You are a wonderful lady with an exciting life in front of you."

"I'm terribly lucky and I'm grateful to all those around me who encourage me. It gives me the energy I need."

"Well, I guess you are on your way."

She gets up and smiles; he stands. "Thanks for your advice Nick."

"Celeste it is been a privilege. Call me anytime."

She presents her cheek, which he kisses.

"Take care, Celeste. I'm here for you if you need me!"

Her emotional memory of a father-like figure that she longed for, governs this moment.

CHAPTER NINE

Primal Instincts

CELESTE ACCEPTS A DATE next Saturday morning to fly with Andy to the San Diego zoo. It's another opportunity to enjoy life. She senses a need to express her liberation from the past. There are so many pent-up frustrations waiting to be exorcized, such as a condescending father, an egotistical boyfriend and a dead-end job. Andy is a jock; so what? She's still attracted to that man who doesn't seem to be bothered with any lingering problem. He seems to be a What You See Is What You Get guy. He's not the type of person who questions anything, he just tries to be fun and to have fun.

Celeste doesn't hesitate to go to a zoo. It isn't the ideal place for animals, but in our world, where humans care little about nature, a zoo is a concrete reminder that we share the earth with other species and we should be aware of their presence and our role as masters of the earth. If it weren't for zoos, many endangered animals would have been irrevocably wiped out. She sincerely believes that there are redeeming advantages that outweigh the callousness of keeping animals in limited enclosures.

As usual, she looks stupendous in her cargo pants and loose blouse. Andy is thrilled to see her again and he kisses her unabashedly. She likes his determination and his confidence.

Soon they're on their way to the San Diego International Airport, next to the zoo. He takes the time to fly around San Diego and to visit over the sights, all the way the Mexican border. They get to destination, take a cab and enter the zoo a few minutes later. She quickly attracts onlookers. "Are you a movie star?" "Where did I see you?" "Could you sign an autograph?" Andy manages to make their way out of the gathering crowd. Derek, Akarsh's photographer, is there, not missing an opportunity.

"What's your favorite animal Andy?" Celeste asks.

"Dogs I guess. Maybe pandas. There are some, a little further." He isn't an animal aficionado.

"Well for me, it's the Macaw. I love those types of parrots, with their pure colors. They're so smart. They get to live up to seventy-five years. The problem is that Macaws are an endangered species and I want to protect them as much as I can. It would be very sad to have them disappear from our planet and it would be as if we let part of our soul die or let some musical note disappear. Wouldn't that be terrible?"

"It sure would."

At least, he didn't disagree.

"We should protect the forests, where the animals live, but poor people want to make money quickly so they cut the trees," Celeste adds.

"Not only poor people!"

"You know what I mean. Even pandas are endangered."

"They come from China don't they?"

He isn't interested in animal survival, but is it that important for their relationship?

Celeste continues: "Yes and they only eat bamboo. I love most animals; however, I don't like insects and reptiles. To me, insects are a nuisance and reptiles are disgusting. I suppose that I should like them, I just don't. The bee would be an exception, after all they pollinate plants. Maybe I could add the beetle bug and the cricket. How about you?"

"I like animals in general. I don't dislike any because apparently they all have a function on earth."

"He might not be that bad after all," she thinks to herself.

"I'd like to protect the endangered animals. Humans have destroyed or changed their natural habitat and that's sad. Animals also should be able to live in a safe environment."

"It's not an easy task."

"No but we have to keep trying."

They don't argue. Though their opinions differ, at least he's not disagreeing. There's room to convince him.

They pass the elephants and the "urban jungle" to see the pandas. Celeste relishes at admiring those beautiful animals. Andy is enthusiastic; he came here mostly to please her and to have a nice day. Apparently, he doesn't want to antagonize her.

"I also love flowers and plants. They hold many secrets," Celeste confides. "For example one-third of the orchids actually mimic insects, such as wasps and bees, by looking like the female that the male will try to copulate with. Some even send an insect sexual odor. Isn't that mindboggling?"

"It's vicious, if you ask me."

"They're not vicious at all. The orchids are only trying to get pollinated. Isn't that worth appreciating?"

"You must particularly like the endangered species."

"How did you guess?" she replies amicably.

"It's an admirable goal! I admit I don't have much interest for that stuff."

"Don't you care about nature?"

"I love nature, but it isn't my business. Many scientists, engineers and politician care for these things. I let them do their job."

"Here are the pandas."

"Everybody loves pandas!"

"Aren't they adorable! To look at them is worth the trip. You had a great idea in coming here."

"You told me you liked nature, so here we are."

She kisses him spontaneously. "You're very thoughtful."

They're both taken by the moment.

He kisses her back while his hands pull her hips towards him.

She feels that his masculinity is being aroused and that stimulates her.

He realizes that he will soon become uncomfortable and so he releases her.

"Hmmm!" he murmurs with satisfaction.

She resumes breathing and gathers her composure. This isn't the place or the time for such an intimate feeling. It was a bit embarrassing being kissed in that way. She hopes Derek didn't catch that episode. She feels good to be kissed by a real man who wants her.

He takes her hand. She lets him do it. His hand is large and he has a firm grip, as if he would never let her go.

They reach the "Northern Frontier".

"The polar bear and the penguins are in peril because of global warming."

"You want to save the world don't you?"

"I might as well try. At least we have to do what we can, don't you think?"

"I'm for that."

She's content that he's beginning to get a sense of the human custodianship of nature.

They walk slowly reflecting more on their burgeoning relationship, than on the animals.

They arrive at the aviary, where they admire a flock of macaws with their blue, green, red and yellow color. It's a delight for everyone.

"I agree that these birds need our protection."

"Once you see the nature's wonders in front of you, your perspective changes."

"I had never considered that seriously."

"Our visit was worthwhile!"

"Sure was."

She's attracted to the smell his manly scent that's intense after their escapade under the Southern California sun.

At the end of the visit Andy tells her:"I've taken the liberty of reserving a table for two at the Hotel Del Coronado restaurant. Since you are new to California, this is a famous place. It looks like a huge cone with a rotunda beneath, where the restaurant is located. It has a breathtaking view of the Pacific Ocean. It has a long history including the filming of Some Like It Hot with Marilyn Monroe. This will be a memorable experience."

"I can't wait!"

They reach the restaurant and sit down to behold a panoramic view of the sea. They start with small talk, but Andy mostly speaks about himself, his home and his ambitions. She listens but she's more interested in the tone of his manly voice, the rhythm of his sentences and his verbal and physical expressions.

Andy takes a small box from his pocket and offers it, "Celeste, I'd like you have this as a reminder of this date."

She takes the box and opens it. It's a gold pendant with an image of a panda.

"Thank you so much Andy," she answers as she kisses him.

Once diner is over, they take a stroll slowly on the beach and watch the sunset slowly drop beneath the horizon, to reveal a star spangled sky. He takes her hand. She feels his powerful grip. She often daydreamed about such an idyllic situation. They walk and breathe in step. She senses the oncoming events and she's uncertain.

As he's about to kiss her, suddenly she runs away giggling. He's surprised and after hesitating, he runs after her. As he nearly reaches her, she avoids him and heads for the sand dunes. He puts more effort and he manages to grab her after awhile. They kiss to the sweet rhythm of the waves reaching the shore, savoring every moment, as if it were eternity. He dares to pull her onto the sand where they continue their amorous courtship. He is on top of her, squeezing her, embracing her and kissing her. Her legs lose their feistiness.

"Let's go to my home."

She doesn't reply.

He gets up and tends his hand. She reaches for him and she gets up. They keep embracing each other all the way to the airport, where they get in the helicopter. They take off and enjoy the nocturnal scenery where the stars of the heavens blend with the stars of Hollywood. It's magic! They can't help but savor every instant and share their love of life.

They head back to Torrance airfield.

They get in his BMW and he drives to his place in Palos Verdes, Malaga Cove district. Sculptured bushes replace the grass to save water. They drive from the street directly in the garage, after waiting for the door to open. Already she's impressed. It's a three level Spanish style property, where the garage is on the bottom floor. They climb to the main floor and a large living room with a fireplace adjoining an unobstructed view on a baseball park across the street and the Pacific Ocean further away awaits them. Her heart is throbbing. The moonlight flickers on all of the rooftops overlooking the coast.

"This is my home," Andy proudly says. "As far as I'm concerned, it's an ideal family home, close to everything, in an exceptionally nice neighborhood. All I need is a wife and kids."

"I never thought of you as a family man!"

"So far, I've been busy with my career. I have to travel extensively and that doesn't help."

"You only meet women at airports," she quips.

"You got it."

She walks around the main floor to a sun porch next to the family room. At the back, a deck with a barbecue and a slope provide much privacy to the backyard. The galley style kitchen has all the commodities and is next to the elegant dining room that gives to the living room.

They sit down on a comfortable sofa.

Andy gets up, puts on soft romantic music and asks, "Do you want something to drink?"

"I suppose some wine would be fine."

He goes to a wine cooler in the dining room, and takes out a bottle of red wine. "I'm sure you'll like this Beringer Private Reserve."

He brings two glasses and pours some wine. "To your health!"

They sip the wine slowly while listening to the music. The living room has huge windows overlooking the bay. The moon is high and its reflection illuminates the waves that gently ripple to shore. He kisses her with passion; his tongue penetrates her mouth and licks her tongue; she shares his quest. He nibbles her ear lobes and it transports her as she hears his tongue splashing and she feels his sweet breath overtaking her.

He unbuttons her blouse and pets her throbbing breasts. He massages her ears with his tongue while telling her that he craves for sex. This goes on for a while.

They take a pause and sip a little more wine.

"Let's go and take a shower together," he proposes.

She follows him. They climb to the second floor and enter the master bedroom. He dims the lights. They undress, but she covers her breasts with her arms.

She doesn't dare look directly at his penis, but she manages to notice that it's already aroused. It's a strong masculine proof of desire.

"Let me go first," she says.

She starts the shower and gets in. The water falls like the rain during a passing summer rainfall and she opens her arms to its gentle water.

He knocks softly at the door: "Can I come in?"

"Come on in!" she responds with a smile, coyly trying to hide her breasts.

They wash individually at first.

"Let me wash your back!" he asks.

She allows him to massage her back.

His hands slowly caress her entire body.

He places her hand on his private parts and she enjoys the feel of his manhood that she cuddles, as she washes. To her contentment, his penis becomes a rigid rod, full of vigor and strength.

He takes her head with his hands and approaches her mouth impatient to kiss her lips as her head tilts back. She feels his erect penis come towards her as the water engulfs them. They lose themselves in a world of sensuality, their hands slowly caressing their partner, discovering and appropriating every part of each other's body.

He pinches her nape with his lips.

He flutters the tip of his tongue on her hair.

He bites her neck, as a wild animal going for the kill; he brands her with a hickey or two.

"Don't do that," she complains.

She can fell his manliness stiffening even more.

He pushes her down gently, signaling that he would like her to give him fellatio. It is a moment she apprehended, yet that pleases her very much. She strokes his virile erect penis gently, while she inserts it as far as she can in and out of her mouth. His moan encourages her and she quickens the rhythm. He grunts in satisfaction. With her other hand she cuddles his scrotum. He puts a hand at the back of her head and he pushes it, as the penis reaches the back of her throat. They are enthralled in an intense sexual union for an indefinite amount of time, for it has no more meaning.

He leads her to get up and hands her a towel.

They look at each other in the eyes, one pair as eager as the other's eyes. Her cheeks are taut and flush. He's ready to lay on her, with his overwhelming desire to make love.

He lights a few candles and an incense stick.

He prepares the bed.

He put on a condom.

They snuggle in and resume kissing and embracing. His hand seeks her firm tits and he deliberately rubs her nipples that swell and stiffen. She watches him, as his mouth seeks to suckle each of her tits, like an eager baby. He ravishes and craves them. While he's squeezing a breast and its nipple, the other hand slides down her body to her waiting vagina. He rubs her lower lips and she can't help but begin to moan. Now her clitoris is empowered and its lips are flush with blood.

His finger penetrates the now thoroughly lubricated vagina. His finger rocks back and forth. She enjoys every stroke.

His head descends and he licks her clitoris, while his finger swings in and out, sometimes reaching the G spot.

"Oh my god! Oh my god!" she cries. A few seconds later, she reaches orgasm and releases a short scream. This pleases him and encourages him to go faster.

"Fuck me! Fuck me!" she begs.

He pulls her towards him and inserts his impatient cock in her slippery vagina.

He fucks her in the missionary position, looking at her face filled with ecstasy and her complete abandonment. His weight pounds her pelvis repeatedly in a constant rhythm until she feels an orgasm, as she shrieks.

He stops and guides her to place herself in the doggy position.

She looks back and sees his big, long and strong cock. She waits with anticipation to be penetrated.

He slaps her butt, making it more sensitive; it pleases her, as her butt becomes more receptive to the oncoming tide and she smiles.

Slowly and forcefully, he fucks her.

He pushes in, as far as he can. She feels a great satisfaction.

He grabs her long hair and he pulls her towards him. Each time he pushes in, he applies more pressure. She shakes in delight. He keeps doing this endlessly until she reaches a second orgasm and releases another blissful scream.

He's persistent and she keeps having more orgasms, till she is drained of her energy:"Please stop." He obliges and quietly lies besides her.

He removes the condom.

He takes her hand and places it on his cock. She strokes it. Then, she gives him a blowjob, sucking his cock, licking it and playing with his balls. She adjusts the rhythm and he becomes all tensed up. He's going to come. She doesn't quit; he shakes and groans until he ejaculates in her mouth. She lets the cum drip away on her neck and breasts.

She looks at him, glad he had a happy ending.

"That was a good fucking session," he remarks.

"You liked fucking me?" she asks with a provoking smile.

"Yeah. You're a great lady."

She smiles.

He gets up and she notices that he gained more self-assurance, as if he made her his and she was his, to do as he wished.

"There's some wine left. Do you want some?"

"I'll just finish my glass."

"You don't want to drink too much because you know what might happen," he says with a laugh.

They finish their glass and they relax.

They get in bed and cuddle up. They are so fired up that they can't go to sleep. Now that their guards are down and they are intimate and trustful, they find comfort in spilling their most private thoughts.

"There's something I've never told anyone," Celeste advances.

"What's that?"

"I hate my mother. I hate her, I hate her. The only thing she's good for is to criticize. She doesn't like this, she doesn't like that. No wonder my father left her, not that he's any better. He must have been frustrated hearing those criticisms day in and day out. Now she watches the news and she doesn't stop rambling from the time I get up until she goes to sleep. I hear this chatter and it gets on my nerves. I can't stand it anymore. I'm sooo glad that I haven't seen her for the past weeks. I wonder how I could ever go back there."

"That was a mouthful!"

"She could have encouraged me, but nooo. She only tells me what I should do, what I should wear, who I should see. Everything is negative. I'll never succeed, I never do what I should and I never say what is right. What on earth did I do to deserve this mother? Every time I go to church, I pray that she might one day reduce her constant negative comments but my prayers go unanswered.

I don't hate my dad, I don't like him, but I kind of love him. He's been nasty with me, sure, but who wouldn't be after living with my mother? I guess he's a little fed up with women, because he would have had a girlfriend by now. He must be frustrated with life in general. Lucky, he has Michael to talk to and comfort him. They're more buddies than father and son. I wish I had a good relationship with my parents. Michael and dad even go to hockey games and to sports bars together. Michael and I get along pretty well. At least, he minds his own business. I treat him like a prince which kind of helps, but he's all right.

Now I never talked about Matt, did I?"

"Your ex-boyfriend?"

"Yeah. He's the kind of guy that make women distrust men. He always took me for granted. Whatever he wanted, I went along. I did whatever he asked, to please him and what did he do? He wanted to dump me; the bastard had a mind to dump me. Did I deserve this? No. Did he deserve me? No. I hate him."

She takes the pillow and beats Andy with it.

"Hey! Hey! I'm not Matt. I'm Andy, remember?"

She keeps on going. He joins the fight, but she's unabashedly aggressive while he defends himself. She gets up and pushes him. She beats him on the floor. He gets up and runs after her. She goes down to the main level and runs around in the living room and in the kitchen where she splashes him with water. He takes a hold of her and makes her stop. He's about to kiss her when she slips away and throws fruits and vegetables at him that were in a bowl. He falls on the floor. "Aw."

She's calms herself and comes close to him. "Does it hurt?"

"My arm."

"Let me look at it."

As she gets within reach, he grabs her. "Come here you."

"You were faking. I should have guessed. That's not fair."

"You've been a bad girl, you need a spanking."

They wrestle and he manages to control her and to spank her on the butt; as he does that, he gets an erection that she senses. The more he hits her, the more rigid he gets and the more submissive she is. When he stops, she says, "Are you finished?"

"Yes."

She turns towards him and gives him a blowjob, sucking as hard as she can. He moans and groans in pleasure. She toys with his balls and his prick. When he's about to come, he get up and turns her in the doggy position, but this time he pushes her chest down, rotating her ass towards the sky. Like a jackhammer, he pushes his cock in her, as if to crush her. She moans her contentment and begs for more.

"Fuck me!"

"Fuck my pussy!" she adds.

He does his utmost to apply as much pressure as he can. She adores it.

He does it relentlessly for as long as he can until he has to take it out and ejaculate on her back.

They are both relieved. They clean up and they go back to the owner's bedroom where they cuddle up and sleep the rest of the night. He snores, but she doesn't mind.

***

Next morning she gets up first and finds Andy's dressing gown. Her makeup is all a mess and she'll have to go back to the Triz. She makes coffee as if it was for her kid brother, Michael, and she prepares breakfast with toast, eggs and bacon.

He wakes up to the wonderful odor of breakfast. He dresses scantily and joins her. He slaps her on the butt.

"Good morning sunshine."

"Good morning, I made breakfast for you. I hope you'll like it."

"Just the smell is enough to put me in a good mood for a week, which is how long I have to go out of town. I'll be back next Sunday morning."

"I'm starting a new job as a shopping channel host. I'm going to present high-end jewelry."

"Good for you. I'm sure you will be great at it!"

They finish breakfast, get dressed and each are on their way.

CHAPTER TEN

Illusions

CELESTE IS WELL prepared to be a host and, most importantly, she feels relaxed and confident when she arrives at the studio. The receptionist invites her to sit down. A minute later, a fortyish blonde woman with a charming smile comes with her hand stretched:

"Celeste, I'm Lori Menier."

"I recognize you from the TV ads."

"Thank you. In a few days, you will be as recognizable as I am. Come on in."

Celeste is already a person with some notoriety, but she wonders what being a celebrity would be like? They go to an office on the second floor where different products cover the walls, with a mention beneath them.

There's a lovely impeccably dressed young girl, with long brown hair and with a "look how great I am!" smile.

"Celeste, this is Diana, who'll you're going to work with."

"Hi!"

"Hey!"

They sit down.

"I understand that you're Jim Farber's protégé!"

"Is that what I am?"

"So far, your progression has been spectacular. I'd like you to continue on that trend. Our studio has a similar impulse and now, we want to attract wealthy clients to purchase luxury products. We believe that you can be our pole of attraction, if you don't mind the expression. Most of the time, you will simply be associated with a product. You'll be above the crowd. You won't be a hawker or a model. You will be like royalty that relishes these products. You will be entitled to own and use these luxury goods. Some of the exceptional products will have your seal of approval, if they are above reproach. We wouldn't want the manufacturer go into bankruptcy, or the product recalled, would we?

Being like royalty isn't as easy as you might expect. Everything you say might be used for you, against you or to some other end. I'll give you an example. In 1907, President Theodore Roosevelt was visiting Andrew Jackson on his estate, The Hermitage in Nashville Tennessee. The party went for lunch at the Maxwell House Hotel that served a blended coffee that was new concept at the time. After President Roosevelt finished a cup, he stated that 'It was good to the last drop', so the manufacturer decided to name the coffee 'Maxwell House Coffee' and used Roosevelt's quote as a slogan.

And, everything you do will be the subject of tabloids. They will probably release all kinds of wild rumors just to get some attention, so don't take it too seriously, but don't give them any cause to add to the muck seekers. Since you will be the talk of the world, everyone will invite you to every event, so be careful to choose the people and the places that won't get you in trouble. Then, some people might be offended by your refusals, so be careful how you do that."

"Mr. Farber's training facility is called The Aquarium and I can now appreciate its full meaning."

"Royalty dwells above the mass, so you will have to be a little bit haughty. When you interact with people you have to let them recognize that you're doing them a favor, so that when they're home, they will be proud to boast they even saw you."

Lori handed her some papers. "Why don't we visit the place where you will be appearing?"

"Lori told us that you're quite the phenom! I look forward to working with you," Diana says.

"Thank you."

It's a relatively small studio with 210 seats but the stage is large and can accommodate two large vehicles.

"This is where you will do your magic," Lori tells Celeste. "As usual, the audience will be warmed up. Then we will dim the lights and we will play the theme music. The spotlights will focus on you as you come in. You will give your signature introduction and you will go and touch each luxury product, as if it were your own. A narrator will describe the product and its qualities as you caress it like your fine possession. Be sensual about it! Then, you leave it to the others to make and close the sales. In other words you're like the showcase that attracts the customer in the shop."

"That should be fun," Celeste replies to her surprise.

"Today, you will have your first rehearsal. Tomorrow there will be another. The premier will be in two days, when you will do it the first time, in front of the live cameras. There will be full coverage on every media, with streaming clips on the Internet and photos in every magazine. A reception will follow with the excitement we can muster. You will become an instant world class celebrity."

"Are you kidding me?"

"Really, every talk show will invite you and everybody will want to meet you. This is a world of instant fame and stardom. Jim gave me one invitation to a talk show tomorrow night and one for an interview on Sunday."

"Lucky girl," Diana remarks.

"Holly smoke!"

Diana looks at Celeste, unsure that she said that.

"So let's get along with it," Lori says, pointing to the stage manager, who nods. They go backstage and wait for the cue. A car is on the stage, along with some props. Then a Philharmonic Orchestra music explodes in the studio, penetrating everyone's heart and soul. Celeste performs her entrance like a pro. She walks like royalty, one foot in front of the other, her arms slowly swinging by her side, her soft smile scanning the audience. She introduces the show with a short message. She approaches every luxury product as if it were an erect phallus, yearning to be caressed. She has the intuition to discreetly blow some air on it. She shocks everyone, but it works.

She passes by Diana, who reacts as if they are lesbians about to make love. She's sexually attracted to Diana and it is nearly an invitation. Diana shares the moment with complicity. Celeste turns back a moment, and expresses her modesty, before leaving the stage.

During a pregnant pause, everyone reflects on what had just happened.

"I'm speechless!" Lori exclaims.

Celeste is stunned that she did these things. How could she flirt with Diana? She isn't a lesbian. She wonders if she has a strong attraction towards her. Perhaps these were hidden feelings. This is embarrassing. She feels the need to go back to the hotel.

"I have to leave," Celeste apologizes.

Celeste is confused. She is not the Celeste she believed she was. There seems to be another Celeste who is emerging and she doesn't recognize her.

At the hotel, she has a session at the spa to settle her feelings. She decides to seek an apartment to change her mind and focus on a practical task.

She scours the Internet to bring out what is available and quickly meets her criteria with three possibilities.

She phones Andy and leaves a message: "See you on Saturday, because I have an interview scheduled with one of the most influential reporters, on Sunday at two o'clock."

She reflects on her choice.

***

Next morning, she arrives on time at the studio. Diana is there with a smile. She's about as tall and has the same build as Celeste; she has long brown flowing hair that she likes to flip on one side or the other. "Hey! You were cool yesterday. You surprised everyone in a good way. We didn't expect that."

"Neither did I!"

"Do the same today, but take your time, don't rush. A little pause, will add a touch of suspense. Trust me."

"How long have you been doing this?"

"About a year. Lori is a great friend of mine. Maybe we should get together after the rehearsal, to get to know one another."

"Yeah, sure!" answers without conviction.

***

The complete rehearsal takes place without a hitch.

Lori approaches the girls with a smile. "Tomorrow and we'll have a blockbuster, believe me!"

"So how about hanging out, to let go?" Diana asks.

"I have to search for an apartment."

"Let's do it together?"

"Why not! Actually I've in mind three apartments on the Internet."

"Do you have your portable? Show me."

"Let's go to a coffee shop on the corner, we'll be more comfortable."

Ten minutes later, they're in a coffee shop where they're being flirted by a bunch of guys, but they aren't bothered.

The girls are conscious of their mutual attraction.

"Tell me about yourself!" Diana asks; Celeste obliges and spill out what she had already confided to Sybil.

"So, your new to Hollywood and you have corporate sponsors that solicit you to live a flashy lifestyle with their money?"

"That's one way to put it."

"Well don't let them down! Lemme see what you selected."

"Look at these images! They each have a spectacular view, all the amenities including swimming pool, exercise area, an up-to-date kitchen, private balcony and concierge service."

"Wow! I'd die if I had your luck!"

"They would be the ultimate luxury, wouldn't it?"

"Girl, why don't we wait till we do our grand opening performance?"

"Why?"

"It's just a couple of days."

"I can do that."

"Where are you staying right now?"

"At the Triz."

"Geez! Do you like it there?"

"Sure, who wouldn't? I've got a junior suite that's very cozy and has a great view."

"They're giving you the treatment! You must be special!"

"That's what my coffee cup says at home."

"Come again?"

"My coffee cup has 'You're special' written on it."

"There you go! You can't fool a coffee cup!"

"You're a crazy girl, you know that?"

"Why, thank you!"

"What are we going to do in the meantime, if we wait before visiting apartments?"

"We could go shopping?"

"I don't need anything."

"We're going shopping that's what girls do; if you don't, you're missing half of your life. Shopping is happiness."

"Is that so!"

"Come on, let's go to Rodeo Drive and at least do some window shopping."

"I have to go apartment hunting."

"Come on girl, let your hair down."

"My hair has to look exactly like this. I couldn't be seen going shopping into places that might be competitors to the lines I represent. I'm sorry!"

"Suit yourself," Diana answers, as she disappears in the crowd.

Celeste goes back to the hotel and makes some calls; then she visits the apartments she chose; it's so easy and convenient with the Internet to find anything your heart desires, so she didn't have the need to visit a gamut of places; one clearly emerges from the rest. She makes a virtual visit. The apartment has the highest standards of conservation and sustainability which are very important to her. It's equipped with the top of the line furniture. It has a very high "walkabibility" score. There are expansive decks terraces for outdoor living with sweeping views of the mountains, the ocean and the city panoramas to entertain guests, as well as a pool and a fireplace. There is a spa and a screening room. The apartment has a gourmet custom kitchen with granite counters. The floors are made of bamboo. The bathroom has a shower with side jets and raindrop head, a long soaker bathtub and two exquisite sinks. Best of all, there is a domestic service, a door attendant, a valet, a concierge and even a botanical service to take total care of the apartment's plants, so that she needs not do any household chores. It will be paradise on earth! Who would want a young and lively woman to stay in a cold and damp castle in the middle of nowhere, when she can live in a full facility urban residence in the heart of glitz and entertainment? She phones back to close the deal. The concierge will give her the keys, whenever she will be ready.

***

Celeste meets Akarsh who is aware of her peregrinations and so, he prepared a high fashion azure tulle dress with a fluttering transparent cape, inspired by a nymph, that will add sparks to Celeste's Hollywood enthronization; it emulates a maiden dwelling in the mountains, forests, rivers and lakes that Celeste is so fond of. A white hip belt enhances her profile and is coordinated with a slim white ceramic smart watch. Navy blue platform pumps adorned with bowknots adorn her feet. Her hair is curled up and bounces freely with every move. Akarsh provides her with a breathtaking diadem that can be converted into a choker made by a well-known jeweler and that symbolizes the Flower of Life, one of the oldest sacred symbols known to man, consisting of a geometrical design made of multiple, evenly-spaced overlapping circles. Akarsh accompanies the diadem with a note that says, "You are a junction of the Flower of Life." Celeste didn't understand the profound meaning of this message. With all this care and attention and Akarsh's unwavering belief in her, she's ready to charm the world with her poise and grace, empowered by some mystical force.

Celeste waits in the stage's left wing. She remembers Nick's counsel to express herself, with as much genuine passion as she can muster. She wonders whether her family is watching; she is certain that Michael and Trish are.

The overflowing audience is impatient.

The music introduces the presentation. Celeste smiles and flows into a thundering applause.

"Welcome to the Prestige Fair, where you will have the opportunity to buy the most exquisite products on the market," she proudly invites the public, in a sweet and provocative voice that she created. As rehearsed, she touches one product after another as if they are her lovers. At the end, she raises her hands to invite Diana to proceed with her part. Then she discreetly leaves the stage.

Backstage, Lori is overjoyed with Celeste. "Super. You were super!" They stay together until the end of the show, when Celeste returns on the stage to receive the audience's enthusiastic reaction. The recorded sales are tremendous and so Celeste acknowledges them with sincere appreciation. "I'd like to thank everyone for making this debut a stunning success. We've been overwhelmed by the public's response."

The program ends on that note. Diana informs the audience members that there are thrilling gifts for them underneath their seats. Meanwhile, the cast and crew are whisked off to a reception hall, where there are caterers and waiters that offer champagne and hors d'oeuvres.

***

Celeste takes a glass of wine, for appearances sake, but she barely sips it to avoid any faux pas. Mr. Farber approaches her. "Celeste I'm so proud of you. I got the latest ratings and they are through the roof. You are the world's new idol. Your success is astounding. I trust that you can deal with that?"

"I'll do my best."

Akarsh has a huge smile, as he marvels upon her ineffable radiance and nods. "I bow to the divine in you," Celeste finds these words rather strange, ignorant that they are common in the Hindu culture.

Her mind is racing and she is confused. By the time she regains composure, he's gone like a vanishing daydream. She tries to locate him, to no avail. She is unsure that the event happened. Perhaps it was a vision. She starts to wonder if everything is a vision. This is too good to be true! She checks around her that indeed she is living this dream.

What did she do to deserve this? Is it fortuitous? She has no answer. She asks herself, what Trish would say to her? Enjoy yourself and stop questioning, she would say. That's what she decides to do; Trish is right!

It isn't long before some roaming males try to catch her attention. She could make some smart or rude replies, but she's polite and firm with them, because she isn't interested at their advances. As for Diana, she lets herself be seduced by their enticing promises and she enjoys trying to put them on the spot.

Sybil comes to her with a triumphant smile. "Celeste, here you are the world's new superstar."

"That a little exaggerated!"

"Not at all. You don't grasp every moment. People are starting to gravitate around you. Gradually, you will be able to influence people, about every aspect of their lives. The media is the new realty and you are its new idol. Do the most with it!"

"I'm so sorry to have to part with you as my mentor; I've evolved so much, thanks to you."

"I'm not going anywhere. I'm still your guide and I trust your confidant. You haven't finished your progression."

"What on earth could be better than this?"

"We have to discuss this, soon."

"I'm looking forward to it."

"I leave you to celebrate your success. Here's a toast to a beautiful life," Sybil lifts her champagne glass in Celeste's honor.

"Here's to our friendship."

***

Celeste meets Sybil at the Magic Castle where professional magicians go to refine their art (and sometimes disappear). It's a suit and tie affair. It isn't a place to be shy, so she dons a flashy red satin dress with matching glossy lipstick. Sybil is dressed in black also with striking crimson lipstick.

The women arrive by limousine for a brunch, in baroque glitz settings. Sybil had to say the magic word before a hidden door opens; (hint it starts with "A").

"Celeste you're becoming a fairy. I'm a certified magician and I'm a master of this subject. You are becoming a fairy."

"Sybil, don't turn this into a joke."

"Do you believe in magic?"

"No. They're tricks. Magicians distract their audience and trick them. There's nothing supernatural about it. People are tricked."

"And they love it."

"Sure."

"You tricked an enormous number of people."

"How's that?"

"You disguised yourself from a simple girl to an astounding beauty and you captured the imagination of the world. Everybody likes you. That's the description of a fairy."

"You're kidding!"

"No. With some makeup, you were able to mesmerize nearly everyone. Many women have had makeovers, but you had a mysterious power few can attain. Some of these special individuals are fairies and you are one of them."

"So what does that mean?"

"A very long time ago, there were many fairies. Artists tend to describe them as short females with wings. The truth is that they look like ordinary women; however, they can exert a power over others. They obtain their power from their unique connection with nature. You're just beginning your role as a fairy and your special powers will grow. Now that you have become initiated to these gifts, you should use them judiciously."

"What powers?"

"Celeste you have the power to make others do what you want them to do."

"I wish I did!"

"You do have that power. You doubt it, and doubt is your worst enemy. You have to become confident that you hold that capability."

"All women are able to do that!"

"To a certain extent, yes. You are much more powerful than most women, especially if you use a spell."

"What spell?"

"Say to them 'I have a desire to fulfill'."

"That's it?"

"Yes. Cast them this spell and they'll ask 'What desire?' You'll then tell them what to do. You have to be convinced when you say that. If you flinch, they'll sense it, so be forceful and impose yourself. "

"You must be kidding!"

"You don't believe me. Try it, that's all I'm asking you."

"What if it doesn't work?"

"It doesn't work on some people, particularly those that are fearful of being influenced."

"Have you tried it yourself?"

"I did try it, without success. I don't have that power. It will work for you because you are a true fairy, a young woman who has this hold on people, whether she is aware of it or not. There are many magic powers, such as guessing what others think, reading with the fingers, whispering to animals or appeasing people. You might have some more powers, that have yet to be shown, but, without a doubt, you have the power to charm people and do what you desire from them."

"Perhaps they simply trust me?"

"Certainly that's part of it."

"Isn't this folklore, old stories for kids?"

"Some people believe that. Demons steal, destroy and crush all they can. The world has witnessed demons and saints and I'm sure you could name many. They aren't fictitious characters, for they existed, as do fairies?"

"I suppose," she replies meekly.

"It's rare to find authentic demons, saints, fairies and other esoteric figures. Nowadays, in the world of science and technology, we dismiss our mystical past that taught us their presence.

I grew up with talented magicians and I'm sensitive to exceptional beings. Perhaps my role is to instruct you on your nature and what you can do for the rest of us."

"Well then, what can I do?"

"You are a force of goodness, a caretaker of nature, of equilibrium, of harmony, of humility, of care, of justice and of hope. It is the incarnation of the Flower of life you were given. You will conquer hearts and you will propagate well-being. You will offer faith in life and contentment of fate."

"That's a lot to take in."

"You'll get used to it. Tell me about nature."

"What do you mean?"

"Talk to me about nature, in your own words."

"Well the first thing that comes to mind is water, because water is the source of life, so much so that we are made essentially of water. Water lingers in the seas and oceans with no apparent purpose, yet bacteria and tiny creatures cling to it, and are carried away to uncertain places at water's whim. Air attaches itself to water and all sea creatures suck in water to capture the attached air. Water may wander aimlessly for eons in those oceans, before it surfaces. It may become warm, soaking the sun's rays, but mostly it sleeps in total darkness amidst the eerie sounds of whales and dolphin clicks. Unexpectedly, it propels upwards by mysterious boiling chimneys spurting mineral clouds from the floor. It may be upset by ruthless nets sweeping the depths in search of some unlucky sea creature or by ships grinding away across the surface. When it surfaces, water swells up and then sinks down at a secret and relentless rhythm, as if the wind was endlessly making love with the water that bursts and breaks up in cresting waves ejecting foam, as it emits an uncontrolled screech. When the wind is devoid of its drive and disappears from whence it came, during the night the moon shines on it, reflecting its subdued light, and during the day the sun heats it, until it rises into the air and it flies to meet awaiting sparse clouds. It travels along, over mountains and valleys, joining with other clouds and it transforms into gigantic carrousels that spin over the earth and spill rain, thunder and havoc. For an eternity, clouds persistently splash across chains of mountains and, disregarding their opposition, have crushed and pulverized them, until these mountain ranges are reduced to fragments. Then water gently attends the resulting humus so as to foster life and help seeds to grow into plants."

"What did I say!"

"I'm flabbergasted at what I said. It's as if, there's another person in me is waking up. I just don't speak that way."

"I agree, there's another person in you that is revealing itself. In a way, this is magic, don't you see. Think of it this way, a woman can be a lover, a wife, a mother, a friend, a parent and a worker while being perfectly genuine. Your role as a protector of nature is emerging from inside you. It's already present, so let it become a greater part of your personality!"

"I'll have to dwell on this."

"Naturally."

"It occurs to me, that I was always concerned about the fate of animals. Animals are paramount to our survival however we take them for granted, simply because we can."

"You are taking this to heart!"

"Yes. I'm tired of waiting for others. Now that I have influence and power, I'm determined to improve our society."

"Do you know the story of Cecil the lion?"

"The word rings a bell. Remind me of its story."

"Cecil was a thirteen years old male Southwest African lion who lived primarily on the Hwange National Park in Matabeleland North, Zimbabwe, in Africa. It was enormous, powerful and regal with a long and shaggy black-fringed mane; it was comfortable with humans, who regularly came in safaris to see him, so much so, that he was nicknamed Cecil, which was unusual, in honor of Cecil Rhodes, the founder of the Rhodes scholarship. Along with another male, it shared two prides of six lionesses and twenty-four cubs. The Oxford University Wildlife Conservation Research Unit studied the lion for about ten years, so it was collared with a GPS locator and the lion was accustomed to people who were delighted to photograph it close by. It wasn't the kind of beast that posed any threat whatsoever to humans.

During June 2015 Walter Palmer, a dentist who was a recreational trophy hunter and member of the Safari Club International, paid an estimated amount of fifty thousand dollars to a professional guide, Theo Bronkhorst, to kill a lion, even though there are fewer than forty thousand lions remaining in the wild. Killing a lion with a GPS collar can't hardly be called a hunt. Presumably, the trophy was part of the 'big five', an African lion, an African elephant, a Cape buffalo, an African leopard and a rhinoceros. After the lion was allegedly lured out of its National Park sanctuary, Dr. Palmer wounded it by shooting an arrow. Presumably, the infamous doctor used a modern composite bow with cams and stabilizer, farfetched from a bushman's bow and arrow version. He tracked the wounded animal for many hours, before fatally shooting and beheaded it. Hunting down an alley cat would have been more challenging.

That killing caused an "uproar", if I may say. Many airlines banned transport of animal parts, such as heads, for trophies. France and the United Kingdom banned their import.

That's the true story."

"How come you know every detail by heart?"

" I have the faculty of clairvoyance. I looked up its story just before joining you."

"You're a good friend to have!"

CHAPTER ELEVEN

Diadem

CELESTE LOOKS LIKE a million. She's wearing a diadem with three rows of pearls, crystals and feathers. She is even more breathtaking than before. She is dressed in teal with slick blue under-soles shoes and a chiffon gown.

Sybil meets Celeste to prep her for her promo tour. "I'm here to give you a few tips for the upcoming Johnny North talk show."

"I thought we'd covered that?"

"I'm sure you'd do well with what we've already taught you, but there are differences between interview and talk shows. Johnny uses the stream of consciousness approach, consisting of conversing with whatever comes to mind, as long as it's amusing. You'll be able to choose the subjects, if you want to. It's up to you, to capture the moment."

"That's interesting."

"It can be. Some guests can hijack the show and do practically whatever they wish, if they're sufficiently funny."

"Do I have to try and be funny?"

"No, but it's the best way to get people attention. Johnny will do his best to keep it entertaining; that's what he does. Try to reveal of some aspects of yourself that will fascinate people."

"What if it gets too intimate?"

"You don't need to go where you don't want to. Be yourself, that's what people most like about you. People love you already, but this prime show will make them adore you even better, after they understand you better. There's nothing to worry about, Johnny will help you."

"Diana suggested that I take half a glass of wine to help me loosen up."

"I'm sure that you can get along without that. You aren't an anxious person to begin with and, as far as I'm concerned, you don't have some weird behavior that might emerge. Has Diana been on the show?"

"Actually yes, and it went very well."

"By the way, don't take yourself too seriously. He might try and have a little fun with you."

"Like what?"

"Well he likes to show some bloopers that will embarrass some guests. If he does, go along."

"Oh my god!"

"You can take a joke. Sure you can."

"It depends!"

"You'll be fine," Sybil reassures her.

"If you say so."

"Try and make the awkward situation your own."

"How would I do that?"

"Well, simply own it. You can also add a personal spin to the moment."

"That might be fun, if I can manage that!"

"At least, you will have the knowhow to deal with it."

"You're the best!"

"Remember you're the star everyone has been waiting for!"

***

The introductory Prestige Fair music plays, while Johnny introduces Celeste. With much aplomb, she waits, until she hears her exact cue to enter. The audience offers her a standing ovation. Celeste bows with true humility, reminding herself of her youth when she was booed. A tear forms in the corner of her eye that the camera is quick to focus on. She's the world's sweetheart!

Johnny encourages the audience to react to her emotional entrance.

They sit down and he hands her a paper tissue that he fetches from a drawer in his desk.

"It isn't often that I make my guests cry!" he apologizes to her.

"I'm sorry about that." She retains her single tear before it drops.

"Tell me, what makes you so sad?" he jokingly says.

She laughs.

"I watched the Prestige Fair you presented so magnificently and I was impressed."

"We're offering the most beautiful things in the whole world. Highly skilled artisans from every region of the globe are producing the best products available and I'm proud to be part of this. Without our Fair, many of these products would not be available and the artists and artisans wouldn't earn a decent living."

"The blogs are talking about your twinkling diadem."

"Isn't it spectacular! You'd be surprised to find out how affordable it is! The thrilling characteristic is that the Flower of Life inspired it. I looked it up on the Internet and it's one of the oldest symbols on earth. Civilizations such as the Egyptians, the Chinese and the Hindus drew it. It has many intersecting circles within a circle that produce a design similar to a flower."

"Is that so?"

"One of my favorite outdoor flowers is the sunflower, because it follows the sun as it travels in the sky. I also like it because its seeds form a design similar to the Flower of Life; isn't this stupendous?"

"Yes," he replies. He likes the direction the talk is going, so he lets her continue.

"The sunflower seeds are very healthy. It makes oil that's cholesterol free. The birds love its seeds. You can attract many songbirds with sunflower seeds. They come in the garden and they sing in the morning. What could be better than that?"

"A mug of cold beer!" he quickly replies, that sends the audience in a hysterical laugh.

After a moment, he agrees. "Kidding aside, I can appreciate what you mean."

"I love birds. At home, I have pictures of parrots. They're so colorful. Many species live and fly together in pairs. They can live for fifty to ninety years, so we should take great care of them. We have to watch what we say because some of them repeat what they hear. If we swear often in front of them, they'll learn to say it and it might become embarrassing."

"Yeah," draws some chuckles since he imitates a parrot's voice.

"I find that the cutest parrots are those that annoy dogs or cats. They bite their legs just for fun and make them back off. I even saw a parrot that barked like a dog. It was so funny."

"Talking about animals, we have some clips we took at the celebration after the Prestige Fair show. Let's roll."

The clip placed itself at the reception. Then it focuses on the young men surrounding Celeste, who are trying to flirt with her. One licks his lips. They play that clip from different angles and they show it repeatedly that provokes laughs.

The clip then shows another young man glancing at Celeste's breasts, but when she turns her head, he quickly raises his eyes. They play this from different angles many times and that makes people smile.

"I want to make it clear that he was looking at Celeste's necklace," Johnny says with a mocking face.

"He must have seen the Flower of Life design," Celeste excuses the young man.

Johnny makes a funny face because she stole his joke.

"Do you like geometry?"

"I like curves, if that's what you mean?"

"Seriously! By trade, I'm a graphic designer, so I'm curious about nature and its shapes. That's what got me interested in the sunflower. Its seeds grow in lovely spirals. We're beginning to understand the connection between geometry and nature. What seemed to be erratic is actually a form of geometry."

"Is that so!" he exclaims in an incredulous way, trying to get a free chuckle.

"Beauty can be analyzed mathematically. It's all about symmetry and the rule of golden proportions."

"When I look at you, I don't have math in mind," Johnny launches and obtains a barrel of laughs.

Celeste lets the audience subside.

"So you like nature."

"Yes. We're using it as if we have an absolute right over it. Just because we can cut down trees and dig humongous holes in the ground doesn't mean that we ought to. We're being very egoistical and this will destroy the earth that we depend on to live comfortably in a bewildering environment. I'm fully committed in helping nature recapture its rights. This will eventually work against our descendents and us, if ignore nature. Humanity has been around only for less than five thousand years. In the history of the world, this isn't even a fraction of an era. If we manage to survive for twenty thousand years, it will be a heartbeat in the history of the world. At the pace we are growing, both in numbers and by encroachment of our resources, not only will humans not survive, we'll eliminate many other life forms that help up subsist. We'll are depleting earth's resources and increasing the planet's temperature so much that there will be no more precipitation."

"That's not funny!" Johnny quips.

"No it isn't. We're transforming potential energy into spent energy. When we are burning fuels of any kind, much of the energy dissipates in the air. What was once a liquid in the earth, burns to heat up the air. In addition, the carbon residues damage our very thin atmosphere. The efficiency of combustion engines is less than fifty percent, which means that most of the energy heats the atmosphere. If we compare that to animals, their efficiency is near one hundred percent. A horse eats grass and yet it can pull heavy cartloads. There is much waiting to be understood about nature. We believe that we have mastered it, but we should be humbled by it."

"You are an apostle of nature."

"Yes and very proud of it."

"What would you change if you could?"

"One issue troubles my heart. It's time we abolish trophy hunting. In the past, some animals were dangerous and it was courageous to hunt and kill them. Wanton killing of animals should stop, particularly hunting for trophies. Too often, that type of sport, if we can call it that, targets vulnerable species. That should end, because we can easily kill all types of animals.

This is a remnant of a bygone era. It has no more purpose in our world."

The audience approves. Upon that note, Johnny invites another guest and his show continues. Celeste is relieved to have overcome that hurdle.

***

Sybil is waiting in the dressing room and her heart is beating fast. "You were astonishing."

Celeste embraces Sybil. "I couldn't be happier that you coached me. I was able to pass on my concerns about the environment. It gave me an unexpected opportunity to expose my beliefs about sustainability and trophy hunting. It was a secret desire of mine that I never expected to share with the world. I'm grateful to you, to Mr. Farber and to Akarsh for having given this chance."

"I'm sure that you'll get more of these opportunities, now that everyone has heard your opinion. At the beginning of the talk show, I didn't expect that you would talk about the Flower of Life."

"I'm intrigued by it."

"We'll talk about it later."

"Why not now?"

"You need some R&R after these hectic days."

"If you say so."

Sybil looks at the security monitor that films the building's exit.

"It would be better to go home right away, before the crowd waiting for you outside becomes too large."

***

As soon as the outside doors open, the waiting admirers rave and chant "Celeste, Celeste, Celeste…" The paparazzi are nervously taking photos, adding to the frenzy. She signs a few autographs in a hurry. The security guards usher her in the waiting limousine. She asks the driver to take her to her new apartment. She phones the concierge and advises him of her arrival.

When she gets out of the limousine, she receives a bouquet

of complimentary roses to add to the ones already in her apartment. The staff salutes with their heads and says, "Welcome Celeste!" in unison. She has an escort to her apartment.

"We've taken the liberty of bringing your belongings from the Triz. We also neatly placed your clothes in their proper location. If you like, I will add our app to your phone," a butler offers. She hands him her phone and it is ready in a second.

"Is there anything else we can do for you?"

"Not for the moment, thank you."

The staff leaves the apartment.

She truly feels like royalty, in the mist of lavish luxury, the world at her feet. As she did when arriving at the Triz, she puts on some music and she dances across all the rooms letting go of her guard, closing her eyes and humming with the music as she twirls around.

After half an hour or so, she gets totally undressed. She lets go her hair and she takes off her makeup. She sets the temperature of her whirlpool bathtub and fills it with water. She slowly soaks in the tub and relaxes her mind and body, listening to some meditation music. To her, life couldn't be better. She has everything that she could want. She'll see Andy, after he comes back home. She is in excellent health, in one of the most beautiful places on Earth, and she is liked or beloved by everyone.

When she's laid-back, she gets up, dries herself, dawns a bathrobe and heads for her bedroom where she takes her phone. She has a list of callers that would like her to phone back. Trish is her first choice.

"Hi Trish, this is Celeste."

"You were terrific on the Johnny North show. I recorded everything and I've been viewing it many times over. You were sublime. Sublime. That hairdo with that diadem! I was so jealous. And that superb gown! Gosh, I wish that I had been there. I swear, if I had known, I would have joined you. It was fantastic. And, the Internet just lit up as soon as the show started. You're even on the local news. They're making a real fuss about it here. I got calls from a dozen girls who know that we're friends and they wanted to be in on all the details. I'm getting popular because of you.

I haven't heard from you for an eternity. What have you been doing? You have to call me more often. I have to go to the social network to get news from you. What's new? Tell me!"

"I finally got an apartment. It's just about in the best location in Hollywood, near everything. It is a full service residence, where I don't have to do a thing. All I have to do is ask for something I'd like and I get it in a blink. It is fantastic.

You can come here whenever you like; I have a guest room, so there's no problem. Just say so and you can stay here."

"What about your boyfriend Andy?"

"Perfect. We made love together at his place and not only is he a hunk, he's a stallion."

"Wow! Does he have a brother?"

"Ha! Ha! Ha!"

"I'd be willing to let my hair down."

"You have to do better than that, Trish. I told you to try a little more."

"I don't have your luck. It was in your cards, not in mine. There's this Flower of Life that you talked about. Where did you get that from?"

"Actually it was a diadem from Akarsh that caught my attention. I Googled it and it explained its meaning. My mentor, Sybil, is familiar with it."

"Who is this Sybil?"

"My agent, Mr. Farber, assigned her as my mentor. She did a wonderful job at prepping me for my job and for the show. I rely on her a great deal."

"What was your mother's reaction?"

"I haven't talked to her yet."

"Well thanks for the phone call."

"Sure."

Next Celeste calls back her mother.

"Hi mom."

"Celeste, it's so good to hear from you. Michael, Mary and I watched the show. We're so proud of you. You were a real gem. I never had any doubt that you would achieve great things in your life. Your appeal about protecting nature was very touching. How are you doing sweetheart?"

"I'm terrific. Things couldn't get any better. How's Michael?"

"He's right next to me. I'll pass him the phone."

"Hi Celeste!"

"Hi Michael. What do you think of your sister now?"

"Great. All my friends want to get to meet you. When are you coming back home?"

"I can't say. I'd love to go back for a visit. Maybe soon."

"Take care sis!"

"You too. Bye."

Andy called, but she didn't want to call him back right away, since she's meeting him tomorrow morning, at her new apartment.

She looked up the list of callers and she didn't see her father's name. That's a heck of a way to finish this otherwise perfect day.

CHAPTER TWELVE

Home

ANDY ARRIVES AT TEN in the morning and the valet parks his car, the door attendant opens the door and the receptionist checks with Celeste to allows him to go to her apartment. She watches him on her smart watch knock on the door; she lets him in. She meets him and they kiss amorously, until they have to catch their breath.

"Jeepers, this is a posh place. How on earth can you afford this?"

"I have very rich sponsors who believe in me."

"I don't doubt that!"

"I've been incredibly lucky and I'm taking advantage of it."

"Why not? Some win the jackpot or inherit a fortune. You are a sweetheart!"

"I don't want to get smug, because this could be wiped away in one day. One earthquake would do the trick."

"Seize the day, as they say."

"So what have you planned for today?"

"This morning, I'd like you to meet my parents. Mother invited us for lunch. Spaghetti and wine. Then, we could go to my place or yours and have torrid sex. After that, when we'll be famished, we'd go to one of the best restaurants where I got a reservation. Finally, we'll go dancing in the most popular nightclub these days, Los Locos. I had to use your name to reserve a place. I'm sure that you'll forgive me for that! If I hadn't used your name, we'd be put on a six months waiting list."

"I'd forgive you anything."

"That's sweet," he replies as he kisses her.

"So let's go to my parents. They live in south LA. They've had a modest bungalow for over fifteen five years. I'm their only child, so I only have my mom and dad. As I told you, I come from the Midwest. They had to sell their property and they moved here. They live a quiet life and they're very happy. Dad likes bowling and mom does the gardening. Sometimes, he helps her out. Her first name is Beatrice, but dad calls her Bea. My father's name is Oscar. I guess that he feels at home here in Hollywood with all the Oscar jokes he gets."

They go with his car. They don't talk much on the way.

He parks on the driveway of his parents' home.

The mother was taking care of the garden when they arrived, "We can't use much water this year."

"Mother I'd like to present Celeste."

"Andy told us to watch your show. You're much more beautiful than on the screen!"

"I'm pleased to meet you Mrs. Czerny."

"Call me Bea, everyone does. We're not very formal. Did Andy say that we come from Lincoln Nebraska?"

"Yes he did."

"We had a farm there, till they bought it to build a highway, then we moved here."

She leads them in the house.

"Oscar," she shouts. "Andy is here with his new girlfriend."

Andy is a bit uneasy at the free comment.

"Dad, I'd like you to meet Celeste."

"Howdy!"

"Please to meet you, sir."

"Andy tells me that you like nature?"

"Yes, very much so."

"I was a farmer for most of my life. I grew corn and wheat. I never farmed this fancy stuff."

"He means soybeans," Andy explains.

"I would have farmed all my life, if it hadn't been for that damn highway. Have you ever been on a farm?"

"I lived in the Niagara peninsula where there are many small farms. When I was a teenager, I used to sell fresh produce in small markets. I love the smell of fruits and vegetables. I like that fresh country scent."

"It was a quiet life; none of the commotion that we have

here. I cherish many memories of that time. When I was young we had horses to help up out. You talked about horses on your show, didn't you?"

"Yes. I love animals."

"I do too. It was a good life. We could rely on horses to do some of the hard work; they didn't break down and they didn't complain. I had no choice but to buy a combine, but I liked working with horses."

He reminisces for the remainder of the morning.

"Lunch is served," Bea shouts from the kitchen.

"We're having spaghetti, I hope you like it?" Bea asks Celeste.

"Yes, I love it."

"Oh you do, do you?"

The room next to the kitchen has a four seats country style dining table where mom and dad take their usual place, one next to the other. The cutlery and the china are basic and practical.

"Celeste, you could tell us a little more about yourself?" Andy proposes.

Celeste obliges, as she sugarcoats her childhood and her path to here.

"What a wonderful story then!" Bea exclaims.

"I have been very fortunate."

"I'm the lucky one," Andy rushes.

"Oh, I suppose," Bea agrees.

"Mom, what have you been doing these days?"

Bea doesn't spare any detail in explaining her gardening and the care she gives to every single plant, flower and bush around the house.

Later, Andy gets up to signal his departure and everyone bids farewell. Andy and Celeste get in the BMW and they drive back to her apartment.

"My parents liked you."

"They're a sweet couple."

"They live a simple life, because they like it that way."

***

It is breathtaking to come home to handsomely dressed valets, door attendant, concierge and receptionist who do their utmost to satisfy all your desires. The couple serenely walks to her apartment. She selects romantic music on her watch.

"Some port perhaps?" she suggests.

"I'll try it," he answers, a little leery, since he usually gulps a cold beer.

She opens the liquor cabinet and takes out a bottle Cabral Caràcter™ with two glasses.

"To health and happiness!" Andy proposes.

"Health and happiness!"

They take a sip. Andy is about to kiss her.

"Let's go to the garden on the roof."

"Let's go!"

A soft breeze brushes their skin while the relentless sun warms it. They walk about the rooftop garden. They're alone. She reserves its access and selects some romantic music.

"It's strange that a few months ago, all that I dreamed of was to live a quiet life in the suburbs, with my husband and children, much like your parents," she confides.

"Look around you, at what you would have missed."

"Now the sky is the limit. It seems that I can achieve anything that I might desire."

"So what are your dreams?"

"I haven't made up my mind yet; I've been caught up with the moment. I see no need to ask for more, I just want to continue enjoying life."

"Would you like to have children?"

"Maybe later? Raising children might jeopardize my lifestyle. I love what I'm living and I want to continue doing so."

"I don't blame you with this setup!"

"How about you?"

"I'd like to have a wife with children in a nice house and go on vacation a couple times a year. I'm pretty conventional."

"I'm done with 'ordinary'. I'm experiencing an extraordinary life and I own it. If I ever have some children, they would have to be extraordinary in some way. I have the means to lead a unique life and I intend to put them to good use."

"My you've changed!"

"Let's make this an extraordinary day!"

Andy takes her in his arms and he gives her an unabashed French kiss. Time is forgotten.

"Let's go skinny dipping poolside," Celeste volunteers.

Small tents border the secluded pool where they slowly strip their pieces of clothing, one by one, until they're in the buff. They finish their glass of port and place them on a pedestal. Andy takes her hand and leads her to the pool's stairway. The water is warm and comfortable. They play catch-me-if-you-can in the water. Andy manages to get a hold of different parts of her body but she manages to wiggle away. She teases him the best she can. She splashes him. He loves to pat every part of her body. She pushes him back and reaches the end of the pool that has a transparent glass overlooking part of the city and the mountains. It's thrilling to be naked and contemplate the view, while being nearly invisible to the outside world. Andy approaches her with a strong erection. They kiss and she drags him underwater; her long hair embraces their heads. He squeezes her towards him and then he guides her hand to make her feel his virility. She strokes him slowly. He feels her erect nipples that he pinches lightly. They're having an unforgettable moment.

They climb out of the pool and they sit on a cushioned lounge chair next to each other, to take the sun and to dry up.

"How about some more wine?" she asks.

"Wine not?"

She's amused at his reply.

She brings the glasses back to the cabana, where there she pulls out two new glasses and a bottle of port. She pours the wine.

"To health and happiness."

"Health and happiness."

They savor the port.

"How many guys have you been with?"

"Just Matt."

"Tell me about him."

"What do you want to know?"

"How was he in bed?"

"At first, he was too uptight to do much. It was frustrating, but I suppose that it might be the same for youngsters without any experience."

"So what happened?"

"Well, he came so quickly that I was baffled. I didn't have any orgasm and he didn't seem to mind. After that, I simply jerked him off. It took little time, but he came. He felt so stoked about it. After that, I gave him blowjobs. When we had intercourse, he came after a few thrusts. I kept thinking 'This is it?' In the corner of my mind, I kept telling myself that it must be better than that. We kept the same routine that he felt comfortable with."

"What routine?"

"After the blowjob he assumed the missionary position and he would come."

"How about you, did you have an orgasm?"

"Once or twice. He didn't care that I came. I didn't mind that much, as long as he was relieved."

"Did you masturbate?"

"Yes, I did it at least once a day."

"Do you use a dildo?"

"Yes, it's reliable and it's just right, but I had to wait till Michael went downstairs, because it made too much noise."

"Did you have fantasies that you wanted to do?"

"One of them was to do it outside, like we just did."

"Have you ever tried it with your girlfriend?"

"Trish? No. She wouldn't."

"Have you ever proposed having sex with her?"

"No." Celeste wasn't about to divulge that Diana was very tempting and that she would have succumbed to her proposal, if she would have made one.

"Come here. You got away from me in the pool but you won't get away from me here."

He pulls her towards him.

"You are irresistible," he tells her, as he starts to dance slowly with her. He looks at her eyes and she avoids his stare. "While I was away, I couldn't stop thinking about you. Not one second passed, that you weren't in my mind. I wanted to hold you like I'm doing, I wanted to grab your ass and pull you towards me and I wanted to make love with you like we did last time."

He makes her lie down beside him. He kisses her while his hand travels to her breasts, then her hips, only to end up at the extremity of her lips. He caresses her and she moans. His fingers test the flowing waters. He gradually ascends to paradise. He kisses her between her lips and she quickly comes. His ardor intensifies and again she comes. He repeats this until she pleads him to stop. He does.

He slides up and assumes the missionary position. He penetrates her like waves, ebbing to the shore. She loses her sense of space. She is floating.

He stops and urges her to turn over. He slaps both sides of her buttocks, to increase their sensibility. She doesn't object to this heightened sexual awareness. He penetrates her from behind; her red buttocks enhance every thrust.

"Oh god!" she cries.

He moans.

"Oh god! Fuck me hard!"

He applies as much pressure as he can.

Every thrust is heavenly.

As he's about to ejaculate, he stops and lets his cum spray her butt. He groans with pleasure. She smiles in satisfaction.

He takes her in his arms and they relax and go to sleep.

A sea breeze awakens them. They kiss. They dress and go back to her apartment.

***

"Dinner is at seven; what do you want to do meanwhile?" Celeste asks.

"We could watch TV and catch up on some games."

"Do you want something to drink?"

"Yeah, I'll have a beer."

"One beer coming up."

She taps her watch and a huge TV screen comes down, the shades darken the room and the living room transforms into a home theater. She gets the cold beer from the kitchen and hands it to Andy, who kisses her in return. They sit down and watch the latest football game. Andy participates with the crowd. Celeste feigns interest, to please him.

"Man, this is total decadence!" Andy says.

CHAPTER THIRTEEN

The Flaw

CELESTE ATTIRES for Dining & Dancing. She also puts on a sandalwood perfume guaranteed to tantalize any mortal into complete submission, not that she needs it! The instant she joins Andy, he's bewitched and he starts kissing her and petting her. "Oh babe, come here."

"Andy we have to go to the restaurant."

"Just a quickie before we go."

"Nooo. Calm down tiger. We have to go and eat. I'm hungry."

"It can wait. I want to make love to you. You're so tempting. I want to fuck you."

"You're a bad boy. Wait until we come back from dancing. I'll be yours all night."

"You're cruel. Look I already have a boner," he points out the bulge in his trousers.

"I just got dressed. You can wait a few hours. It'll be even better then."

"How can you do this to me?" he squeezes her.

"Whoa! Be patient." as she manages to wiggle away.

He gets on all fours and tries to catch her legs. She escapes.

"Andy, I promise to do whatever you want when we come back. Get up."

"Oh babe!" He stands up unzips his fly and lets his dick stick out.

"Andy, cool off. We don't have time for this."

"I can't. Blow me."

"OK we'll do this quickly." She gets on her knees and sucks his cock. He pulls her head back and forth. When he's about to come, he pulls her in and she starts to gag. Nirvana arrives and he explodes. She lets the cum ooze out of her mouth. He groans in ecstasy. "Oh babe, that was good!"

He falls back.

She goes to the bathroom, washes and retouches her makeup. She brings a wet towel to Andy. "What were you saying? You want to have dinner?"

"I thought you didn't understand!"

"OK babe, let's go."

The two are on their way.

***

"I brought you to my favorite restaurant, Chuck wagon Steakhouse. They serve real food here, none of this fancy pansy stuff."

"Andy Czerny," Andy murmurs to the maitre d for the table he reserved, as he slips some dollar bills.

They enter the restaurant and, noticing that Celeste is spectacular, the maitre d places them in a center table to be admired by everyone.

They read the menu.

"Would you like something to drink?" the waiter asks.

"I'll have a coffee with my meal," Celeste says.

"I'll have a beer on tap."

They read the menu. The waiter brings the drinks.

"I'll have a twelve once rib with fries."

"I'll have a filet mignon with a Caesar salad."

Celeste is stared at and Andy is proud as a lion for dining with her. "We're the center of attraction."

"I'm accustomed to it."

"Frankly, I find it a little annoying. I can't stand your photographer, Derek over there, but that's about it."

"You'll have to get used to it. The more exposure I'll have, the more people will want to get my attention."

"I don't know whether I could handle that. I sort of cherish my private life."

"I'm pretty much committed to living a public life. There's always a downside to everything; I gained fame but I lost some privacy. We have to cope with that."

"As long as they don't get in my way."

"You'll have to get used to it."

"We'll see about that," Andy replies, as he senses that his "territory" is being challenged.

The rest of the meal goes smoothly.

***

She summons the limousine that takes them to the nightclub, Los Locos. A large crowd surrounds the entrance, where a huge bouncer controls the access, like Cerberus at the gate of Hades. In the crowd, there are paparazzi waiting to capture any potential gossip. Since Andy used Celeste's name for the reservation, the paparazzi are on high alert. The limousine is a sure sign that someone important is about to emerge. The driver opens the rear door and Andy gets out, tending a hand to Celeste. The second she gets out someone shouts "Celeste. Celeste."

Every paparazzo takes as many photos as he can; their flashes light up the night sky like fireworks.

Andy feels aggressed. He pushes them aside to let Celeste pass. Celeste keeps her composure and smiles. The couple slowly makes his way towards the entrance. A paparazzo gets in their way to take a frontal shot. Andy instinctively shoves him aside.

"Get out of the way, you fucking rodents." Andy warns.

The paparazzo falls on the ground.

"That's where you belong, you fucking piece of shit."

A frenzy of flashes, like piranhas charges at a prey.

The entrance guard recognizes Celeste, so he lets the couple in.

Once inside, they are led to a small table, where they order a beer and a Shirley Temple.

"Andy, why did you knock down the paparazzo? This is bound to make the news, bad news. You didn't have to do that, he was doing his job."

"He got in the way. He might have hurt you, so I pushed him aside."

"You shouldn't have done that!"

"Now they learned their lesson not to get in your way."

"You might get in trouble for this."

"For clearing the path?"

"Yes."

"Let's have fun and forget that incident. Let's dance, that's what we came for."

She consents and they walk to the floor and let her inhibitions down.

Andy isn't much of a dancer, but tries he does.

Celeste encourages him to move freely and let his instincts drive him.

She has fun making silly moves in rhythm with the music. He's too awkward to respond. He drinks another beer to free his hesitations. He does better.

Another man incites Celeste to dance with him and she accepts. In a heartbeat, they dance in unison. Andy concedes and goes back to the table, as he watches his date become the center of attraction with that Fred Astaire. Celeste releases her energy and her fears and abandons herself to the moves of that dancer.

Meanwhile there is a raucous at the entrance. Three men scan the place and go to Andy's table.

The paparazzo that was thrust to the ground says:"That's him. He did it."

The two other men identify themselves to Andy. "Police. You are under arrest. You have the right to remain silent. Anything you say will be used against you in a court of law. You have a right to an attorney during interrogation. If you cannot afford an attorney, one will be appointed to you. Follow us."

"What for?"

"Assault and battery on this man."

"I just pushed him because he threatened us."

"You can explain that at the station."

"I have to inform Celeste."

"Come with us now. Don't make any trouble."

"I just want to tell my date."

"Never mind that," the police officer orders as he grabs Andy by the arm and walks out of the nightclub. He cuffs him and directs him to the waiting police car where Andy takes a place in the back.

Celeste watched the whole scenario. She keeps on dancing, not wanting the attention to revert to her. She goes back to her table. Someone tells her: "Your boyfriend was arrested. He was taken by the police."

She takes her purse, pays the bill and she heads for the exit. She gets in the limousine that takes her back to her apartment.

Celeste isn't unduly concerned about Andy, because it was a minor incident. He was surely going to ward it off, so she waits for Andy's call and eventually goes to bed.

Next morning, she meets Sybil who prepares her for the huge interview with the gossip columnist Elaine Mitchell.

"Today is a big day. Dozens of millions will be watching the Mitchell interview, so after this, you'll be famous everywhere. If you thought that you were popular before, this will advance you to the forefront of the scene. You've already done very well, but this interview is the clincher, because the rest of your life will be under the microscope. Whatever you say or do, will catch the attention of the public."

"Goodbye anonymity."

"Mitchell is famous because she has the knack to go to the core of the matter. Given the recent incident, she will undoubtedly focus on your boyfriend's prank last night, so we might as well talk about it."

"Where did you hear that?"

"It's in the local news. Don't you watch it?"

"Sometimes I do, but I haven't done so today."

"They've got many viewpoints. Your boyfriend was swearing at the photographer."

"He was protecting me."

"That's not how he's being portrayed. They call him a brute, a bully."

"That can't be!"

"Luckily, you weren't directly involved. I think the best would be for you to distance yourself from him."

"I can't disavow him, he's my boyfriend!"

"You didn't intervene in any way. It's important for your future that you not defend him. Act like a bystander that watched it happen."

"I can't deny that we were together."

"Of course not, but don't excuse his brutality."

"He brushed him aside. That's not a crime."

"The paparazzo filed a formal complaint against him for being attacked without any provocation."

"We were provoked, the guy purposely got in our way."

"You can't say that. Be careful Celeste or the press will chew you up."

"I won't dissociate myself from him. He's a nice guy and I like him."

"Are you in love with him?"

"No but he's a terrific guy. Sure he looks rough and tough, but he's a sweet guy."

"We're not dealing with whom he is, we're confronted with the perception the public will have of him. A few seconds of his life have made him out to be a brute without scruples. You can't let your own image be affected by his. Position yourself as a spectator to this event. Don't implicate yourself."

"Won't people say that I'm not loyal to him?"

"Just explain what they see. You stood by him which is great, but you didn't involve yourself in any way in beating up the guy."

"Frankly I'll have to consider this."

"That's perfectly natural. At least you're warned."

The Elaine Mitchell interview is taking place in a studio. Intimate and personal, the ace interviewer is in her sixties, a veteran of countless one to one confrontations, tries to make Celeste at ease. "It's great to meet you Celeste."

"The pleasure is mine."

Elaine can immediately sense that Celeste has been prepped and that the answers are canned, so she intends to disrupt the programmed reactions.

The show starts quickly as the Celeste sits in front of Elaine.

"I'm privileged to have Celeste on our set, the host of the new show Prestige Fair. Your rise to stardom has been meteoric. How did you manage that?"

This is an obvious cue to praise her sponsors.

"When I went to the Dyann Winter show, the fashion designer Akarsh helped me to launch my career by having me promote his fashion ware. Then my agent, Jim Farber, took me under his wing, to hone my entertainment skills. I'm truly indebted to them."

"Last night, you made the news for another reason. It seems that your boyfriend pushed a paparazzo. He was charged with aggravated assault."

"It was a total shock to me and I'm very sorry that it turned into a scandal."

"Has he been brutal with you? Is he violent with you?"

"No. He's always been very gentle with me. This was an utter surprise to me."

"He isn't out of the woods yet, not by a long shot."

"I expect to see him shortly."

"Aren't you aware that he didn't make bail?"

"No. How could he not for such a minor incident?"

"It seems that you haven't been informed that he's facing twenty-five years to life in jail!"

"That's impossible."

"You're obviously in the dark. Your boyfriend already had two prior felony convictions, one for shoplifting and the other for possession of narcotics. Since this is a third offence, he is subject to the law that forces the court to punish him with the twenty-five to life conviction, the three strikes law. This time it appears to be a crime against a person, which is very serious."

"You're kidding!"

"I'm as serious as I can be. Apparently, you're not about to be with him for a long time. That's why he was denied bail."

Celeste is shocked and speechless.

"I'm sorry I had to break this news to you, but I couldn't avoid it!"

"I'm upset. I'm ending this interview."

"Well good luck!"

Celeste walks out to the media horde that awaits her.

"No comments," she says as she cries and enters the limousine.

***

As she heads to her apartment, she tries to contact Andy who doesn't answer, so she leaves a message to call her back.

She phones Sybil: "Hi! Why didn't you warn me about Andy?"

"I would have told you, but the news just broke out, as the interview was beginning."

"I was ambushed by Elaine Mitchell."

"She couldn't avoid it. She had a scoop and she used it. Nevertheless, you did very well Celeste and that's the essential."

"She even suggested that he was violent towards me. That's absurd."

"This is how she gets her rating."

"Meanwhile, I took the brunt of the shock."

"Show business has its dark side."

"But Andy is a nice guy. Now he looks like a hardened criminal."

"I'm sure that he'll get a good lawyer that'll free him."

"He has to. This is ludicrous."

"What can I say?"

"Bye."

***

At her apartment, she phones Nick. "Hi, this is Celeste, how are you?"

"I'm great thank you."

"I suppose you know why I'm calling you?"

"No I don't."

"My boyfriend has been accused under the mandatory jail law and he's facing twenty-five years to life, because he pushed a paparazzo aside."

"That's too bad. I don't follow that kind of news. What can I do to help?"

"Well I'd like to talk to him. I don't know where he's jailed and how I can reach him."

"All right I'll get on it and I'll call you back."

"Thanks Nick."

***

Nick calls back and gives her Andy's phone number. Celeste hurries, "Andy, what on earth happened?"

"Boy, am I glad you called! The police arrested me in the

nightclub. Before they took me, I asked to speak with you, but they refused. I was booked at the police station because I pushed that photographer at the club's entrance. I thought that it was no big deal, but then they read my file and they realized that this was my third arrest and a violent crime. Violent my ass! If I wanted to be violent, I would have shoved my fist in his face. Anyhow, I was allowed only one phone call, so I got in touch with my lawyer. He tried to get me out on bail but it was refused because of the three strikes law. I'm in trouble. I managed to get a message to my parents; they're all confused. They can't grasp what is happening. They'll take care of my home, while I'm gone. My lawyer told me that we have a good chance that the charges will be dropped.

I sure hope so. It would be preposterous to be jailed for such a petty incident."

"It wasn't even a brawl. You just pushed him aside; unfortunately he fell on the concrete border."

"Apparently, he broke his camera. I'll pay for the damn thing if that's all that it takes."

"Tell me, what were the two preceding crimes?"

"When I was eighteen, a buddy of mine dared me to steal something. I had never done so before, and I didn't have any idea how to do it. It was a dare; I had to do it. I went to a restaurant and stole a rare fish in the aquarium. The owner caught me, I pleaded guilty to grand theft, and I had to do a month of community service and I returned the fish. That wasn't a big deal.

A few years later, I was in a college party with a bunch of guys. We were drinking and smoking pot. The guys chose me to get some more pot to keep the party going, so I went on the street and bought some pot from a guy6 who happened to be an undercover policeman who targeted the student crowd. I got six months probation plus community work. Again, no big deal. They can't put me away for these dinky crimes; it would be outrageous. My lawyer told me that he will try to expunge the shoplifting condemnation from my rap sheet."

"Come again?"

"In other words, the charge of shoplifting could be scratched off, so I would have only two convictions. He would also attempt this for the possession of drugs conviction."

"My lawyer believes that I'll receive a light sentence with these procedures."

"Let's hope so. Is there any chance that they'll set bail?"

"I'm afraid not. We won't see each other for a while. Go on with your life, I will be OK."

"I'd like to visit you."

"That would be kind, but don't go to the trouble. I just have to wait it out and everything will work out fine."

"If you need anything, just tell me."

"Sure will. Take care babe!"

"Keep cool."

"Bye."

CHAPTER FOURTEEN

Mystical Geometry

SYBIL WANTS TO MEET Celeste. To avoid being in public, Sybil invites Celeste to her home. It is a small townhouse in south LA. The inside is full of decorations made from seashells, dried flowers with geometric forms, crystals and the like. A scent of perfumed incense sweetens the air and the sound of Nepalese priests reciting mantras atone foreign noises.

"As you can witness, I also love nature and their endless variety of geometric forms. I thrive with these forms and symbols. This is why I invited you here. I want you to witness that I'm a true believer in the secrets of nature. They have deep spiritual meanings to me."

"I can attest that you're serious," Celeste agrees.

"Do you want some tea? Please take a seat"

"That would be nice."

Sybil goes in the kitchen to make the tea.

The furniture is comfortable and practical. The place is clean and in order. There is a pot of fresh flowers on a side table.

There are some man's shoes, next to the door. The worn shoes would have significance for Trish. They must surely belong to Sybil's husband or boyfriend.

Sybil serves the tea and asks, "So how's it going with your boyfriend?"

"It's up to his lawyer. We just have to wait and it'll turn out fine."

"Let's hope so. I'd like to talk to you about The Flower of Life and its meanings.

"I looked it up on the Internet and it's full of mathematical meanings, such as the Fibonacci series and the Metatron cube. It is also compared to the Seed of life, the Tree of Life, the Egg of Life and the Fruit of Life."

"Right on. I'm not here to talk about geometry I'm interested in the Spirit of it."

"Go on."

Would you agree that the Flower of Life is beautiful?"

"No doubt about it."

"Why is it beautiful?"

"It is made of circles everyone likes."

"Circles are feminine traits."

"Soft and symmetrical."

"Excellent. This brings me to talk about another concept, that of outer beauty and inner beauty. You are a perfect example of external beauty, as shown by your growing popularity. This exterior beauty should be symmetrical to your inner beauty. Let me explain. Inner beauty is the notion that a person shouldn't be motivated by strong negative emotions. For example, if someone is anxious and worried, he might have a tendency to frown or if the person has pent-up anger, he might be rude or irritable and tense up his body. In other words, that person who nurtures negative feelings might exteriorize his emotions that would taint his beauty, both internal and external. That's why it is important to address that aspect."

"I understand."

"In Asia they call it the Ki. It is a measure of one's equilibrium."

"The masseuse told me that my Ki was not in equilibrium. I didn't press her to explain."

"Well, from what I understand, your relations with your parents are a bit tenuous?"

"I have to admit that they aren't the best. I get along quite well with my brother, though."

"Most young adults have a rocky relationship with their parents, because it is part of growing up to break the bond with our parents. However, the link must be reestablished and preferably strengthened between mature children and their parents.

The idea is not to change the parents' behavior, but to adapt your own attitude towards your parents."

"I doubt that I could easily do that!"

"I'm not saying that it will be effortless, but I'm sure that you can do it. It's important for you as a person, because you'll reduce some negative reactions that hinder you progress."

"So what do you recommend?"

"I suggest that you go back home periodically and attempt to improve your ties with both of your parents. Again, don't attempt to change your parents, because they won't change, unless they want to change. Improve your communications with them, be patient and forgiving."

"That would be difficult. My parents have their little routine and nothing else preoccupies them. I wouldn't know where to start."

"Remember that you want to improve your own relationship with your father and mother. It will take some effort, but it'll be worthwhile. When we are young, our parents determined what and how we communicate. When we become teenagers, we rebel against that. Oftentimes, communications stay that way for the rest of their lives, which is deplorable, unless the parents are fundamentally toxic. Some children simply accept what the parents established. A fully mature person will restore communications, using their own tone and rules. I'm inviting you to meditate on how to improve your contacts with your parents so that you do not carry negative feelings throughout your life. Find some common ground where both will be comfortable. You take the initiative; don't rely on your parents to make the first step. They did their best and now it's up to you to initiate your progress."

"I suppose that I could try that."

"Now what other characteristic would you say the Flower of Life has that makes it beautiful?"

"The lines flow from one point to another."

"Yes. The points are linked, within the circle of consciousness. This is an essential trait. In human terms, it is the concepts of linking one thought to another. This ability can be a form of social network, which is important to build links with people and with your environment. I encourage you to get to know people from all lifestyles. You never can tell when a person might help you.

"Proportionality is another trait of beauty. Everything should be proportional. This means that you shouldn't exaggerate in anything, whether it is our emotions, our behavior or the thoughts that flow in our mind. Physically we grow fat if we eat too much, emotionally we can somber into depression, if we grieve excessively or we can become obsessive, if we continually rehash some pet peeve, for example."

"I'll try that," Celeste agrees reluctantly.

"Given your present situation what are your goals in life? Have you modified them since you came here?"

"Yes, I've adapted them to my condition. Even though I'd like to marry and have children, I intend to wait and experience opportunities that have become accessible. I want to become a mature woman that has lived what she can achieve."

"I'm impressed," Sybil recognizes the maturity and the wisdom of the answer.

"Tell me more about yourself. You seem to be a complex person with many layers," Celeste releases some intriguing questions that she yearned to ask.

"My father had a lot of influence on me. As I told you, he was a magician who was fascinated by esoteric subjects, such as the Flower of Life. Much of his magic was to suggest things to the audience. I was eager to gobble up all his tricks. Our family traveled regularly to different cities, where my father would perform his magic. This forced me to become introspective. I meditated and spent much time reading on spirituality. In one city, papa brought me to see a ballet, Swan Lake by Tchaikovsky, which was certainly the most beautiful spectacle that I witnessed in my life. This incited me to dance to music, whenever I could. I liked going in nature to imitate the foliage that sways with the wind, or the ripples of a cackling brook. If I got lucky and saw a swan, I would become one. My life was set. I practiced out of the sheer love of dancing. This led me to become a student in some of the best places in the world. Finally, I danced with a troupe, until I unfortunately hurt my foot so badly that I had to stop. The worst wound was to my spirit, that lost its sense of purpose. I became severely depressed and contemplated suicide. At that point, Mr. Farber herd about me and offered me to coach and mentor to promising youngsters. After a bit of encouragement, I accepted and here I am."

"I'm lucky to have you as my mentor," Celeste admits with admiration.

"Thank you."

"Have you rebelled against your parents?"

"That's a good question." Sybil takes a sip of tea to regain her composure, before dealing with that delicate subject. "When I was in my teens and twenties, I didn't get along with my mother, not that she wasn't a good mother." Sybil braces herself, as she is about to divulge some of her vulnerabilities. "My mother wanted to know everything that I did. She wanted me to detail everything, from the people I met, to the places I went to and to what I thought. She believed that she was nurturing. I felt that she was trying to control me. I avoided her as much as possible, but she always found a way to meddle in my affairs. She would listen to my phone conversation and question me afterwards. She provided me with her opinions whenever she could. My room was never as tidy as she wanted. My clothes were never to her liking. My friends were never good enough. She truly believed that she was trying to help me, but I didn't want her opinions, because I wasn't a child anymore. It seemed that every encounter escalated to become confrontational. She would succeed in making me so upset that I slammed a door or that I started crying. She counseled me relentlessly on my clothes, on my hair or on my boyfriends. We were like enemies.

At least, my father and I got along well. He wasn't interested in how I looked and who my friends were. His world revolved around his work, fooling people that something that wasn't real. To him, the world was an illusion and reality was inaccessible. He viewed business and politics in the same way. Life was an appearance that was different from reality and he tried to guess what the real facts were.

I absorbed my father's outlook on life. That's why I like my work, where I can convert somebody into appearing as someone else. It is a form of magic."

"It's eerie the way you described your relationship with your mother. It's as if you were in my place, with my mother. Did you ever reconcile with your mother?"

"Yes I did. At a certain point, I was about to shut off and ignore her. I decided that this was not the proper solution and that I should establish a better way to deal with her; after all, she would remain my mother for the rest of my life and then some. I realized that I could not change my mother's behavior towards me; I only had the control of my own behavior. Furthermore, I didn't want to hurt her in any way, I just wanted to build a better rapport between us. I could have made some snide remarks or become rude to her, but I avoided that."

"I admit that I avoid my mother. That's how I choose to deal with her. I simply avoid her comments. It seems to work."

"This is a common reaction, but it isn't satisfying, for either mother or daughter. The main solution consisted of warding off any emotion. This is particularly difficult when the comment is an attempt to wound me in some way. For example, if she said that I have no taste, my answer should be 'Our tastes are different' and if I'm too hurt to give that answer, it was best to be quiet and cool off before answering. I didn't want to escalate the fight by replying 'You're old fashioned,' for example. I didn't want to ignore her. I wanted to neutralize her comments. This is easy to say, but it is difficult especially at the beginning. Eventually she realized that I had a right to my opinions, my tastes and my life."

"I gather that the key notion is 'neutralize'."

"Right on."

"I'm not sure that I could do that."

"You should try, for your own peace of mind. You owe it to yourself to become appealing on the inside as you are in your exterior. I will help you, as best as I can."

"I'll meditate on that. It's been a pleasure."

They kiss on the cheek and they part.

***

In the limousine, Celeste takes a phone call from Nick:"Hey Celeste, did you reach Andy?"

"Yes and he explained what is going on. He was denied bail, so he's going to have to stay in jail. His lawyer seems to have a way to get him out, but it'll take time."

"That's somewhat good news. Listen I'd like you to join me in my yacht the 'Finally'. I invited Sean Beck, a bachelor from a reality show; you might be interested in meeting them."

"When?"

"Saturday. We'll be leaving the California Yacht Cabrillo Marina, Whalers' Walk in San Pedro at nine for Santa Catalina Island. It's a day of fun and relaxation. It'll change your mind and you'll probably make some friends. If you've got some snorkeling or scuba gear, bring it along."

"Can I bring along a girlfriend of mine? Her name is Diana. She's a fun girl."

"Sure."

"Great. Saturday at nine."

Celeste doesn't grasp Nick's motivation. He likes being with Celeste, a beautiful woman about half his age that must flatter his ego, but he never made a pass at her. He even invited a potential rival on the cruise, Sean. He never mentioned that he had a girl friend, that he was married or that he has children. It doesn't seem that he's homophobic either. She could enquire; he might construe that she's prying into his privacy. Better leave the puzzle remain an enigma.

***

Celeste phones Diana from the limousine.

"Diana this is Celeste. How are you?"

"Celeste, what a surprise! I'm great."

"Are you free on Saturday?"

"That depends."

"It depends on what?"

"What do you have in mind?"

"A yacht to Santa Catalina with Sean Beck and...."

"Not THE Sean Beck?"

"Yeah."

"For him I'll make room."

"Can you be at the California Yacht Cabrillo Marina in San

Pedro, Whalers' Walk at nine o'clock."

"Sure can."

"All right e."

"Wait. Whatever happened to your boyfriend? Is he in jail?"

"Yeah. He should have been more careful. He didn't have to push that photographer, after all he already had two prior convictions; that was careless."

"What do you mean?"

"He being charged under the mandatory jail law."

"Oh my god!"

"You can say that again."

"Do you love him?"

"I like him. He's good in bed."

"Do you love him?" Diana insists.

"I can't say that I love him, but I like him an awful lot. I never said it to him and he never said it to me."

"Guys don't say it much."

"Well he didn't. We like each other and we like having sex."

"That's a pretty good start."

"I'm hot, I love sex and I'm not ashamed of it."

"Same here."

"We'll see what happens, meanwhile I'm going on with my life."

"Yeah, now let's have some fun."

"Fun it will be."

CHAPTER FIFTEEN

Dolphin

SATURDAY NINEISH and everyone in the group is allowed to pass the marina's gate onto the dock cart manned by a crew member who takes them to the yacht, Finally. One by one, they board by the gangway. Celeste and Diana arrive together. Diana flinches at the sight of her hero, Sean Beck, standing on the yacht.

Nick proceeds. "Welcome on board."

He salutes with his right hand in the manner of the officer in charge. Sean Beck doesn't need any introduction; he's the darling of the media of considerable charm and charisma who conquers everyone with a hint of a smile. His private life is the subject of every entertainment show. He is at the top of the A list and this is a good occasion to get away from it all. His chauffeur will wait for him, alongside Celeste's one; perhaps they will share anecdotes. He moves with fluidity.

"This is Celeste with her photographer Derek and her friend...?"

"Diana. It's a delight to meet you all. Sorry Derek, no photos on this trip," Nick admonishes.

Celeste wasn't about to contradict Nick. Derek is glad that he has a free day to himself.

"I'm Nick Dash."

Over here, is our lovelorn bachelor, Sean Beck. For those who don't watch reality shows, Sean was turned down by a beautiful young woman, who on the final day of the series; it was found out that she was pregnant from a previous lover."

This sparks some chuckles.

In the past, Celeste, Trish and Diana watched the reality series with anticipation. In the latest series, Sean was the darling. He started as an actor, but then he was selected for a reality show. He has a marked masculine demeanor, with a sleek muscular body women dream of. He truly was in love with Nathalie. Sean is the kind of guy that is quick to appeal to women, because he looks charming and reserved and these characteristics becomes even more enticing with time. He's straightforward sweet, sincere and tender. He doesn't shy away from making sweet talk; he got in trouble during the show because the other contestants made fun of him, but he enchanted the predominantly female audience. His father told him "If you have something good to say, don't hesitate but if you have something bad to spill, keep it in your mouth". He is good at sports, particularly tennis that he often practices.

Back on the Finally, two crew members take the diving gear and stow it away in the tender.

Nick nods his head and points the way. "We can go on the flying bridge, while the crew casts off. We'll be able to see the maneuvers, the port and the cityscape. If you want to change clothes, just head inside and choose any cabin."

Celeste and Diana bring their tote bag and head for the main cabin. The magnificent owner's bedroom, with en-suite, is made of spotless dark polished teak and mocha colored upholstery. They change into their skimpy bathing suits, recommended by Akarsh.

By the time Celeste and Diana climb the spiral staircase to the Flying bridge to find a seat next to each other, the ship is on its way.

"Would you like a drink?" a lovely waitress, scantily dressed in marine suit proposes.

"A Shirley Temple," Celeste accepts.

"I'll have a screwdriver," Diana asks.

One can't help but to imagine naughty thoughts Sean and Nick have, as their look slide along her silky legs, begging to be gawked at. Then they check out Celeste who is sitting properly with her legs crossed and attired with the latest you've-got-to-be-kidding emerald bathing suit and matching boater with a trailing ribbon, teasing the breeze.

Sean sighs and Celeste senses it, but unlike Nick, it is not the look of lust, but the longing of a lost love that lingers.

Nick breaks the ice: "Sean? You don't mind that I call you Sean?"

"That's my name. I suppose everyone is on a first name basis."

"How's your film career? I hear you will make a movie?"

"Yes. It'll probably hit the screen in a year or two. Right after this cruise, I'll be promoting the film, an adult romance called 'Remorse and regrets'."

"Are you the one with remorse and regrets?" Diana intervenes.

"Ha, ha. I'm the one who causes them!"

"You've got the best role!"

"Well I AM the hero."

"I can't wait to see it."

"You should be in the movies. Have you been to casting auditions?"

"No. Right now, I have a contract with Prestige Fair. I work with Celeste."

"I heard about that. So, you two are the talk of the town."

"The talk of the world," Diana proudly insists, frowning.

"Yes the world." Sean smiles and opens his arms in the shape of the world.

"The universe," Celeste jokes, shaking her head.

"Her boyfriend just got in trouble protecting her," Nick adds while shaking his head.

"A pretty girl like you needs protection," Sean asserts.

"Thank you," Celeste warms to the compliment.

Turning to Sean: "How are you getting over your rejection?"

"You mean on the reality show?"

"Yes."

"I'm pretty much over it. For me, it ended three weeks ago, but it was aired only last week."

"Did you love her that much?" Celeste is a bit skeptical.

"Yes I did. It's a risk I assumed and I have to accept the consequences. Most guys were dumped, but that's the game."

Celeste asks Sean, "Do you think that love is a game?"

"To a certain extent, I do. Courtship is a means to test your potential partner."

"For you, love isn't serious then?"

"I didn't say that. See, you're playing a game with me. You're testing me."

"Am I?"

"You can be serious about love and play games, after all games are fun."

"So love is fun?"

"It should be. Couples should have fun with one another and games are part of that fun."

"So Natalie played with you!"

"Yep and she won. I learned a lot about myself."

"And so did we. You're a nice talker."

"That's kind of you to say."

"Tell me, how do you feel about this experience?"

"Are we talking about the reality show or about this boat trip?"

"Both I guess!"

"I still love Nathalie. I was duped and I still feel that way."

"Why? You knew what you were getting yourself into."

"I could sense that she felt for someone else. I was never going to win."

"So you wanted to win?"

"I mean that, from the beginning I didn't have a chance."

"Why didn't you leave?"

"I wanted to be sure. She's an awfully good looking girl and she's so sweet."

"You wanted a tease then?"

"I had to try my luck."

"Admit it, you wanted a tease. You knew she'd fallen for this other guy, but you wanted to flirt with her and you liked that she played along?"

"Maybe I could have seduced her?"

"The odds were against you."

"Perhaps, but I had to try."

"You liked the thrill of the chase?"

"Yes. Celeste, how about your boyfriend? It was all over the news."

"That's his problem. I'm getting along with my life."

"Do you love him?"

"I like him, but I'm not in love with him. We're very good friends. I'll support him, but I don't know what our future will be like."

"I must be difficult for you?"

"Yes. Things didn't turn out as I'd like, but that's destiny. On the other hand, I couldn't have predicted what my life was going to be like. Now, I let fate present me with surprises."

"Destiny led us here."

"I wonder what fate will present me with, in the future."

"At least you don't have a broken heart, unlike me!"

"I may not be broken-hearted, but my heart still aches for Andy. He doesn't deserve to be in jail for such an insignificant act. He's a good guy. We had a great time together. He showed me the city by helicopter. He's a helicopter salesman. If it wasn't for the mandatory jail law, he'd be having fun with us here."

"He's lucky to have a woman like you!"

"Thank you."

"I guess that we're on the same boat! Our love interests are both far away and we're here sharing our feelings talking about our pain."

"Can't argue with that!"

Nick announces, "Ladies and gentlemen, for those who aren't in the know, we are taking a cruise to Catalina Island for the day. A buffet waits for you in the dining quarters. If you need anything, just ask for it in the galley or from any of my staff."

Sean confides to Celeste: "Last time I went on a cruise was with Nathalie."

Celeste doesn't reply, keeping hidden that she'd never been on a cruise before.

"Let's have some fun!" Diana enticers Celeste, who senses that Diana is up to something.

The girls go on deck, and Diana lies face down on a lounge chair.

"Oil me up!" she tells Celeste, as she hands her a bottle of tanning lotion.

"Do it with prestige!" she says with a smile.

Celeste smiles back, as she understands the meaning of the invitation. She palms a bit of lotion that she rubs with both hands slowly, sensually. She starts with Di's neck and shoulders that she squeezes gently.

"That feels good," hushes Di.

Delicately Celeste's hands strike Di's arms back and forth. Nobody ushers a word as the oil glisten in the sun's reflection.

Methodically Celeste travels down Di's back to the delight of the onlookers.

Di lets out a slight moan to exacerbate the tension.

Celeste reaches the legs sensing every curve, till all of Di's back is done.

"I'll finish the rest," thanks Di as she takes the bottle.

Celeste relaxes in a waiting lounge chair with her cocktail glass. Nick is pleased to join them, as if an invisible force pulled him.

Sean roams about the ship.

So this is the life of a Hollywood star, Celeste ponders! Heaven must have a reason to bestow such a destiny upon her. Perhaps she is destined to accomplish something important. What will the future bring? What does heaven have in store for her?

She has more than she wished for, yet she feels that something is missing. It seems that whatever we have, we still lack something or other.

What could be better? Some lucky people could take this kind of lifestyle for granted, but she is humbled and grateful for everything that is happening to her. She appreciates every second of it.

The fresh sea wind flows past her. She has never been so close to an ocean before. Some seagulls circle overhead, some shrieking for no apparent reason. As the yacht hits the combers in succession, she dozes off.

She wakes up to a hustle-bustle of people preparing to leave the ship. They're already moored at the Santa Catalina Avalon marina, where ships are lined up like a bunch of sardines in a tin can.

"Are you going ashore?" asks Nick.

"Sure."

"We're going to do some snorkeling at Two Harbors. Do you want to come with us?"

"I've never done some snorkeling before."

"You can swim don't you?"

"Sure."

"Snorkeling is a cinch. I'll show you how."

"But I don't have any gear!"

"It's all taken care of. Wait till we get there!"

"I might as well go."

"All right then!" Nick likes her gumption.

Nick, Sean and Celeste leave the ship by its gangway, to their dinghy that shuttles them to port, while Diane remains on the ship. The crew is busy carrying the gear and dealing with the local firms that have arranged every detail of their adventure.

Celeste feels somewhat uncomfortable surrounded by two alpha males. She isn't the kind to complain or even comment.

A pelican is perched on a piling post and watches the scene.

Most people on Santa Cat use golf carts to travel back and forth and so they board a cart, Nick driving. The crew takes other carts to cater the gear. The caravan is on its way.

The town was built in the 1930s and many building have retained their initial styles, such as the casino that kept its Art Deco aspect. Many homes are in the Craftsman's style with earthy colors and paned windows and doors. Most have verandas or a porch overlooking the bay. Palm trees rest peacefully.

The land is arid and there are cacti here and there.

"Look, there's a bison," Nick points out at the animal.

Nick makes the remark that many Americans talk about "buffalo" when they should say "bison".

Celeste replies, "That's a good 'Jeopardy' question!'" referring to the popular TV program.

Nick smiles.

They arrive at the Two Harbors campground, where a Park Ranger welcomes them, orients them and points out the services he provided.

In little time, some tents are set up along with chairs, barbecue, coolers and so forth.

"This isn't quite roughing it!" Sean remarks.

"For me it is," Nick chuckles.

The snorkeling equipment is spread out on a table.

"I suppose that I have the pink equipment?" Celeste jokes.

"Yep," Nick grins. "Your snorkel has a top valve, so it'll stop any water from entering it.

Put on your vest, but don't inflate it with the manual inflator; use it only if you have to."

"Yes captain," Celeste replies.

"Watch out whom you call 'Captain!'"

"You're the admiral," Celeste manages to figure out.

Everything fits perfectly.

Sean is already in the water.

Celeste smears herself with some sun lotion. "Can you rub some on my back?" she asks Nick.

"Sure thing."

After obliging Celeste, Nick puts on his wetsuit, he tests and puts on his scuba gear and loads it on his diving kayak, shaped like a mini catamaran to enable it to remain stable when diving.

Celeste and Nick also suit up.

"I'll stay with Celeste, since it's she's a novice," Sean tells Nick who paddles his way out towards Fisherman's Cove.

"Nick did a stint in the Navy!"

"Did he!" Celeste is truly impressed!

Celeste follows Nick; it's her first time in seawater. Everything goes well. There are hundreds of small fishes to observe, since the visibility is at least fifty feet. The water is clear and clean.

There is the orange Garibaldi, Calico bass, blue smelts, silver barracuda... between the kelp forest and rocky shallow seashore. They have a very pleasant afternoon.

When everyone is tired of swimming, they get out of their wetsuits and gather around the campfire where they warm up. They eat some barbecue meat. Celeste lets herself be tempted by a beer. They exchange what experiences they have just had. Nick mingled in a rookery of harbor seals.

Celeste tells her story: "There was this fish swimming alone beside me, as if it was following me. At first, I didn't make anything of it. Then, just for fun, I swam towards it but it ran away. A moment later, it came back and this time I tried to catch it. I think it was playing hide-and-seek with me. That went on for quite a while, till I quit."

"You're making this up?" Nick quickly responds.

"No, this is a true story. It was a small dolphin."

"They travel in groups," Nick adds.

"So, it is a story?" Sean point out.

"It's true. It happened."

Nobody wants to pursue this argument, but she has the benefit of the doubt. She will never confide this incident to anyone, yet it will remain one of her fondest memories.

Nick must have done something, because the staff began to pack.

The group mounts the gear in the golf carts and they're on their way back.

Not much is said, as everyone seems to go over the day's events and reminisce in order to memorize them in a beautiful place.

Oddly, the bison seemed to be in about the same place, but turned around in the opposite direction, towards Avalon.

They arrive at the town's extremity, the group steps down on the Via Casino, and they wander towards the pier.

"Do you want to buy some souvenir?" Nick asks Celeste next to him.

"Maybe we could stop by and take a look?"

Sean waits outside and talks with Nick.

"Sure."

They browse in a spacious souvenir shop, where she buys a dolphin charm for a souvenir bracelet.

"Good choice," Nick smiles.

One by one, they wind up on the Finally. Nick takes a nap in his stateroom. Sean and Diane converse. Celeste enjoys the scenery.

Evening sets in, and the ship lights up and glows to the soft classical music in the background. The ship heads for Cabrillo Beach where they anchor.

"You must be hungry," Nick asks rhetorically.

The crew sets up a dining table cover and colorful porcelain.

"Champaign everyone?" Nick proposes and nobody refuses.

The chitchat begins.

Sean proposes a toast to Nick and it is with delight that the guests embrace it.

The day is a complete success.

A slight sea breeze send shivers on Celeste, who cringes.

"Let me get a throw blanket," Sean proposes.

"I'll get one," Nick intervenes and is quick to find and wrap around Celeste, since he is the owner of the Finally and is privy to all the nooks.

Celeste likes the attention of both men seeking her favors. Her self-worth has just risen to a level never experienced before. She wants more. She flicks her hair back, looks up at the sparkling sky, and takes a sip of sparkling Champaign. It now seems that, for some unknown reason, she deserves a sparkling life.

She listens to the beat of the waves on the ship's side. In the distance, Los Angeles glows. On board, people joke and have fun, but she is detached in a world of contemplation.

They finish supper and the ship heads back to a catlike purr.

Celeste relishes at the distant connection she had with the seagulls, the bison and the pelican. The bison just stood there in her mind, without a care and without a friend, as if it were waiting to be immortalized in a picture or on a coin, by some unexpected passerby. The pelican on the other hand, seemed to question whether people had a good time or not, as if it were a welcoming door attendant. Well, are you having a good time it insisted? Most of all, she tried to figure out whether her experience with the dolphin was real. After all, the people around her doubted that it happened. Perhaps that particular dolphin had some previous contact with humans. Perhaps it had been trained. Dolphins have been mixing with humans since the beginning of civilization. Did it have a meaning? Did the dolphin want to communicate something by buddying up with her? At any event, she felt something uncommon after having lived that moment.

CHAPTER SIXTEEN

Amends

N HOUR AFTER she gets home, she fortuitously gets a call.

"Hi, this is Nick."

"Nick?" Celeste recognizes his voice.

"How are you?"

"Couldn't be better," she refrains from echoing the question.

"How is your boyfriend doing?"

"You mean Andy?"

"Of course."

"I'm going to see him tomorrow."

"Well I hope he's doing fine, given the circumstances."

"That's kind of you."

"Tell me, if I can help you."

"I will."

"What are you doing this weekend?"

"I'm going back home to see my parents. I haven't seen them for a while. I've set aside some time to see my mother and my brother."

"You live in Canada?"

"Yes, in a suburb of Toronto."

"Let my join you. I have a private jet that's just waiting to take off. We could be there in no time. You could introduce me to your mother, I'm sure she'd be thrilled to meet me."

"That's too much. I couldn't do that."

"And why not?"

"Will Diana come with us?"

"She told me that she already had plans for this weekend, so no, she won't come," Nick says, as convincingly as possible.

"I couldn't accept your offer. I don't know you that well."

"We'll have a whole flight to talk about ourselves."

"Still!"

"Ok, I'll tell you about myself. You must think that I'm a womanizer and that I'm constantly on the hunt?"

"That crossed my mind."

"I admit, women are attracted to me and I respond to their flirts. That's perfectly normal, as far as I'm concerned. Don't you think?"

"I suppose."

"There you are.

So how about my offer to fly you home?"

Celeste wasn't certain that she could handle him. She hesitates but then she gets an idea.

"Could I ask you for a favor?"

"Ask."

"Could we bring Sean along? He's so lonesome and it would do him good."

"The more people the more fun," he replies reluctantly.

"You're a great guy."

"How about Friday evening at five at the Bob Hope Executive airfield?"

"Fine."

She's got some phoning to do.

"Sean?"

"Is this Celeste?"

"Yes."

"What a pleasant surprise."

"Get a hold of this, Nick offered to fly me home this weekend. I thought that it would be great if you could come also. Would you come?"

"That is a surprise. Let me see. For the whole weekend?"

"Yes. You could visit Toronto, if you've never been there."

"Yeah, I could make it work."

"Friday evening at five, at the Burbank airfield."

"Perfect."

She's thrilled to bring along two triple A celebrities.

She can't wait to call Trish.

"Hi."

"It's been so long since you called!

How's life?" They recognized each other's voice without any preamble.

"Hectic. You wouldn't believe what is happening," she throws a teaser.

"Tell me, tell me."

"I'm going home for the weekend."

"Aaand?"

"On an executive jet."

"Aaand?"

"With Nick Dash."

"Noooooo!"

"Yeees!"

"Wait for the best part."

"There can't be a better part."

"Oh, but there is."

"What is it?"

"I'm bringing along Sean."

"Sean?"

"Yes, Sean."

"You don't mean Sean?"

"Yes, Sean."

"You're messing with me!"

"No I'm not."

"How is that ever possible?"

"Listen, I want mother to meet them. I'd like you to organize a get-together with all her parents, friends and acquaintances. Can you do that?"

"I'll do my best."

"Most of all you've got to keep it secret. Ask Michael to help you. Don't worry about the cost, I'll foot the bills, but it must accommodate a lot of people and be first rate, top of the line."

"What's the occasion?"

"I just want to show mother what I've become."

"You are pulling my leg?"

"No. It's important to me.

Will you do it?"

"It'll be a challenge, but you must introduce me to Nick and Sean."

"Naturally. Now I have to get in touch with mother so that she'll be there on Saturday morning."

"I'll set the wheels in motion. Don't you worry."

"Mother?" Celeste asks on the phone.

"Hi sis," Michael answers, instead of their mother.

"Michael you'll get a phone call from Trish. Please do as she'll ask you."

"Sure. What is this hush-hush?"

"Please, just get mom on the phone."

"Sure. Keep cool!"

An instant later, "Hi dear!" Alice says, with her sweetest voice.

"Hi mom, how are you?"

"All right, I guess. I'm concerned about you."

"You shouldn't be. I get along quite well.

 Listen, I'm going home for the weekend and I'd like to introduce you to some of my friends."

"That would be wonderful, but I promised Martha I'd go shopping with her."

"Please do me a favor and postpone your shopping. You can ask your sister to come and also meet my friends."

 "That could be arranged, after all, we seldom see you."

"Thanks mother."

"Bye," Alice was aware that it was important to Celeste when she called her 'mother', rather than 'mom'. There was something unusual about this demand. Celeste had never done that before.

Alice wanted their relation to evolve because she didn't relish the regular confrontations they had when they stayed together. Alice was open to a new rapport between them and this might be the occasion for such an improvement.

CHAPTER SEVENTEEN

Oblivion

ANDY IS BUNKED up with another inmate, Josiah, a veteran who doesn't seem to realize what happened and what was going on; another inmate told Andy that Josiah was a crackhead whose brain was fried. Josiah is harmless most of the time, but when it comes to sleeping, he snores and his bad breadth, due to his rotten teeth, infiltrates everything in the cell. Inmates take every opportunity to "crack" jokes about him.

One of the first things Andy learns is not to be polite in any way. He doesn't say that he's sorry, because someone might construe it to mean that he's weak. He has to seem tough and sometimes he has to be tough. It helps to admit that he "was in" because of a charge of assault and battery and he readily admits that he's guilty of the crime. However, he can't get his mind to wrap around the fact that his sentence is so harsh. Sure, he was aware of that law, but it seemed unreal. He doesn't regret having shoved that idiot, but he does anguish that he was so foolish, so careless, so naïve to put in peril his liberty and all that goes along with it, including his relationships with his parents, his friends and fellow workers and mostly with Celeste. He rehashes the incident over and over in his head.

Every morning, Andy awakens at six o'clock, he's cramped and he feels sick. Josiah gets up and, as a wild animal pent up in a cage, he walks back and forth with a blank stare, waiting for death to come; it doesn't. Andy has become indifferent of this being, now that he's accepted the daily routine. They do their bed and arrange their locker according to regulations, but Andy has to clean the place up. At first, he tried to engage a conversation with that sorry being. Then he tried to convince him to do something else, anything else, in vain. Now, his cellmate is a zombie, a paltry remnant shell of a human being, in an empty and utterly careless world. They go to the showers to wash up, but Josiah still walks back and forth until a guard or a prisoner pushes him in under a shower; Andy learned to do this in such a way as not to anger Josiah. Then the inmates go to the refectory and have their morning breakfast, served by a separate group of jailbirds.

Every day, Andy's feet become sore, because he forces them to hurt by prying them back or against an object. He would rather feel those particular pains than suffer the thoughts of having harmed the people around him that he liked or loved.

He was assigned to a work detail, assembling some mattresses, so he does it, in total resignation. He talks to as few people as possible.

He tries to remain fit by doing some daily exercises, in the hope that he'll someday be able to be released from this ordeal. He clings to this, to avoid becoming forgotten by humanity.

Every night, when he tries to overcome the stench in his cell, he remembers the lovemaking with Celeste and he jerks off, to release the pent up frustrations that continually pester him.

Even though he isn't religious, in case there is a heaven, he mutters some pleas to God, in solace. Sometimes, when Josiah hears Andy's prayers, Josiah moans and laments.

While Josiah suffers of the despair that nobody will ever visit him or communicate with him, Andy awaits with uneasiness Celeste's visit, for he feels mortified at having loaded this burden onto her.

To him, Celeste is like an angel, travelling from heaven to hell. She had just feasted with some of the most blessed people on this planet and now, she must enter the somber corridors of society, where men are locked up to spend their remaining lives in eternal damnation; she is an angel that has the ability to enchant both cherubs and demons. He recognizes that she is drawn to the task in order to provide some reverie to a man she made love to, who relies on her to provide some sort of sense of the absurd situation he's in. While she may have unwittingly been the cause of Andy's demise, Andy doesn't partake any responsibility with her.

***

As she travels towards this hell, she dwells on the reason that she was attracted to him. Is he a bad boy women find so appealing, because he can thrill her and incite her to do things she would have never attempted by herself? One thing is for sure, he isn't the boring type that'll give her roses and chocolates.

She can attest that he's great in bed. His muscles are strong and firm. When he grabs and penetrates her endlessly, in every way, he abounds of masculinity, the kind she yearns for.

He likes danger; he takes risks because he dared make advances to her, when she appeared uninterested in him. Maybe it's his cockiness and arrogance or maybe even his aggressive and possessive drive towards her that are so appealing, or his "You belong to me" attitude. He doesn't readily reveal his deep emotions and she want to find them, behind that cool front. He wants to look like he's a nature guy; she's not fooled by this facade.

She has a sense that he's a challenge, a masterpiece waiting to be revealed, HER masterpiece. She feels that her influence will smooth out his flaws and imperfections. She will become his redeeming angel.

She dresses soberly, not to provoke him too much, like the "nobody look" that conforms to the accepted prison dress code; Akarsh okays it.

As she enters the portal of infamy, her name is ticked off a list. She passes the security measures with great discomfort.

He's already waiting for her, after the official morning count. Normally, he would have greeted her with a smile, however he's stressed out, and his shame prevents him from showing it. She kisses him warmly and he cherishes it, as long as he can. They sit at a small table. Everything is clean and sanitized as if it were a hospital room.

She waits for his cue.

"Every day, every hour I envision this moment in my head."

"I miss you too."

"It's such a relief that you are actually here, after having been treated as a gear in a machine."

"What do you mean?"

"I'm merely a part in a machine that keeps on turning, day and night, and my role is to fit in perfectly, to be in tune, so that I don't upset it in any way. I'm under constant surveillance. I'm under the control of this mechanism that dictates every move and that censures every thought. There is a whole series of things I'm not allowed to do and I can't deviate from, under the threat of punishment. Not only is my liberty to act spontaneously stinted, they monitor every move and they even forbid me to dream; instead they provoke nightmares that haunt my sleep."

"Poor thing!"

"You said it; I've become a thing, a public nuisance, that they lock up in a cage and do everything in their power to keep me there. I'm lucky to have you occasionally console me; otherwise, I would attempt suicide. We're like weeds that you just can't get rid of."

"I didn't mean that. I meant that I'm so sorry for the mess you got yourself mixed up in. I share your despair and your need of me. I'll keep on visiting you and helping you in any way possible. You're very much like a child confined in his playpen that I have to comfort and support.

I'm here for you Andy."

"You're wasting your life for me. You should leave and forget me. You're young, beautiful and successful. Don't put that in peril because of me. I should have been more careful. There is no sense in ruining your life over me. My life is in shambles. I wish you all the luck in the world. Let go of me and leave me to my fate."

"I couldn't do that. What kind of woman would do that? What kind of woman would drop his man, when he needs her the most? I'm not that kind of a woman. I'm here to help you and I'll be here to help you throughout your ordeal. I'm sure that if I were in trouble that you would stand by me. Why should I do otherwise?

You have to hang tight. You will get out and regain your freedom. I have powerful friends that will help me. I won't let you stay in here forever. You must believe me."

"Celeste, you're an angel. What did I do to deserve you?

Listen, could you send me a picture of you? Maybe you could wear the outfits you had when we were in the zoo! I would appreciate that very much."

"Certainly. Do you need anything else? Some money perhaps."

"No thanks, I have all the dough I need and I can buy the things I want at the commissary. Of course, what I really want is forbidden."

"What did your lawyer say?"

"He's doing his best, but the repeat offender law is harsh. He suggested that I try other means, such as the court of public opinion. Sometimes reporters can be motivated to do stories on cases that resonate in the media."

"I'll see what I can do."

"That would be great."

"Have your parent visited you?"

"Yes, my father and mother came last week. I have their full support. My mother can't quite convince herself that I'm here. My condemnation broke her heart. I don't want to worsen the situation by insisting that she come."

"I understand.

Listen, I'll try and get public support."

"Thanks Celeste."

They get up and kiss.

CHAPTER EIGHTEEN

Flight

DEREK IS THE FIRST one to arrive at the airbase, because he'll capture the three most prominent showstoppers of the day, Celeste, Sean and Nick together at the same time, at the same place. The others arrive in succession. There are no queues and the limos arrive on the tarmac.

Before they board the plane, Sean questions, "Why do we need a photographer to tag along?"

Celeste comes to his rescue: "He goes where I go. His presence is required in my contract and the reason is very simple, Mr. Farber wants to control the pictures that are to be published. He wants the paparazzi to have as little leeway as possible."

"Ok, since it's in your contract," Sean accepts, somewhat vexed that he doesn't have Nick's authority.

Derek blinks at Celeste. Derek unpacks a portable drone that takes pictures from the air.

Sean greets the pilots and the sexy flight attendant who confirms that everything is in order. Everyone boards the plane. Since it's a wide body executive jet, they have enough space to carry on comfortably a group conversation. They taxi on the ramp and the plane takes off and heads towards the east. The sunset splashes on the Rockies and makes them glimmer in a myriad of bright hues.

The captain announces, "We'll be landing at the Burlington Executive airport at nine thirty."

The flight attendant offer drinks and food. Celeste delights herself with some California sparkling wine. She holds up her flute glass: "I propose a toast to Nick for inviting us here. A true Hollywood gentleman!"

"Hail!" Sean salutes.

Derek is busy taking shots from everywhere he can sneak in. He's somewhat of a contortionist who can take angle shots from the weirdest places.

Celeste closes her eyelids and ponders over her incredible adventure. Not long ago, she was an ordinary girl, going about her daily routine, ignored by most people and now, she is literally soaring above millions of fans who are idolizing her. She is bringing home two of the most admired men to present to her mother. She is astonished. She longs to show her parents who and what she has become. She wishes to remodel her relationships with them.

The hot flight attendant bends towards Sean, given his reputation, and looks at both men in succession and proposes: "Would you gentlemen desire anything else?"

The men don't succumb to the veiled invitation of joining the mile-high club, by going in a secluded compartment, as they are acutely aware of Derek's ubiquitous cameras.

Celeste keeps an innocent look, without flinching.

"Celeste you dodn't know much about me. Now is your chance to prod my past," Sean says.

"You're right.

Let me see. As you know, before going to the reality show, I was an actor.

What was the character I portrayed that you liked best?"

"I could say that it was that of Ernest Hemingway, because it got me the most prestigious awards."

"You got an Oscar for that, didn't you?" Nick interjects.

"Yes.

I suppose it was the most glorious moment of my life.

Actually, the character that I cherish most was that of Dr. Owens. That character won over a place in the heart of people, regardless of age and sex. Everybody loves a doctor who saves lives and cares about patients. There are people to this day that call me Dr. Owens.

I'll tell you a few anecdotes. During the series, I often had to shuttle by regular planes and more and more people recognized me. On one occasion, a passenger became sick on the plane. Wouldn't you know it? A woman summoned me to examine the passenger. I said that I wasn't a real doctor, but the woman would have heard nothing of it. People around her began insisting that I do something. Fortunately, a real nurse offered her services and comforted the sick passenger.

I must admit, however, that being thought of as a doctor did have some advantages. One day, I met a lovely young woman who seemed to be attracted to me. I told her that she looked pale and I asked to examine her. I took her hand and checked her pulse that was rapid. I looked closely in her eyes and I asked her to stick out her tongue, which she readily did. I told her that I thought that I found out what was troubling her and that I would need to do a thorough examination. She didn't object at all and I led her to a private area where I completed my examination. My diagnostic revealed that she was healthy and all she needed was some tender loving care that I gave her profusely."

"You're joking?" Nick says.

"It's a true story. In fact, I had a few comparable encounters with similar results."

"Sean, you confessed to the whole world that you couldn't find love. Come on. I've heard of ploys before but that's a beauty. Poor Sean all the women were pleading, he can't find his love. You have to help this poor soul!"

"These were my true feelings. I swear. I'm not faking."

"You're lucky, in a few days you'll have all women at your feet wanting to satisfy you," Nick says. "It's a great script. I wish I always had writers like you have."

"That's how I feel man!"

Celeste steps in: "So Sean, what's been your most embarrassing moment?"

"My most embarrassing moment?

I was doing a movie. It was a beach love scene. Just when I was about to kiss my beautiful costar, a seagull decided to relieve itself on my head. The editor cut the scene. Apparently the studio kept it as a possible blooper."

"Tell us about something that people usually don't know about you."

"I'm not an actor. What I mean by that is that I don't have learned any acting skills. I've never been in acting school. As a youngster in Hollywood, I sometimes would be part of the crowd in the street traffic. It was quick and easy money. By some fluke, they asked me to play a bouncer. I guess that they liked it. An agent contacted me and offered to represent me. I told him that I was not an actor. He replied that it didn't matter and that all I had to do is act natural. I did it and it worked. I'm still not an actor. I don't try to imitate someone else I just become that person, whoever he is. If they tell me that I'm Ronald Reagan, I become him. I am him."

"It's method acting," Nick adds.

"So they tell me," answers Sean. "I guess that I'm a natural method actor."

"Do you have any secret skill?"

"Nobody ever asks me that. Why yes, I'm a ventriloquist. Not only that, but I can imitate the sound of many birds and animals." He takes a cushion and he imitates a parrot: "Give me a kiss. Give me a kiss."

Celeste breaks up in laughter and can't help herself but kiss him.

She turns to Sean: "How about you, do you have any hidden skill?"

"I can also imitate a parrot."

"You've got to be better than that!"

"I make custom golf putters."

"Really?"

"It's my hobby."

"Great surprise," Celeste says.

"How about you Celeste?" Sean asks.

"I grow orchids; they must have two colors. They're wonderful plants that keep their flowers for a long time. They don't require much maintenance and they're so pretty. I just love them."

"Is that so?" enquires Sean.

"They're one of the most beautiful flowers in the world, as far as I'm concerned. I look at them whenever I can in and I count my blessings."

There is an instant of relief.

"There is one thing I can't get my mind off," Celeste admits.

"It must be Andy," Nick immediately responds.

"Yes. I visited him yesterday in jail and he's rather pessimistic. His lawyer talked about publicizing his story, rather than aggressively pursuing the legal approach."

"Oh boy!" Nick lets out.

"He's in serious trouble," Nick reinforces.

"I'm afraid so."

"Celeste, I should not say this, but maybe you should back off. He seems like a looser and you'll waste your time and life fighting for him," Nick warns.

"That has been troubling me for some time. Andy also told me that. On the other hand, I do like him and we do have an affinity between us. I can't let him go when he needs me the most. What would people say of me? More importantly, what would I think of myself? He's like a little kid that got himself in trouble and he's expecting me to help him and to support him. He's part of my life. I don't know if I'll ever love him and whether we'll share life together, at any rate I have to stand by him for now."

"Your life has begun, don't let him take too great a part of your life," Nick adds. "I think that he's toxic and that the more time you spend for him, the more you will get poisoned by him."

"Oh, I already had the experience of a toxic boyfriend, so I'm acutely mindful of that. Nevertheless, I decided to help him. I went out with him before he went to prison and he seems to be a good guy."

"It seems that you pity him. He did commit three crimes so he should be punished," Nick comments.

"Prison should not be about retribution and punishment; it should be about rehabilitation. Can Andy live in our society without threatening people? Just because he shoved a paparazzi doesn't warrant serving a life sentence. That's laughable. He's not a dangerous member of society. Come on!"

"So what are you going to do about it, now that he's locked up?" Sean asks.

"I was going to ask you the same question. What would you do if you were in my place?"

"Your lawyer said that the case should be publicized," Nick echoes. "I suppose that he has a good reason for saying that."

"How would I do that?"

"I guess the first thing would be to post the story on social media," Nick says.

"I'm not very good at this."

"There are professionals that can do that job. They'll start a Web site and they'll create a buzz in a mouse click. They'll send newsletters, answer Emails and do all of that stuff."

"That sounds good."

Nick takes smartphone and surfs the Internet.

"Here's a prisoner's blog that has a touching story of an inmate who wrote while in prison. In a nutshell, he writes that when he was eighteen years old he was sentenced to life without the possibility of parole for lending his car to a friend who was convicted of murdering a man. What is ludicrous is that the murder conviction of his friend was eventually overturned, but not his. In any kind of logic the two felonies were inexorably linked and if the one convicted of murder is exonerated and freed, obviously his 'accomplice' should also have been freed, especially when he wasn't even present at the murder scene."

"What is wrong?" Celeste deplores.

"Some people can get away with murder and others are harshly punished and nobody seems to care?"

"That's just the point, nobody cares," Nick steps in. "You have to make the right people care. You have to win the sympathy of people. I have a friend who investigates such case, if the story is worthy of broadcasting. That's the key to freedom. Is your friend, Andy, catchy and exciting or is he boring? Andy has to be media friendly. Can he manage that? Only then will he have a hint of a chance at appealing to people."

CHAPTER NINETEEN

Harmony

THE PLANE LANDED on time and the limos were waiting, one for Nick and Sean that would drive them to a boutique hotel in Port Credit's waterfront and the other that would drive Celeste to her family home.

Alice greets Celeste with warmth, and she reciprocates. Once Celeste is settled, she joins her mother in the kitchen. Alice and Trish are up to date on Celeste tumultuous life, since Celeste phoned them regularly.

"It's nice to come back home in my old room," Celeste says with a smile. "I'm so glad that you took care of my plants and my flowers."

"It will always be your room dear."

"It's so peaceful and worry-free here."

"That's what a home should be."

"My L.A. apartment is so much more luxurious, still I feel more at home here."

"It must be stressful having to constantly mind of your image."

"Then there's Andy. I went to see him just before coming here and he's in a bind. He seems to think that he won't be able to get out because of the legal system and that he has to resort to marshalling public opinion. I wish I didn't have to deal with that."

"You were the quiet and shy girl when you lived here."

"I kind of miss this place."

"Are you homesick sometimes?"

"Yes. I shouldn't say that, I know. Here and then, when I'm alone in bed, I think of this place and I cry, as I wonder what I got myself into."

"I'm sure your life will get better as time passes. Your life here wasn't very promising before you left. You had just broken up with Matt and your career had stalled. Now you can be optimistic. Life has hardships, whoever and wherever we are. You have a much better chance to be happy and successful now."

"I keep telling that to myself, yet I love this place. I love you, I love Michael, I love dad and I even love Gyp. By the way, where is he, I haven't seen him?

"I didn't want to tell you this dear, but I'm afraid I had to have him put down. He was very sick and in pain."

"That stupid dog. Why did he have to do that?" Celeste cries and retires to her room for the night.

Saturday morning, Celeste gets up lazily after the clock's second ring. She puts on her dressing gown and heads for the bathroom, glad that her brother Michael has not yet occupied it; she locks him out and disregards his complaints when he arrives. She brushes her teeth that also freshens her mouth and her mood. The shower is next, being careful to keep her thick hair dry. After she gets out and dries, she combs her long, plush, satiny, sepia mane that she fixes it with a barrette. She reminisces over that hair strand aptly nicknamed "Mickey" that took pleasure in annoying Celeste by obstructing part of her face.

Back in her room, she searches her trunk to choose what she was assigned as most fashionable for today's reception. She feels dazzling. Then, she adds a stunning piece of jewelry to attract attention, with matching circular earrings. She likes her glam look. Now that she's ready, she climbs down to the eat-in kitchen.

Alice is waiting for Celeste. "Did you sleep well honey?"

"You aren't looking at the news?"

"I've stopped doing that in the morning. The only news I listen to are those of you and Michael,"

Celeste pours two cups of coffee her mother brewed and she prepares two breakfasts of eggs and toast for herself and a bigger portion for her brother who kisses her on the cheek, as he arrives to eat, "Thanks sis!"

Celeste drinks her coffee from her preferred "You're special" mug.

Her mother purchased some new furniture and had the house redecorated.

"I like the new look of our home," Celeste is pleased to say.

"The time had come to change my outlook of life. When you stayed with me, I held on to my past. It was safe and reliable. Then you went away and I could think of my needs, rather than yours and Michael's. I started experimenting. At first, I just bought a little flower vase made of crystal, just because I liked it. I kept looking at it and it made me realize that I had put my life on hold to raise you. It was time to break out of my cocoon, as it were. I set aside my old life, as some animals shed their skin, in order to grow.

When you were young, I dedicated my life to you and Michael. That's all that I cared about, night and day, from the instant I woke up, to the time that I slept. It was fine. I tried to watch everything you did and protect you from any harm that might come your way. When you became teenagers, that perpetual surveillance must have been troublesome for both of you and you showed me your displeasure. After you left home, my role changed, simply because you weren't there anymore.

I started doing other activities, like playing cards with a group of women. I started gardening. I take walks with my friends and I have to admit, that they do me much good. I even followed some cooking classes. I was finished with the 'mac and cheese', the hamburgers and fries. I wanted to eat better.

Well, that about sums it up."

"Good for you mom. You are a surprise that I would have never expected. To tell you frankly, you've become the mom I always wished I had."

"Thank you dear, but I did that for myself, not for you."

Celeste smiles: "That's fine with me."

"Well dear, why do we have this celebration today? Is there some sort of event?"

"No, we're just celebrating life. Life can be fun, so why not enjoy it while we can?"

"Let's do that."

Michael explains to Celeste that they rented an entire modern open space restaurant with a large patio and ample parking space, called Jerry's Landing. It is located downtown Oakville. It serves different buffets and it has open, alcohol-free bars. There are ribbons and balloons galore and pleasant background music. All the napkins, tablecloths, wine glasses are eco-friendly throwaways and there are enough kitchen helpers to keep the area nice and tidy all the time. The personnel are dressed in black-tie uniforms. It is going to be a classy event.

The air smells of perfume with delicious culinary odors. You can hear the hustle and bustle of the staff making sure that everything is perfect. Trish and Michael are at their best, ensuring that the flowers, mostly orchids, are placed in strategic places and that the lighting is at the proper intensity and adds to the atmosphere. The ventilation is calibrated to make everyone comfortable. At the entrance, there are small souvenirs, with distinct written proverbs that people can read and use to start a conversation and that will be cherished as a reminder of this occasion. Photographers offer to take pictures at designated well-lit enclosures. There is a valet ready to park the guest's car. A master of ceremony waits at the door to announce the arrival of each guest in the loud speaker, much like royalty. A nametag is available to encourage the guests to fraternize. Each guest receives an orchid corsage or a boutonniere. A concierge is available that will cater to any demand.

Michael and Trish told Celeste that they invited all the notables of the place, as were the wannabes and their families including the children. Some people did not respond or were unavailable. Though Michael invited the incumbent priest to the celebration, he won't attend. Brent, Celeste's father, also responded that he wouldn't attend. Nobody insisted that he come, out of respect for his choice.

Some hungry guests were already munching some appetizers. The pair heads for Trish and Michael and exchange kisses and hugs.

"It's so good to see you two," Celeste tells them. "Wow, this is wonderful!"

"Thanks," Trish and Michael say in unison.

Trish whispers to Celeste's ear, "When will they be here?"

"Be patient."

Guests arrive more frequently. Pedestrians on the sidewalk slow down to admire the well-dressed people entering the restaurant. A greeting team identifies the guests, asks whether they wanted to check-in some of their garb, place the orchid and name identification, announce the guests' names and give them a souvenir that can easily be stored in a pocket or handbag. Servers lead them to an advantageous spot in the restaurant and recite the offered services.

Some hired clowns invite the children to come to the playground that had been set up especially for them. Magicians would play tricks and acrobats would help them go through the maze and slide in and around the castle.

When practically everyone has arrived, the MC declares with the loudspeaker, "Whoever said that there's no such thing as a free lunch was wrong. You are invited to eat what you can and if you want something, just ask for it! Sorry, but we don't serve alcohol because we'd like all of you to be able to go back home when it will be over. Thank you for your understanding"

People chat in mini groups.

Trish warns the MC that THE limousine has been spotted; the MC cuts the music and switches to the Los Fabulosos Cadillac "Matador" music that stirs the crowd. "Ladies and gentlemen, could you welcome two of the most famous personalities, Nick Dash" He waits for the cheers and applause to crest. "and Sean Beck." The cheers intensify to a frenzy. Bodyguards have to limit the crowd. Discrete cameras broadcast their arrival and some announcers address their particular channels.

The two men sign autographs, pose for selfies and shake hands.

Eventually, they enter the restaurant and reach Celeste.

"That's quite a gathering for a small town," Sean says.

"Sean, Sean, I'd like to present you my mother," Celeste says.

"You've got a very beautiful and resourceful daughter ma'am," Sean says.

"She's the pride of my life."

Michael could have felt slighted, but on the contrary he agreed wholeheartedly.

"And this is my brother Michael."

"Nice to meet you."

"Hi."

"Hi."

We're at some chitchat about this and that.

Celeste and Alice meet as many guests as possible. Celeste is inundated with compliments, flooded with thanks and submerged with admiration. When they've finished their round, they ease their way to Nick and Sean. Nick raises his hand to say: "We thought of leaving tomorrow, however I spoke to Sean about what we could do concerning your problem and we figured that we should stay one more day."

"You mean Andy?"

"Yes. I have a contact that might help you out and he has a vacation home near here in the Thousand Islands. I phoned him and he's willing to hear us out. I told him that we had a case of a damsel in distress. He figured that I was joking, but then I told him about you. Well he's a reporter, so he follows many of these stories. He's willing to meet with us tomorrow late in the afternoon."

"That couldn't be better."

The celebration winds up after Nick and Sean leave in their limousines. Celeste and Alice go home with Martha while Tess and Michael see to the cleanup of the place and to the last guests' demand for doggy bags for food leftovers.

***

"Well that was a morning to remember," Alice remarks.

"Mom, you'll have to excuse me, because I'd like to go and see dad."

"Go ahead dear, I'm not stopping you."

CHAPTER TWENTY

Understanding

SHE DRESSES CASUALLY to attract as little attention as possible. Celeste enters her father's apartment building. Today, somebody has been cooking steak. She rings at the door. Brent is kind of expecting her.

"If it isn't the princess!" he can't help but spew out a sarcastic comment, as he kisses her on the cheek.

He goes to the living room where they sit.

"How did your get-together go?"

"It went hunky-dory."

"There you go with those fancy words. You can't say that it went well?"

"Isn't it the same thing?"

"No."

"Anyhow, mom was more than happy with me and she was enchanted at meeting Nick Dash and Sean Beck."

"If you're trying to impress me, stop. They're all show."

"You say that because you don't understand them. For example, Sean is an Oscar winning actor. I'm proud to mix with these people."

"I suppose that you're ashamed of mixing with me?"

"Not for a second, after all I invited you to my party. You didn't come of your own accord."

"I didn't go because everything is artificial. You're masquerading as a celebrity. You're just a small city girl with a great deal of makeup and pretty clothes. Don't try to be someone else. And don't try to fool me; I'm too old for that."

"Dad, how could I possibly fool you. You brought me up. When I was young, I was teased and even bullied because I was plain. I've overcome that. Sure, I put on makeup and beautiful clothes, because that works. Now, I'm admired because of what I look like. Don't you think that's better, or would you have me be plain like before? Well, I sure the heck don't want to go back there anymore."

"You were always a nice girl."

"Well now I'm nicer."

"Your self-esteem is what bothers you, not what you look like."

"Now, I don't get any snide remarks about my appearance, in fact it's quite the opposite. And now, I get to be with the crème of society. I'll bet you that I could be introduced to anyone I wished, if I set my mind to it."

"I don't doubt it. You look like what others want you to look like. Don't you get that? Others govern your life. You're their hostage. If you don't do exactly what they want, you'll lose your lifestyle and you'll go into oblivion. You're a person of their making. You sold your integrity, your identity."

"Dad, I don't mind becoming another person, because I didn't like what I was before. I'm a much better person now that I've ever been. I'm much less vulnerable and I'm much more in control of my destiny than before, when I was an unknown identity that nobody cared for much. True, others modeled a part of me, but I think that's everyone's destiny in a society to a certain extent.

Take mom for example, she took the role of a mother when Michael and I were born and she stuck with that until recently. It finally dawned on her that she didn't have to keep that role anymore, now that Michael and I were adults that didn't need her anymore as a doting mother. I'm astounded that during the past few months she took the role of the patriarch. She redecorated her house, renewed her clothes and started other activities. She isn't the same. She doesn't criticize me or try to tell me what to do anymore."

"But I do, you're saying! Sure, I'm telling you what you should do because that's the role of a father. If your mother let go of the role of a counselor to her children, she coped out of her responsibilities. That's what I think and I'm not about to change."

"I'm not telling you what to do, dad. It seems to me that you aren't very happy and I'm trying to help you, by discharging you from being our educator. That's all I'm saying. Michael and I are adults, and we're making our own decision, good or bad, as any adult will do. You don't need to burden yourself with that load anymore."

"Michael still needs me. Celeste you obviously surrounded yourself with a bunch of folks who tell you what to do, but Michael only has me to counsel him and he comes often to talk to me and ask for my advice. If you don't want my opinion, fine, but I'll still put my two cents worth."

"Don't get me wrong, your suggestions are welcome, but don't feel that you have to tell them all of the time. There's something else that bugging me."

"What's that?"

"I'd like to be treated with more respect. It hurts me every time when you make those unkind remarks on me."

"Now you want me to treat you like a princess!"

"There you go. That type of comment is hurtful. Don't you get that?"

"How could it be hurtful, I just called you a princess! If you don't want to be called a princess, I won't do it."

"You don't get it, do you?"

"It's just a joke. I like to make jokes. You should know that by now, after all, as you said, you're an adult."

"There you go again!"

"What?"

"You're constantly degrading me and you don't even realize it."

"How's that?"

"You're making fun of me, because I'm asserting myself."

"Since you are an adult, you should be able to take a joke."

"Dad, would you say that to your boss? If you were at work, would you say that to your boss?"

"No, because you don't joke with bosses."

"Could you please talk to me as if I were your boss."

"You must be kidding! You want me to talk to you as if you are my boss. This is the world upside down. Now days, children want the parents to consider their own children as their boss! Did you get that in Hollywood?"

"You can't stop yourself, can you?"

"You're making this ridiculous accusation and you don't want me to joke about it?"

"That's not what I'm saying. Please, don't joke about me. Could you please do that?"

"With pleasure. You don't have a sense of humor. Neither does your mother."

"There you go again."

"It's difficult being serious all the time, especially in the family."

"That's the point. Don't joke with us. Any of us. We aren't fair game anymore."

"I'll try."

"That's all I ask."

They had some snacks and drinks and talked about the current events. Nonetheless, Celeste leaves in good terms.

CHAPTER TWENTY-ONE

Temples of Love

IT'S SPRINGTIME SUNDAY morning. Birds are chirping, the sky is clear and pure, the air is brisk and fresh, and hearts are light and merry.

Celeste gets ready to go to church. She puts on a monochromatic blue-grey print dress, the kind that does not solicit inquiry, but is chic and swell. A simple purple ribbon with a fresh garden daisy keeps her hair from displaying their wanderlust. No jewelry. Anyone with a keen eye would marvel at her comely beauty, punctuated with a homely smile. It's with pleasure that she prepares the family's breakfast.

"Mother, I've had something on my mind for quite some time."

"What is it dear?"

"Remember when I was fourteen and you thought that your favorite perfume had soured?"

"Yes, I remember it quite well. If I'm not mistaken the day before, you were sore at me because I grounded you for a week."

"It was me, I put some vinegar in your perfume bottle because I was mad at you." Celeste takes out a gift box she had hidden and she presents it to her mother. "I want to make it up to you with a brand new bottle."

"That's very kind of you dear," Alice says, as she takes the gift and unwraps it. She kisses Celeste on the cheek.

"Did you guess that I was the culprit?"

"Oh yes, I knew it all along. I made the whole story about perfume souring by keeping it too long. I gave you the opportunity to confess, but kept your prank to yourself until this morning. It must have been troublesome, feeling guilty during so many years for such a trivial sin."

"Oh mother!" Celeste says as she hugs her mother. "You could have scolded me?"

"You punished yourself dear and it was much harsher than I would have done. I forgave you; that what parents do!"

"Mother!" Celeste says as she squeezes her mother.

At a quarter to ten, they take the car and drive to Saint Simon's Anglican Church where they quickly mingle with their fellow parishioners on the parvis. Since most parishioners have been at Celeste's celebration, they greet Celeste and Alice with thankfulness. Celeste and Alice make their way in the church, where they pray with devotion and listen to the inspiring sermon on the parable of the prodigal son. Celeste wonders if it was inspired by her return home. Anyway, she ponders on the spiritual meaning of that story, given that some of the last words from her mother were on the subject of forgiveness. This sequence of events seems to include some kind of uncanny coincidence. Obviously, her mother is a true believer and that accounts for her Christian behavior. Moreover, this coincidence suggests that there was an intervention from an external force. This revives her faith.

At the end of the service, Celeste shakes the priest's hand and wholeheartedly thanks the priest for his stirring sermon.

Celeste changed her outfit early that afternoon to meet Nick and Sean who planned to visit the reporter Nick had mentioned. The Thousand Islands are far enough away that Nick rented a Cessna 180 hydroplane. The three take off and head for Alexandria bay, home of the famed Boldt 'castle' where they moor the hydroplane. Upon landing, they phone the US Border authority and clear Immigration and Customs.

***

A guide tells the trio that George K. Boldt was born in island of Bergen auf Rugen in Germany. At 13, he immigrated by himself to the United States and started to work in the kitchen, while applying to medical schools. His dream of becoming a surgeon was impossible. With his savings, he bought a ranch in Texas, but that venture was also thwarted by a flood that swept everything he owned, including his dream. He went back to New

York and at 25, he was invited to manage the exclusive Clover Club in Philadelphia where he fell in love with the boss's daughter, Louise Kehrer who he married. They were an uncanny team. They catered to the so-called "robber barons" that cheated and robbed investors, ruthlessly crushed their competition to create monopolies and unashamedly charged consumers exorbitant prices, corrupted government officials and in general carried on predatory activities to make colossal fortunes that they ostensibly spent. The Boldts took advantage of these super-rich, by charging them outrageous prices for fulfilling their luxurious eccentricities and in the process, they became part of them. They started the "room service", providing morning newspapers, adorning the suites and restaurants with flowers and answering all requests. They became co-proprietor to the Waldorf hotel that he merged with the adjacent Astoria hotel in New York to become the Waldorf-Astoria Hotel where they introduced the now ubiquitous "Thousand Islands" salad dressing.

For several summers, the Boldt family enjoyed a frame cottage on picturesque Hart Island in front of Alexandria Bay, that the couple expanded. George Boldt changed the name of 'Hart Island' to 'Heart Island' and he made many decorations accordingly, as he renovated the place; he altered the shape of the island to resemble the shape of a heart as a token to the love for his wife. In 1900, he launched an ambitious construction campaign, by building a grandiose masonry structure, one of the largest private homes in America. He engaged an architectural firm to conceive a six-story Rhineland style "castle", as an eventual grandiose present to his cherished wife; after all, he owed her his good fortune. He wanted to impress even royalty. He hired three hundred workers including stonemasons, carpenters, and artists to fashion the six story, hundred and twenty seven room castle, including thirty bathrooms, with a servants' passage with a tramway, a powerhouse, Italian gardens, a drawbridge, the Alster tower similar to towers on the Alster river in Germany that served as a playground, the Hennery, or Dove-Cote, that contained a water reservoir, the unfinished peristyle Arch, that was to constitute the formal entry with rare ducks and swans enclosed in the pond, the gazebo and the power house with tower chimes replicating Westminster's tower. The Alster tower's basement housed a bowling alley and plans for the upper floors contained a billiard room, library, bedrooms, cafe, grill and kitchen. There is also a huge yacht house on a neighboring island, where Boldt had another summer home, and a vast estate that included farms, canals, a golf course, tennis courts, stables, and a polo field.

Tragically in January 1904, a year and a half before the "castle's" completion, his wife died at age forty two, after a long illness. Having the dream of giving this exceptional tribute on a Valentine's day to his wife, shattered by fate, he ordered that the construction immediately stop and that everybody vacate the site; he never returned there, for fear of constantly being reminded of that heartbreaking fairy tale in the making. He abandoned the island, as fate abandoned his latest dream. Nobody ever lived in the main building and in that respect it, unfortunately stands more as a mausoleum than a mansion.

Generations of dream believers are pursuing the love project, since Boldt's own family left it in tatters and ruins.

***

The guide compares this story to the one of the Taj Majal, in India, built by Emperor Shah Jahan as a memorial for his wife, Mumtaz Mahal, who died during childbirth, at thirty-seven years old, after having borne fourteen children. He was stricken with grief and had weeping fits.

The tomb is the representation of the house of the queen in Paradise; its foundation was set on the palace gardens of the great nobles estates that lined both sides of the river at Agra. It was constructed in white marble by twenty thousand workers for twenty-two years and remains to this day, one of the marvels of architecture. In muslin tradition, humans are not depicted, so it is adorned with vines, flowers and leaves to remind the beholder of nature's loveliness. Profound calligraphic verses from the Quran decorate its walls. As in classical Greek architecture, the shapes are slightly changed as to be perceived harmoniously as perfection; for example, the upper scriptures are larger, so as to reduce the skewing effect as seen from below. It is a truth that reality has to be delicately altered, in order to be perceived as pure beauty. Imperfections are part of beauty and it would be sacrilegious to attain and even to strive for absolute perfection.

The third oldest son deposed Shah Jahan, who was then imprisoned nearby, in fort Agra for eight years; so he spent all of this time admiring from afar the testimonial to his love of his deceased wife.

***

The three tour the island without much ado. It is an interesting way to pass the afternoon. They stay mostly outside, on the quay and the garden.

They board the hydroplane that take them to another private island not far away. As they disembark, a woman who was basking in the sun greets them. She gets up as she recognized Nick and Sean.

"Hi, I'm Greta Georgiou," offering her hand.

"Nick Dash, please to meet you."

"Sean Beck, my pleasure."

"Hi, Celeste McCawley."

"Haven't I seen you somewhere. I can't quite grasp where I saw you!"

"I was on the Dyann Winter show."

"Of course, the Cinderella girl."

"That's me."

"I'll call Ari, he'll be right over," she says as she summons him with her phone.

A minute later, he trots in and they resume the introductions.

"So what has made you come all the way from Hollywood to see me?"

Nick doesn't want to spoil Ari's sense of importance, so he adlibs: "Celeste has a problem with her boyfriend that we believe you are in a good position to solve this predicament."

"Is that right?" Ari answers flattered.

Ari is a nonchalant fellow, with a gravel sounding voice that seems to have scooped up the graves of humanity.

Celeste confesses Andy's narrative.

"I understand," is Ari's remark.

"It's an injustice to have him perish in jail, while he's not a menace to society."

"It is a form of justice. Who knows what he might do next? After all, he did attack someone. He didn't hurt him, but he did attack him."

"The punishment is excessive. He shouldn't get life."

"The supreme court judged otherwise in cases similar to his."

"I'm sure that with some anger counseling, that he could manage his aggressive manner."

"He isn't the only one in such a situation."

"Isn't there something you can do?"

"You'd like me to attract public interest I gather?"

"Yes, that seems to be the only solution."

"I'd have to convince the producers first."

"Could you at least talk to them."

"There's no harm talking about it."

Sean intervenes:" "Can we count on you Ari?"

"Yeah, I'll talk to them."

"Great!" Nick says with a smile.

"Have you visited the region, it's magnificent?"

"Before landing here we went to Boldt castle," Nick answers.

"Isn't that something!"

The three have some drinks and leave soon after, by hydroplane that flies to the original airfield where they switch planes and fly back to L.A.

CHAPTER TWENTY-TWO

Revelation

SHE MEETS NICK at his office. He gives her a friendly kiss on the cheek and accompanies it with a compliment he kept in reserve: "You look good."

"Thank you." Celeste is accustomed to compliments and is somewhat indifferent.

"How was did you enjoy your escapade?"

"Fruitful. Ari Georgiou is an influential reporter and he consented to make an investigation of Andy's case."

"You have a powerful ally. Are you sure that he will help you out? Those people are awfully busy and sometimes they promise things they can't deliver."

"I'll make sure he comes through with his word."

"You're a determined young lady!"

"If the roles were reversed and I was imprisoned, I'm sure that Andy would do his best to free me. It's my duty to do so."

"You are aware that he might freeze your life, in quest of this goal?"

"Yes. I'm willing to take the chance."

"I like that. You're the kind of friend everyone should have!"

"You are a man with impeccable connections. I came to you to put pressure on Ari to investigate Andy's case, if that's possible."

"Honestly, I don't think so. My association with Andy might blemish my image and that is not going to happen."

"What if it were to polish your image?"

"That would be a tour de force. I'm not about to place myself in a risky position of having to make that choice. I won't take the risk where the reward is practically insignificant, while the risk is potentially great. I'm a poker player and I calculate everything, as if it were a bet. Having invited you to Santa Catalina was a win-win bet; you are now indebted to me, at least to a certain extent. I can brag of being pal with you and Sean, and I solidified my links with the media that is paramount to my success."

"What could convince you?"

"Nothing."

"I have this desire to fulfill," she dares test the spell Sybil told her.

"What desire is that?"

"Please use your influence to have Ari Georgiou investigate Andy's unjust conviction."

Nick suddenly feels troubled.

"Say again!"

"Please use your influence to have Ari Georgiou investigate Andy's unjust conviction."

Nick stares at her in stupefaction.

"Please use your influence to have Ari Georgiou investigate Andy's unjust conviction."

Nick presses a button and says: "Call Michaelovitch."

"Yes sir."

A light signal alerts Nick to speak to the phone:

"Michaelovitch, Nick speaking...

Fine. Do me a favor and have Georgiou do an investigation of the three strikes you're out conviction."

Nick sits puts the phone down and there, as if he had just been knocked out, wondering what just happened.

Celeste smiles, gets up and shakes hand with Nick. Apparently, she does have the power to convince people to do what she wants. She walks out.

***

Celeste is on her way back to her limousine. She is floored.

The spell did work.

As Sybil predicted.

The meaning of her life has changed in a few minutes.

She must be a fairy.

A real fairy, otherwise the spell wouldn't have been true.

She proved that she holds that power.

She wonders what she can do with it.

To make sure, she wants to try it out, one more time. She doesn't want to be nefarious and take something from someone without his consent. She could ask someone to do something he wouldn't normally do.

As she looks outside, they pass a local baseball field.

"Please stop at the curb," she orders.

After it stops, Celeste rolls down her window and watches people pass by. She spots a businessman holding a pouch who has a quick step.

"Excuse me."

"Who me?"

"Yes. I noticed that there's a lot of garbage along the baseball diamond. Could you pick it up and throw it in the garbage pail!"

"Excuse me!"

"There's a lot of rubbish along the baseball diamond. Could you pick it up and throw it in the garbage pail!"

"I'm not a garbage collector."

"It's unsightly. Please pick it up and throw it in the garbage pail!"

"Anyhow, I'm in a hurry. I don't have time for this crap."

"I have a desire to fulfill."

"What is it?" he replies dumbfounded.

"Pick up the garbage and throw it in the garbage pail!"

"With pleasure!" he answers as he starts doing it.

Celeste is astounded. She does have that power.

***

Celeste and Sybil are in a bistro, having a coffee.

"You didn't believe me, did you?"

"It was so farfetched."

"Now, do you believe in yourself?"

"You mean in the formula?"

"I mean in yourself. Truly. Without hesitation. Unconditionally."

"It can't be!"

"It is so and for the rest of your life. Nobody can take that away from you. You are a fairy. Nature's fairy."

"You haven't been wrong so far!"

"This is the time for 'the talk'. You could use that power to get whatever you want. For example, to free Andy you could just ask the prison guards to release him. You could do it that way, but as soon as you do, some clever people will notice. Once they do, they'll try to use your power for their own interest. Some might try to amass colossal fortune, either by misleading you or by threatening you or your family. You wouldn't want that would you?"

"I certainly don't want to."

"No. I saw you telling a man to clean a baseball diamond. That was a laudable request, still you are making yourself vulnerable to being exposed."

"How did you see that?"

"I have the gift of clairvoyance. As I told you, you are under constant surveillance."

"Wow!

Are you a fairy?"

"No, that is not my destiny. I use my powers mostly to recruit and train spirits who will improve humanity, such as yours. There are very few, unfortunately."

"Is that so!"

"Let me also warn you on evil. Some persons are evil and you won't be able to use your spell on them. In addition, if you try, they'll immediately identify you as a fairy and they will do everything in their power to destroy you."

"What power do they have?"

"Some have the power to convince people, just as you have, but they will lie, cheat and be ruthless, often causing death and destruction in their path. Beware of them. These are the most dangerous."

"I'm curious; do I have any other power?"

"That remains to be proven. I can't tell you for the moment."

"So, I'm a nature fairy with one power!"

"You don't have to use your spell if you don't want to. This is a very special gift that you should use wisely."

"Is this a secret between you and me?"

"I wouldn't tell everyone that I'm a fairy, if that's what you're asking! Close parents might better understand and be discrete about it, while strangers might surmise that there is something wrong with you."

"That's understandable. I'll be cautious."

CHAPTER TWENTY-THREE

Reconciliation

BRENT CALLS CELESTE that evening. Luckily she's is home and switches his image to her large TV screen.

"I was going to say 'How are you princess?' but I don't want to do that anymore."

"Hi dad. Good to hear from you."

"You were right. I did belittle you before. I don't want to do that anymore. You are a successful young woman and I want to share my life with you. You're my only daughter and I'm very proud of you. I'm getting old and I want to have you in my life. I'm truly sorry for the way that I acted before. It wasn't called for. I should have been a better father and I should have supported you, but I didn't. Sure, I could make excuses, but I recognize my errors. I'm truly sorry for the harm I've done to you."

Celeste is crying her heart out at the other end of the call.

They wait for the tears to stop, yet they keep coming.

After a while, she gathers her self-control.

"That's what I've been wanting to hear all of my life. I love you dad."

"I love you too Celeste. I always did, in my way. I wanted you to be better. I pushed you to improve. Silly of me. You've surpassed every dream I ever had about you. You've become far better than I could have expected."

"That means a great deal to me."

"Do remind me to respect you, if ever I go astray again."

"I'm sure I won't have to.
I should have gone to your celebration and meet your friends."

"That's in the past. Listen, I'd like you to come and visit me. You could come this weekend if you'd like?"

"I'd like that very much. It would be a great occasion for us to bond."

"I'll forward you the plane tickets."

"Great."

***

It's a glorious day and the smog has just lifted in L.A. It's Brent's first trip here. Celeste welcomes him in the airport's VIP lounge. They chitchat about the trip, the weather and all the petty stuff of daily life. The chauffeur opens the limousine door and they get in. Brent lets the good waves soak in, without uttering any of the sour grapes lingering in his throat. He's making the first steps to becoming a better man and a better father.

The limousine winds and wiggles the roads, this quiet Saturday morning, when everyone is resting from the frantic weekday traffic. The chauffeur points out the usual attractions, as a well-informed travel guide would do.

They arrive at Celeste's apartment building, where they whisk away to her place. Celeste shows him the views and the amenities. He absorbs these surroundings with amazements. She offers him a beer that he quickly accepts. They sit down in her living room.

"Celeste, I'm amazed by this luxury."

"Before, you would have said that this is artificial and it's true, in one way. Sure, these are things that can perish and that might not represent anything special. To me however, they represent my new life and they are real as it can be. You might not appreciate them the way I do and that's OK."

"I didn't say that."

"You didn't, but it must be in the back of your mind."

"Perhaps it is. Now, I'm accepting you for the way you are, not by what I feel you should be. I look at your decorations and they represent you in every way. You decorated your home with animals and plants. That's what you did in your room in Ontario and you are true to yourself. I fully understand that. In fact, I must compliment you in being genuine."

"That's quite a transformation from your usual discourse!"

"You've made me grasp that I was harming you and that the last thing I wanted. I had to change, there was no alternative."

"Dad, I've just become conscious of something. I need to confide in someone and I'd like to reveal something about myself and I'd like to keep it to you."

"You have my word."

"All these decorations based on nature aren't there by accident. I chose them because they are part of me. Even as a child, nature was a part of me with good reason. You might not believe in spiritual beings, but I recently understood that I'm a very special being. Part of me is spiritual. I'm linked in a hallowed way to nature and it's my goal in life to foster nature so as to make it prosper and grow."

"For me, it isn't a surprise!"

"I told you that I had the responsibility to free Andy from a disproportionately harsh condemnation."

"Yes, you explained it all."

"Well that triggered a concern in me. Surfacing in my soul, I always pained that humans imprison animals simply for our entertainment. Centuries ago, the only way people could acquaint themselves with nature was to gawk at animals in zoos. That era has passed. Now documentaries on just about all types of animals are available of the media and it's simple to look at them and appreciate their lives.

I've made it my mission to respect animal lives. Animal shelters should protect animals that simply wouldn't survive otherwise. However, animals that could live in nature should have the right to live in their habitat. We shouldn't 'harvest' them, mainly as a challenge.

I'm about to start a crusade to halt trophy hunting."

"You want to become evangelist for nature?"

"Yes. Ever since my childhood, I tried to help nature in any way possible. I wouldn't step on insects if I could avoid them, I didn't hurt of even tease animals and if possible, I would help them. I felt bad when some stupid kid hurt them, just for the kicks of it. I don't take care to look where I'm walking, in order to sidestep insects, but if I do see one, even spiders that I hate, I simply avoid them. We slaughter millions of animals for food, but we should do it with dignity. I remind myself that bees won't sting if I don't provoke them, yet they work tirelessly to pollinate the plants that will help us eat and prosper. If our work and our lives is worthy of respect, so should theirs."

"That's quite a goal!"

"So far, I've focused my life on myself. Now that I've established that I have extraordinary powers, I'll use them to protect nature and the preservation of wild animals is my first quest."

"You make it sound like it's becoming a sacred pursuit!"

"It has. We've taken nature for granted. It was there for the taking, and it was our right to do whatever we wanted with it. True, we have helped nature in many ways, by channeling the course of rivers and improving breeds of plants, animals and humans among others. On the other hand, we've also destroyed huge forests, overexploited the seas and oceans, and in many ways, disregarded animals' right to survive.

I'll do what I can to better our relation with nature."

"That's quite an aspiration!"

"My goal will become actions."

"I offer you all of my best wishes. I couldn't be prouder of you!"

"Your support means a great deal to me dad."

Brent returned home that Sunday afternoon, brimming with satisfaction and happiness, due to the new perspective on his own life and that of his cherished Celeste.

***

Next Sunday evening, Celeste calls Sybil and later they meet at a cafe.

"Sybil, I just had to talk to you. My father came over this weekend and I have to confide in you."

"Go ahead, I'm listening."

"Dad came as a new father. During my entire life, he treated me badly, as if I lacked something. Last time I met him, I confronted him with that behavior. Apparently, not only did he understand me and agree with me, he decided to become a better father and encourage me. He did it. During his stay, he became the affectionate father I had wanted throughout my life. This in itself was wonderful and unexpected."

"What a tremendous development! You could have turned your back on him or continued to be abused by his attitude. Then again, you could have lashed him with your comments. Instead, you challenged what he was doing and you made him recognize his damaging demeanor. Instead of being a constant victim of verbal abuse, you took charge and explained what he did to you. Before you were passive, you are becoming energetic. You aren't the same as you were. Not only did your makeover make you beautiful externally, it gave you self-confidence and allowed you improve your life. That was the essence of your transformation."

"There's something else."

"What is it, I'm eager to find out."

"I revealed a belief that was deep inside me. I hadn't planned it. I wasn't even conscious that I held such a strong affinity to animals. Suddenly it flowed out of my mouth to my surprise and astonishment. Did you ever experience such a happening?"

"Yes, I call it a realization."

"Well, more than ever I will do my best to help nature. My first task is to halt trophy hunting."

"That is quite a objective since there are many individuals that make their living at this."

"I have to try."

CHAPTER TWENTY-FOUR

Runaround

CELESTE GETS A CALL from Nick.

"Hi Celeste."

"Hi Nick, good to hear from you," Celeste answers as she has read the source of the incoming call.

"Listen regarding your boyfriend Andy, you should meet Chuck Wegener. He's a state representative."

"Sure, why not!"

A few days later, she goes to Chuck Wegener's office in his district where she is welcomed.

The representative's office door has his nameplate fixed in brass letters. Inside the office two large flags standing guard in front of the wall, the United States of America flag and the California State flag, confront you. On each side, there are bookshelves garnished with serial legal volumes and antiquated furniture furnishes the office. The representative has an imposing chair behind his desk. Celeste sits on a wooden antique chair suitable for short conversations. The lighting is subdued. You can hear the buzz of a ventilator stirring the hot air in the background as if it was a harmful insect waiting to pounce.

He's a tall good looking guy, who has a pleasant demeanor.

"Celeste McCawley."

"Chuck. Pleased to meet you. Nick told me about you. You're from Canada I hear!"

The implied message being that he wouldn't care one dot what she was about to say, since she was not from his district, a Californian nor an American.

"Yes, my friend Andy Czerny is an American. He's been condemned under the three strikes law. I was wondering whether you could do something about it. His sentence is twenty-five to life, just for having shoved a reporter. The sentence is very tough for such a minor incident."

"I can understand your plea. The poor fellow just pushed a reporter and now he has to spend his remaining life in jail. Obviously, you want to get him out.

On the other hand, it is a third offense. Who knows whether he'll commit another felony? The Supreme Court upheld these types of convictions, because habitual criminals were getting off with light sentences. It is a measure to protect the people."

"He's not a habitual criminal at all. These were minor incidents."

"He did three distinct crimes. However, there is no doubt that incidents were not very serious. Nonetheless, a law is in effect that settles the matter."

"I was told that there are other ways that he could be freed."

"You're on the button, to use a poker expression. The state of California could commute his sentence. You would first have to file a petition. Let me read the official procedure:

'Once the applicant has the application and notice of intent, the applicant should complete the APPLICATION FOR EXECUTIVE CLEMENCY and have it notarized. The Notice of Intent to Apply for Executive Clemency should be sent via regular or certified mail to the District Attorney of each county in which the applicant was convicted of a felony.

The Acknowledgement of Receipt portion of the notice form must be completed and signed by the District Attorney. Both the application and the completed notice must then be submitted to the Governor's Office, along with a full statement of any compensation paid to any person for assisting in the procurement of a commutation of sentence.

Once the formal application is received, the Governor refers it to the Board of Prison Terms (BPT). BPT will conduct an investigation to determine whether the applicant meets the standards set forth in California Penal Code section 4852.05, which states, "During the period of rehabilitation the person shall live an honest and upright life, shall conduct himself or herself with sobriety and industry, shall exhibit a good moral character, and shall conform to and obey the laws of the land."

After the investigation, the case is presented to the Executive Board of the Board of Prison Terms which decides whether to recommend to the Governor that a commutation of sentence be granted. The applicant is notified of when the Board will be considering his or her case, and he or she is given the opportunity to forward any additional information, if desired.

Commutation applicants do not attend the commutation consideration meeting. Following the meeting, the application, investigation report, and the Board's recommendation are sent to the Governor. Notification of the meeting result is also sent to the applicant.

The Governor reviews the information and decides whether to grant a commutation of sentence. If the applicant has been convicted of more than one felony in separate proceedings, the California Supreme Court must also approve the grant of a commutation of sentence.

In the California Supreme Court an application for a recommendation for executive clemency is treated as a court proceeding. Applications are filed by the Clerk's Office and given a file number. A memorandum is then circulated among the justices and each justice indicates his or her recommendation on an accompanying voting sheet. Applications will be denied unless four or more justices vote to recommend that clemency be granted. The Chief Justice will inform the Governor by letter of the court's recommendation.

There is no requirement that the Governor issue a commutation of sentence to an applicant, and the length of time needed for the completion of the commutation process cannot be predicted.

When a commutation is granted, the California Department of Justice and the Federal Bureau of Investigation are notified. These agencies' records are then updated to show that a commutation has been granted in regard to the conviction.

A commutation of sentence is filed with the Secretary of State, reported to the Legislature, and becomes a matter of public record. Although no effort is made to publicize the commutation application or issuance, there is no guarantee that the issuance of a commutation to a particular person will not become known to the public.

Every effort has been made to make this information accurate and up-to-date. Errors are inevitable and changes occur frequently. We would appreciate learning of any errors or inaccuracies regarding any information on this Webpage as soon as possible. '

If Andy is not eligible for such a petition, the other recourse would be a gubernatorial pardon. The procedure is as follows:

' *The applicant should first complete the Application for Executive Clemency. Then the applicant must send the Notice of Intent to Apply for Executive Clemency to the District Attorney of each county in which the applicant was convicted so that each District Attorney receives the legally-required notice. The District Attorney acknowledges receipt of the Notice of Intent and returns the notice to the Governor's Office. Finally, the applicant should return the completed application to the Governor's Office There is no requirement that the Governor take any action on an application for a pardon. Once a Certificate of Rehabilitation or a completed direct pardon application is received by the Governor's Office, the Office typically forwards the application to the Board of Parole Hearings. The Board may conduct a background investigation and make a recommendation on whether a pardon should be granted. The Board may contact the District Attorney, investigating law enforcement agency, and other persons with relevant information on the applicant. If the applicant has been convicted of more than one felony, the California Supreme Court must recommend granting a pardon before the Governor may do so. However, there is no obligation that the Governor seek a recommendation from the Supreme Court, in the first instance. The length of time needed to complete the pardon process cannot be predicted. Once a completed application has been received by the Governor's Office, it is not necessary to contact the Governor's Office to check on the status of an application. If the Governor takes action on an application, the applicant will be notified. Applicants should notify the Governor's Office in writing if their mailing address changes.*'

That doesn't mean that his criminal offense would be stricken off his record. For that, he would have to petition for an expungement. Once you have reached that stage, I will be happy to explain the applicable procedures.

Does that answer your question?"

"I suppose. It seems so complicated."

"If I may be candid, laws are complicated; laws are made by lawyers for lawyers. That's how they make their living! Ordinary people should not try to infiltrate that world."

"Let me put it in another way. I have a desire to fulfill."

"What is your desire?"

"I want to free Andy."

"I'm sure that can be done. Give me his lawyer's name."

"Here it is," Celeste writes Andy's lawyer name and hands it to Chuck.

With a great big smile, he responds: "Thank you for your visit."

CHAPTER TWENTY-FIVE

Public Appeal

ARI AND CELESTE introduces the investigation to the media.

"For many years, a few states have enforced the so-called '3 strikes' law where a person condemned of three felonies automatically receives a sentenced of twenty-five years to life in prison. The Supreme Court upheld these sentences.

In one case, Leandro Andrade was sentenced to two twenty-five to life sentences for shoplifting nine children's videotapes worth $153.34, including 'Snow White' and 'Cinderella', that he stole to give at Christmas to his nieces,. These are excerpts from that case that aired back then: 'I'm not a killer. I'm not a rapist. I'm not a bad person once you get to know me,' says Leandro Andrade, the 44-year-old convicted of this felony. 'Do I deserve to be locked up for the rest of my life, because of the three strikes law?' Andrade will be 87 before being eligible for parole.

'I understand what I did was wrong. I knew I had to be punished. I have to pay for that crime, and for the mistakes that I made in life,' says Andrade. 'But I wasn't aware that for that little mistake I was going to receive a 25-to-life sentence.'

'For a petty theft, it carries, maximum three years,' says Andrade. 'That's what I believe I should be doing for petty theft ... because I didn't kill anybody. I didn't hurt anybody.'

The law passed in 1993 in California, triggered by the vicious murder of Polly Klass, then twelve, who was snatched from her home, raped and strangled to death by a drifter named Richard Allan Davis, who had a long and violent criminal record.

'The law was about putting the Richard Allan Davises behind bars for life, not the shoplifters,' Andrade's lawyer says.

'The eighth amendment to the constitution prohibits cruel and unusual punishment. For at least a century, the Supreme Court has said that grossly disproportionate penalties violate the cruel-

and-unusual-punishment clause,' a law professor at the University of Southern California says. 'If any punishment is grossly disproportionate, it's stealing $150 worth of video tapes and getting 50 years to life in prison.'

However, 'It's not cruel and unusual, because we are not punishing him for what upfront might appear to be a minor crime, the theft of the video tapes. We are punishing him for failing to heed the lessons of his prior history,' says Grover Merritt, the California prosecutor fighting to keep Andrade in prison and pointing out that Andrade has a long list of crimes on his rap sheet: 'He's been a thief, he's been a burglar and he's crept into people's homes. He dealt marijuana in sufficient quantity to get arrested and prosecuted by the federal government, twice. He escaped from a federal prison. And after that, he still committed a petty theft in Orange County, and then he came here to steal from our KMarts.'

The law professor adds, 'It's when it becomes 50 years in prison that it's undesirable. I mean, the California law is irrational. If Andrade's prior offenses had been rape and murder, the most he could have received as a sentence for stealing videotapes was a year in jail. Because the prior crimes had been property offenses, he got 50 years in prison. That's just irrational.'

A person in Andrade's jury said: 'There are people in prison that have committed murder that are serving less years than this man is for selling videotapes,' says Freeman, 'I mean, it's ludicrous... I think that it is cruel and unusual punishment, 50 to life, for stealing videotapes.'"

Ari introduces the new subject: "Andy Czerny was also recently condemned under that law after he had been condemned for three minor felonies, including theft, possession of narcotics and aggravated assault. Andy could you explain?"

Andy is dressed in an orange overall with CDCR letters in the back and is standing in the prison's cafeteria where the interview is taking place.

"When I was eighteen, a friend of mine dared me to do steal a fish from a restaurant's aquarium. I had never shoplifted before and I didn't have any idea how to do it. I went to the Chinese restaurant and stole a fish in the aquarium. I got caught and I had to do a month of community service and I returned the fish. It was merely a prank. It turned out that the fish was a Clarion Angelfish worth many thousands of dollars, so I was charged and plea-bargained a felony in exchange for probation instead of a prison sentence.

A few years later, I was in a college party with some buddies. While we were drinking and smoking pot, the guys asked me to get some more pot to keep the party going, so I went on the street and bought some pot. Unfortunately, an undercover police officer targeted the student crowd and I was caught. I got six months probation plus community work that time.

The third time was for aggravated assault. I was going to a restaurant with Celeste when a paparazzo blocked our way, so I pushed him aside and he fell, spraining his ankle. I didn't want to hurt him, I simply meant to protect Celeste from being threatened and harassed. The Court didn't see it that way and, since someone recorded the whole scene, I was condemned for aggravated assault and battery. That time, I got twenty-five years to life. Is that just?"

CHAPTER TWENTY-SIX

Sanctuary

CELESTE MEETS Sybil in an animal sanctuary in Southern California. Sybil is dressed in outdoor clothes, with pockets galore. Her bush hat protects her from the sun. Celeste also wears loose fashionable sportswear.

Sybil explains:"I spend most of my free time here. I find it rewarding helping these helpless creatures. I learned many stories that you might find to your liking.

Many circuses are shutting down or eliminating their animal acts because of an increase of public awareness of the plight of animals. Unfortunately, circus animal owners eventually retire the animals that they used for decades to earn money, but are given to the care of sanctuaries such as this one.

There's the story of Anne the elephant brought from Sri Lanka who was part of a circus in Britain. At that time, poachers rounded up elephants and killed the adults. As the helpless youngsters nuzzled up against their dead parents, the poachers would trap them and carry them away. The youngsters were then 'broken' by confining them to a small pen, a 'crush', and denied food until they became submissive. They trained Anne to stand on her hind legs and turn around in a pirouette to delight the spectators. A video of Anne shows the world that she and other animals were viciously beaten by workers for no apparent reason and chained for many hours. The owner, whose family had displayed circus animals for seven generations, was sued by the government; he received only a conditional discharge of three years probation, after much legal haggling. The public outcry triggered public fundraising that managed to raise a substantial sum for her survival. Sanctuaries were hesitant to take the solitary elephant, but eventually she was transferred to a 'Safari Park' where she finally lives in posh elephant comfort.

There is the story of Swing, a female chimpanzee who was used to test some vaccines in a pharmaceutical research program, because monkeys share ninety eight percent of our DNA. They have a lifespan of forty to fifty years. She was kept in a cage, where her health was regularly monitored. Meanwhile, she would be administered some medication for testing purposes and she was anaesthetized countless times. After six years of such treatment, the program ended; she was taken outside, where she had a first glimpse of the sun. Having never been free to roam, she just stood there in a daze, terrified to walk out of the transportation cage. She huddled in the doorway until a caretaker coaxed her gently out on the grass. For the next four years, that caretaker re-educated the chimp in an animal sanctuary. The caretaker then had to work elsewhere, however eighteen years later she returned to the sanctuary to check out how the chimp was getting along. She got close to the chimp and reached out her hand asking: 'Do you remember me?' After a while, the chimp gave a smile from ear to ear and hugged the caretaker.

Countless rescues are made by all kinds of organizations. They require human intervention after the harm we do to them, with our nets, our fast cars and our encroachment of their habitat."

Celeste is impressed at Sybil's involvement, "I've always loved animals, but I never implicated myself in preserving nature. I'm very lucky and successful and I'd like to add some meaning to my life my actively contributing to nature."

" Since you are a celebrity, you could use your talents to convince others to join in."

"I'd like to stop trophy killing. This is a remnant of a bygone time, when it was a dangerous challenge for a hunter to track down a ferocious animal, that could react by attacking or that could flee out of range. Approaching a dangerous animal sufficiently enough and using basic weapons required skill to kill the animal cleanly. Now they preys are located electronically with the GPS, approached with elaborate camouflage gear and wounded with sophisticated weapons requiring minimal skill and little risk.

There should be an international ban on trophy hunting."

"I couldn't agree more. Perhaps you will succeed."

"Now killing any animal is easy. What is difficult is to insure that the earth can and will insure their survival of all species of animals. Praise should be awarded to those who protect and improve animal life."

"That's a great idea."

"I'll talk to some people about that."

"I must warn you that you will have to face a fierce opponent."

"Who is he?"

"Her name is Melinda Yeager. She's very well funded and she'll use any means to stop you."

"I have my secret weapons also."

"Don't underestimate her. Once you show your intentions, she'll try to destroy you. She takes pleasure in destroying people's lives, as much as animals. You'll be her prize that she'll display to everyone on her Internet page."

"Tell me more about her."

"She has a show on hardcore hunting, where she revels at every animal someone took down. It's as if animals are her enemies. Weapon manufacturers sponsor the show. Her Internet page boasts of her 'harvesting' a lion, a zebra, a deer, a leopard, a giraffe, a brown bear, various antelopes and even a crocodile that is hanged by its neck; she's posters a great big smile, next to the spoils of her hunt. She's boasts of having killed animals at sixty yards, more than half a football field away, with a powerful rifle having a telescopic sight. Sometimes, she does her deed with a bow and arrows; the composite bow has cams, balancing counterweights and a telescopic sight. In Alaska, thousands of miles away from her home, she might call a bear with a predator sound and makes it approach her by curiosity until it stops and becomes a perfect target, at which time she releases the arrow in its throat. She is stoked with a sense of accomplishment after having killed it.

At home, she has a trophy room where she displays many animal heads stuffed to look as lively and as threatening as possible. She makes no apology, always mentioning that she always hunt according to the local laws. She justifies herself by having given the meat to the local population that is very grateful. She doesn't do it to feed her own family.

We humans act as if nature belongs to us. Just because we master it and we can do pretty much as we please with it, doesn't mean that we should do whatever we want. Nature has proven that on the long run it will prevail, even if by means of a cataclysmic event. Dinosaurs, however powerful they were, disappeared from the earth in little time and never reappeared again. The human race might suffer the same fate. We should treat nature with the utmost respect."

***

Celeste is enthusiastic. She looks at the flowers and plants in her apartment and they have taken a new meaning. They are a legacy of nature that might very well be the key to our survival. She takes a deep breath of air, grateful of to be able to replenish her energy so simply.

CHAPTER TWENTY-SEVEN

Influence

ANDY IS DEPRESSED when he phones Celeste. She, on the other hand, is confident in her abilities and her future. In truth, Andy has become somewhat more distant from her, since her role in life has taken a turn and has become of a much greater significance. Still, he's very much like a child in distress that she has to care for.

"Celeste, I'm discouraged.

I give up. My lawyers just informed me that their petition to obtain a commutation of my sentence, has just failed. The Board of parole rejected it."

"Andy, don't despair. There is a way out and I'm working on it."

"What else can you do? I have good lawyers and they just can't seem to come up with a solution."

"I'm trying to get a gubernatorial pardon."

"Yeah, my lawyers talked about it but they admit that it's one chance in a million. The current Governor is a badass and he want to retain that image."

"I have ways."

Andy is suspicious that she would try and seduce the Governor or other high rank official.

"I don't want you to compromise your integrity Celeste. It's not worth it."

"I swear I won't. Don't worry about that."

"Celeste, I don't want you to waste your life for me. I'm not worth it."

"Hush, you are worth a great deal to me."

"You're trying to encourage me and I admire you for it, but I made my peace with God and I accept my fate. Don't waste your life on me. Torrance Helicopter let me go and I won't get my job back. They had to replace me, 'cause they couldn't wait any longer. I lost my job, my house and all my savings to pay for my lawyers. And you tell me I have no reason to despair?"

"Andy. Have confidence in me."

"All right. I dream of you all the time, you're my guardian angel.

I have to go. So long." He doesn't dare say, "I love you." because he doesn't want to have to live with a broken heart.

"So long!" She doesn't reply, "I love you" because she cares for him true enough, but she doesn't want to mislead him into dreaming of a lifelong relationship.

***

Nick calls Celeste and asks her to meet him at another popular watering hole, for a cocktail. He relishes at dressing up and going places where he'll be seen with her and be the object of gossips. She likes to be admired with him, a dapper gentleman who helps her in a chivalrous manner in front of the crowd.

"How very wonderful to see you here Celeste!" he proclaims as he pulls a chair to let her sit in front of him, at a corner table.

She smiles without any verbal reply. After all, she is doing him a favor for accompanying him.

"Andy called me; he seemed in bad shape. His lawyers couldn't get any relief and he lost his job. He doesn't want to fight anymore, it seems. That worries me. I'm afraid he might do something stupid."

"Do you think that he would kill himself?"

"Not sure. Regardless of all the legal proceedings, I'm doing my best to keep up his morale."

"I want to talk about that. You met Chuck and he informed you of the bureaucracy involved. I got a taste of that also. Well yesterday, he told me that Andy's demand for a pardon has landed on the governor's desk. He said that you were very persuasive;

in fact, he wonders why he ever bothered with Andy's case. I would guess it's your charm!"

"I suppose so."

"Anyhow, it's in the governor's hands. Maybe you're in luck after all. This is the governor's end of term and traditionally when governors finish their term, they grant pardons. We shall see."

"Is there any way we can insist that the Governor sign the pardon? He has a badass reputation to uphold to and he might bypass this unique occasion."

"Actually, I expected that and I Invited the Governor to join us. In fact that's the reason I invited you here. He should be joining us shortly."

"You're a darling Nick. How can I ever repay you?"

" I might take you up on that. Let's chalk it up."

Celeste wasn't in that Nick had gotten a job for the governor's son, so the governor owed it to Nick to come meet Celeste.

He arrived along with his security guard posted at the door. He is ushered to Nick's corner table.

"Dave, this is Celeste McCawley. Celeste this is Dave Johnston, our governor."

"Pleased to meet you sir."

"Call me Dave. Some people have called me worst," the governor jests without much success.

"How are things going?" Nick says, to initiate a dialog.

"Well as you know, I'll be ending my political life soon. I've been looking at different avenues. I haven't made up my mind of what I'll be doing." Dave was fishing for any opportunity Nick might propose. Of course, Nick had prepared the way.

"My firm might have an opening. We need someone like you, as a Vice-President to link up with governmental agencies of all kinds. You'd be exactly the person we need." Nick already chalked one for the offer, whether Dave would or not accept.

"Thanks for that invitation, I'll think about it."

"Did you know that Celeste is a good friend of Andy Czerny?"

"Who?"

"Andy Czerny. He's in jail under the three strikes law. He submitted a demand for pardon."

"Oh, I don't even look at these things. The law is there for hardened criminals and I'm not about to let any out."

"Celeste, could you continue?"

"Andy is not a habitual criminal by any means. The last thing he was condemned for is shoving an obnoxious and obtrusive paparazzo. I was with him when it happened and I'm glad he tried to defend me. I'm sure that you would the same if it happened to your partner. It's a gentlemanly thing to do."

"Nobody would dare!"

"You are well protected with your body guards, but I'm sure you would take their place, if anybody would menace your lady."

"Perhaps, but your friend committed other crimes."

"A petty theft he did, as a dare, when he was in college and buying some pot for his friends. Did you ever try pot?"

"I'm not on trial. Anyhow pot isn't the big deal it once was."

"There you go. I'm sure that if you take the time to examine Andy's file that you'll agree to grant him a pardon, before you leave. It'll add to your image as being compassionate and magnanimous."

"I'll examine the file. I'll do that."

"It's a question of justice."

"No, it's a question of law."

"Have you looked at Ari Georgiou's show where he does an exposé on that law?"

"No, I don't watch that garbage."

"Well, he must have touched a sensitive chord because he seems to have stirred public support for Andy in particular."

"I'll have to consult my advisor, Chuck, on that."

"I'm certain that Chuck Wegener will confer," Celeste says with assurance.

They have diner and part their way, Celeste having omitted to speak to Nick about her newfound mission in life, judging that it would be better to discuss it at another time.

CHAPTER TWENTY-EIGHT

Cat Fight

CELESTE CALLS NICK for a meeting at a quiet cocktail bar. A woman sings old lingering melodies at a piano bar. The atmosphere is that of Rick's bar in the film Casablanca. Celeste pays attention to the music, waiting for the 'As Time Goes By' song that will never be played. Nick kisses her on the cheek when he arrives. She relates what happened with Andy, she explains her new vocation and then she discusses what is on her mind.

"Nick, you're a great organizer and I need your talents."

"Flattery is always a good beginning," he smirks as he takes a sip of Drambuie.

"As is a stiff drink," Celeste fails to reply, but adds "I want people to become concerned about the plight of animals. We share this earth with them and we shouldn't bully nature around simply because we're stronger."

"I'm with you and I adhere to that worthy cause. I've been busy, but I fully support yours. I'm willing to help you out as much as I can. You wish to muster public support. The best way to create a buzz is to as people to sign a petition. Put it up on the Web with some video and people will join your cause."

"Where can I get a video that will catch people's attention?"

"I don't know. From what I gather, it's best to make a video with ordinary people. And you need music."

"You've given me an idea. I'm sure that Ari could help me. I'll ask him."

"That sounds good."

"How do I get exposure?"

"Ask Ari, I'm sure that he'll get an audience to watch."

"Cool."

***

Celeste phones Ari.

"Ari, it's me, Celeste."

"Hey. What's up?"

"Could you make me a video? Something about animals. I want to attract a following against trophy animal hunting and I'd put it on YouTube™."

"That's easy. The most popular one are about babies and animals."

"Well I'd like one that would make fun of trophy hunters."

"Trophy hunters?"

"Yeah, hunters that kill endangered animal for fun."

"I suppose. I'm sure I can figure something out."

"I'd like that."

***

Ari uses a video that has been on YouTube™ for a long time to produce a show featuring Celeste.

"Many years ago two Australians 'Ace' Bourke and John Rendall, travelled to London, England. A visit to Harrods, the legendary high-end department store that purported to sell everything, was mandatory. There, the youngsters encountered a baby lion in a cage acquired from a zoo park, and they bought it and lived with it in their apartment. They named it Christian. When it got cumbersome, they kept it in a cellar most of the time, but would take morning walks in the Moravian church graveyard. Sometimes they would bring it to the seaside. Presumably, people would consider them as being a bit eccentric.

The young men kept a furniture store in London. Word spread that their lion was becoming quite large and difficult to manage properly. They reluctantly gave up the lion to a Kenyan conservationist who transferred it to Africa, where it belonged. There the conservationist and his wife introduced Christian to an older lion to learn the ways of the bush. Eventually he integrated successfully Christian to the wild, as he had previously done with a lioness.

Celeste, why don't you continue the story?"

"With pleasure. A year later, the young men travelled five thousand miles to Kenya in an attempt to witness Christian's evolution. I invite you to look at the true story of the amazing YouTube™ video, Christian the lion. Christian's pride appeared on the horizon. At first, it hesitated and approached slowly. Then, as he recognized his protectors, he embraced each of them with overwhelming affection, as would a long lost friend.

The pair returned a year later. Christian again recognized the pair, but this time he was majestic; he greeted the pair, befriended them, but then he was on his way never to be seen anymore.

Tell me, is this the kind of animal you would track, kill, disembowel, chop off its head, stuff it and hang as a trophy over the mantle place? If you wouldn't do that, please sign the following petition to ban trophy hunting.

Thank you."

***

The video goes viral. Millions sign the online petition. The movement to protect animals from trophy hunting spreads like wildfire. People add comments and replies stating that this is a barbaric practice. They are outraged that this is still accepted. Remarks and replies denouncing sport killings clutter blogs and newscasts. Some groups form to object at this form of entertainment. This becomes the main subject of talk shows. Poets and artists make new songs and even bring back old melodies like Born Free and The Lion Sleeps Tonight.

***

Melinda Yeager, dressed in a camouflage suit, appears on the media to quickly react and issue her point of view.

"Celeste uses her notoriety to accuse full-fledged prize hunters of easy hunts. It's obvious that she hasn't tried hunting, other than in bars. She would have hunters take selfies with animals rather than hunting animals in the wild. She is foolish, because people have been hunting since the beginning of time. We survived and prospered as a species by hunting and killing animals. I'm following a timeless human tradition that requires many abilities. Taking a selfie is easy, just point and click. Hunting animals requires tracking the animal in all kinds of terrains, whether in savannah, in snow, in the desert, the jungle or thick forest. I doubt very much that pretty Celeste has even been in any of these places, much less tracked animals in swamps and during storms.

Authentic hunters have ethics that we scrupulously follow. We promote a fair chase. Most importantly, we obtain permits from the local authorities so that we hunt in complete legality. We never poach or trap animals in any way, not in deep snow, water or ice. We don't hunt in places, where it would be illegal to do so.

Celeste is a Canadian, well Canada is the country where Americans do most of the hunting. In fact, it doesn't even compare to other hunting countries such as South Africa or Zimbabwe. She should aim her criticisms to the Canadian government, not to the hunters.

Secondly, we don't bait animals. For example, some amateur hunters place blocks of salt to attract the animal, so when they come to hunt, the animals are already located near the salt. We don't shine lights at night to paralyze animals. We do not use tranquilizers or poisons. We hunt in free ranges, without fences, to enable animals to escape. We don't farm wild animals.

We don't use electronic devices to attract, locate or pursue animals.

We seek out the biggest animals that are generally, imposing males. Unlike amateur hunter, we don't hunt small animals to replenish out meat reserves. We seek "book" animals that are quickly replaced by younger ones. Prize hunters use accredited organizations to classify their kill according to an official measurer. All animal meat is harvested.

We spend a great deal of money for travel, for outfitter services often in remote places and for government licenses and permits. Many remote inhabitants rely on us to provide them a decent living."

***

Following Melinda's webcast, Celeste is understandably upset. Sybil meets Celeste at their favorite watering hole.

"Well Sybil, that Melinda came hunting for me!"

"That's what she does best!"

"I wonder how I should reply."

"I wouldn't if I were you because she's a bad spirit. Your powers are useless with her. She has negative forces that you can't overcome. I would avoid her altogether and pursue my own agenda."

"I've always followed your advices and they've served me well."

CHAPTER TWENTY-NINE

Bondage

CELESTE IS SUMMONED to Chuck Wegener's office, this time in Sacramento. She passes the security checks and she follows the directions to go to Rep. Wegener's office where she is welcomed and asked to wait; she declines the offer for a coffee. The secretary ushers her in, "Representative Wegener will see you now."

"Thank you."

Representative Wegener is standing, pointing at the chair in front of his desk where Celeste takes a seat.

"Your schedule must be very busy, so I'm grateful for your concern."

"I try my best to be of service to my constituents. As you suspected, I have convened you to talk about Andy Czerny's case. It isn't an easy case, because the law is very constraining, so I had to work very hard for Andy. I'm pleased to inform you that he should be pardoned shortly."

"That is wonderful news. I am grateful for the attention you have given this case."

"The governor doesn't usually issue pardons, so he should have most of the credit."

"I will always remember who I'm indebted to, including the governor."

"There is a small concern that has to be addressed."

"What is it?"

"Pardons are very delicate, because they circumvent the normal legal route. It would be annoying if a crowd acclaimed Andy's pardon. It should be a discrete operation; few people should participate in its proclamation. After all, we wouldn't want the public to have the impression that the legal process was avoided in any way."

"I give you my assurance that the few people involved with a pardon, will be as discrete as possible."

"Well then, I think that we have concluded an agreement to the satisfaction of all parties involved," Chuck ends while standing up and offering a handshake.

***

Celeste is itching to tell everyone that Andy will receive his pardon, but she can't. It would have been great to inform Andy, Sybil, Trish, Andy's parents, Nick and everyone else. Perhaps Chuck will check with Nick, Andy or by other means. Anyhow, she gave her word that she will be as inconspicuous as possible. She has to keep this news to herself.

She rejoices by going to a posh restaurant and ordering a diner in honor of Andy's release. She is a winner. She is a success. Her powers of persuasion have achieved the impossible. Her self-confidence has reached another level. She senses that she can achieve anything that she set her mind on. She is becoming important, not only in the lives of people around her, but also in society as a whole. She has righted a wrong. She has become a champion of justice. She feels more than proud of herself, she feel a sense of wonderment that she has overcome these difficult obstacles. Her role as a fairy is gaining credibility. She has the certainty of being a genuine advocate for justice and for goodness. She has goose bumps.

***

Andy calls Celeste. "Hi Celeste, can you come and get me tomorrow morning at nine?"

"Hi Andy. What do you mean?" she answers feigning a surprise.

"I'm getting out of jail. I received my pardon. I'm being freed."

"Congratulations. I'll be there at nine."

"Bye."

***

Celeste is waiting for him in the prison's entrance hall that holds echoes of the sighs of innumerable visitors and inmates of the past, fraught with pain or relief. She is wearing a sober outfit that contrasts with her glowing beauty and effervescence.

The main interior door opens, and Andy appears in the same civilian clothes he wore when he came here. He can't believe his eyes; Celeste appears in front of him as a guardian angel that has come to rescue him from the perils of life. The door closes with a heavy thump behind him, as if it sealed away his troubles. In a fraction of a second, his eyes scan her face, her eyes, her nose, her smile, the contour of her hair, of her dress, only to do it again, this time with attention to the detailed brow, the eyelashes, the flushed cheeks, the sensual lips, the sparkling teeth, the curls in her hair and the pendant with the engraved parrot he give her at the SanDiego restaurant. He wonders what will be her reaction. Did she make another boyfriend and will that news shatter him, he wonders. Does she like him as much as she did, he asks himself. Are there any changes in her life? He tries to guess the answers by her attitude.

***

Celeste hears the creaking of the main interior door as it opens. There he is the object of all her efforts. He doesn't realize all the energy she had to put to get him out of this door. At last, he is free from his legal entanglements. He is wearing his old clothes; he didn't have enough time to request new ones that she would have gladly brought. He didn't gain weight and he looks like he kept up his athletic shape. He is looking her over, so she does her best to be as warm and inviting as possible. He must be hungry; he will undoubtedly want to have sex after that prolonged abstinence.

He advances towards her, his arms slightly extended, his face pleading for some long awaited affection. She extends her arms reassuringly. They embrace while shutting their eyes and taking deep breaths. They stand there, absorbing the moment that will mark a profound imprint on their lives. A chapter of each of their stories is being closed and another one is about to begin.

"Let's enjoy our freedom!" Andy is delighted to say.

She responds by following him at a fast pace into the morning air, that brushes their face while the rising sun twinkles through the sparse clouds. It is as if they are flying together, like a pair of doves returning in sync to their nest.

They say not a word during the ride home. Celeste doesn't ask any question about the conditions of his incarceration.

The limousine lets them out at Celeste building. Without a single word, they step in the elevator and enter her apartment.

"Do you want a drink?" she asks to make him relax, sensing that he's tensed up.

"How about a whiskey on the rocks," he asks.

"I'll join you," she answers.

She makes the drinks and they sip it on the sofa. She puts on some music, to entice him to have sex.

"Are you hungry? Do you want to eat something?"

"No. I'd like to eat you. Every night, I thought about us making love. It seemed impossible, but it fed my desire to live."

"What did you dream about?"

"I wanted to see you take your clothes off, one by one, teasing me, taunting me, torturing me."

Celeste gets up and enacts what he described to the rhythm of the background music.

"You mean like this?"

"Yes babe"

She rolls her hips while her hands cusp her breasts, captivating his lusty look. Her hands cajole her breasts, her belly, her hips and her mound with gentle and regular movements. He can feel his own hands replacing hers as she meanders along her body. Her right hand reaches her back and unzips her dress with its distinctive sound as she turn around to expose her back. She bends her ass back and forward repeatedly in a provocative motion.

He strokes his hand over his penis that bulges in his trousers. His breath is shorter.

She slides off her dress and looks at him with a languishing look. She throws her dress away.

He looks up and down her body. His hand applies more pressure on his bulge.

She faces him, while squeezing her breasts in her bra, letting them protrude. She unclasps the bra in the middle and replaces the bra's cups with her hands that hide her erect nipples. She turns around, hiding her nipples with one hand while the other takes off her panties.

He takes off his shirt, his pants and underwear. He has the urge to fuck her as quickly as he can. He takes one hand around her waist and he swings her on the sofa. He spreads her legs. His rock-hard penis sweeps her vagina up and down. He enters her gently, but with determination.

She likes to have his penis inside of her. It's been a long time.

He rams it in and out, to her delight.

She moans, "Yes, yes. Fuck me!"

He applies himself to the task, for he has the need to prove his masculinity by performing well.

She waits for him.

He decides to change position by lying on the bed.

She reacts by adopting the cowgirl position that gives her the most mobility. She does her best to stimulate him by grinding her hips against his groin.

He yearns to let go, yet he's tensed-up. After a while, he directs her to reverse position, which she does. Again, he tries to release his seed in vain, so he signals that he would like the doggy position. She obliges willingly. When they had made love previously, he relieved himself at this stage. Though he tries his best, he can't release his cum.

He wants a blowjob. She submits to his demand and she proceeds with vigor and sensuality. She persists but he can't oblige, "Stop. I can't come."

"That happens," she replies with comprehension.

He lies back, crushed, after the countless night when he dreamed of this.

"We'll try it again later. You're all tensed-up. We'll do it again when you're relaxed."

"This is the first time that this happened to me."

"You've been alone in jail for a long time. Give it time, it'll come back."

She hands him a bathrobe. He retreats in silence, somewhat ashamed of not having been able to prove his manhood.

She understands what he's going through and she wants him to regain confidence. "Let's eat. You must be famished."

"Let's order a pizza."

"Great idea!" she replies, as she hustles to find the best choice and orders it.

She lets things settle.

The pizza is delivered and they eat it with shared pleasure.

***

"Celeste, I'd like to try it again."

She approaches him and combs his hair with her hands. "Would you like me to do anything special?"

"Well there is one thing that I'd like, but I kind of didn't dare ask you."

"Go ahead and ask me."

"I'd like to tie you up. All that time in jail, I wish that I could control others, as I felt controlled. Now I want to regain control of the situation. I'd like to have you at my mercy, to do what I want, when I want. You don't have to do it. It's up to you"

"If that's what'll make you happy, I'll do it with pleasure. Please let me speak and don't tape my mouth. There are some ropes in the dresser's top drawer that you might find useful." Celeste had bought all kinds of sex toys in case of such games.

"Get undressed and lye spread eagle on the bed."

She obliges in a lingering manner, deliberately teasing him.

He takes out the thick rope from the drawer and he ties her to the bed convincingly. He takes some massage oil, that he delicately sprays on her and he rubs it on her waiting body while her eyes shut in abandonment. He massages her breasts and her erect nipples. He reaches her clitoris and her lower lips and caresses them. He inserts his finger in her vagina slowly, followed by another finger while the other hand continues to feel he clitoris. He keeps this up until she whines.

His penis is rigid. He gets on his knees between her yearning legs. He inserts his prick in her cunt and he reams her in. He fucks her with all the vigor and ardor he can muster. In and out relentlessly. He wants to ejaculate. He needs to ejaculate. He can't miss this second chance. He pulls on her shoulders with his hands, thrusting his cock in her cunt as hard as he can.

"Oh God! Fuck me," she encourages him, as she thrills at having an orgasm. He wants to join in her pleasure. He speeds up his motion. She wails in bliss. She shudders from orgasms. He grabs her buttocks with both his hands and squeezes them as much as he can, in despair.

"I have a desire to fulfill," she tells him.

"What is it?"

"Spill it out! Let yourself go!"

He crisps all of his muscles, he groans loudly and he floods her with an endless stream of the milk of life.

She is hurting from his clasped hands, but she doesn't complain.

Finally, he releases his grip on her and collapses beside her. His daydreams and his nightmares are resolved.

"I knew that I could do it," he boasts as he unties her.

***

They each take a shower and life feels anew.

"I don't know whether I mentioned my mentor, Sybil."

"Not that I recall."

"Sybil is a spiritual being. I mean that she has a special relation with the world, such as being a clairvoyant that can vision the world with a different perspective. She saw in me that I have a unique relationship with nature. This is nothing new to you, but it goes much farther than a liking of nature, or even a nature lover. She told me that I have a role in protecting nature. I intend to embrace that role to its fullest.

I have recently been engaged in stopping humans from trophy hunting, especially for vulnerable or endangered species. This is becoming more than a passion; it is growing into a mission. I will devote my life to it and I'd like you to endorse me and to contribute to my quest.

Many people are making money from trophy hunting and they will fight against any change. Me, I will do everything I can to overcome any difficulty that might hinder me.

Will on you to join me in this?"

"You're taking me by surprise. I don't have a mind for this, to tell you frankly. I barely got out of prison and all I want is to enjoy my regained freedom. I can appreciate that you are committed to this mission, as you call it, but for me this is too much. I have to rebuild my life that is shattered. I do appreciate that you helped me, but I simply can't devote my life to your cause. Maybe in a few years, after I have a good job, with a home I will reconsider your request."

"I sympathize with you however I wanted you to get where I'm at and where I'm going."

"All right then."

CHAPTER THIRTY

Hunted

MELINDA IS ON THE DEFENSIVE and uses the media to disseminate a worldwide reply. She is perplexed by Celeste's attack on her favorite pastime. Usually, she is the hunter, not the hunted, and usually, the prey is taken by surprise, because it doesn't realize that it's being hunted. Melinda replies with all the cunning of the most dangerous living predator on earth, the human. She replies on her show:

"Recently there was an investigative report concerning animal trophy hunting. Celeste, a Hollywood doll accustomed to hair salons and beauty shops, partly hosted that special report. Her notoriety incited many individuals to sign a petition against prize animal harvesting. That show was one-sided and it didn't explain that hunters are serious and responsible in their sport nor did it say that these hunters act within the laws.

She made it look like hunters harvest tame animals that wouldn't hurt the hunters. Let me tell you that this is not the case. Powerful wild animals can wound and maul humans. They are dangerous and hunters must beware. Obviously, she hasn't tracked in thick forests or jungles full of dangers. It takes skill to be able to handle weapons and to find animals, skills she doesn't have. It also takes stamina and a good deal of effort to follow quick animals in the wild. She doesn't know what she's talking about.

Celeste would rather tour cocktail bars and have fun with her boyfriend who happens to be a repeat criminal. Apparently, she gets her thrills with that jailbird who attacked a photographer. Perhaps I should post a petition against people who can't control their anger and lash out at the first person that gets on their way. She should try to contain his rage, instead of accusing responsible sports hunters. We are not the criminals. We follow the law however three times offenders, such as her boyfriend, should stay in prison because they are a threat to society. On the other hand, society should let law-abiding hunters provide jobs to outfitters and businesses that provide the equipment and the services for legitimate hunting.

Celeste is also deceitful about herself because she isn't genuine. She's a product of Hollywood. If she wasn't dressed in her high fashion clothes, if she didn't have her perfectly cut hair trimmed by experts and if she weren't wearing all kinds of beauty products, she'd be a very ordinary woman. When she was young, she was nickednamed 'pizza face' and nobody wanted to be near her. Underneath that facade, she's probably a monster. Don't listen to her."

***

Chuck Wegener isn't pleased either, as he summons Celeste to his office.

"Celeste, I trusted you when you agreed to keep quiet on this Andy Czerny affair. Now this Melinda Yeager is broadcasting to everyone that the governor pardoned a habitual criminal. What have you got to say for yourself?"

"I held my part of the bargain. I told nobody, not even within my family. That woman is getting back at me by making a personal attack. I had nothing to do with it. She's furious because of my success. Millions of people signed up and agreed with me.

Now, we can't ignore her comments. We must fight back. We can't be on the defensive and simply try to rebuke her."

"So what do you intend to do?"

"As for myself, I'll dress in plain clothes, ordinary hairdo and simple makeup. Now, I have enough confidence in me to exhibit the person I've become. I felt meek and humble before, but that changed. I'm another person who feels great about herself. That's what I'll do."

Chuck is in a quandary. Celeste will fight for what she believes in. He can't let that Melinda woman get away with her vindictiveness.

CHAPTER THIRTY

Winner

A FAMILIAR VOICE shouts " Here's Dyannnnnn!" announcing the queen of the media.

Dyann Winter walks quickly among the cheering crowd to the stage. She has a Hollywood smile, as she waives to the people.

"Good afternoon. What a wonderful audience!" she says, as the applause sign lights up and people cheer and applaud.

"Today we have a special show. Remember some time ago three young women we chosen for a makeover. The audience acclaimed one of them by her complete transformation; it was Celeste. She then became a celebrity by her own rights. It's my pleasure to welcome her back on the stage."

As she had promised Chuck, Celeste comes in a plain white dress, with her normal flowing hair and basic makeup. The audience immediately recognizes the modification, yet it is subdued by Celeste angel-like appearance and it applauds her in approval.

"Tell me Celeste, what made you revert to a simple look?"

"Well I made a public appeal to people to join my cause to abolish trophy hunting. Millions of people signed up to stop this antiquated custom. Melinda Yeager is a well-known trophy hunter. Like a wounded animal, she attacked me personally with all that she has. She said that I wouldn't look beautiful if I didn't have a makeover, so I came here as plainly as I can. Do you like it?" she asks the audience with a tremendous smile.

Everyone claps and cheers with enthusiasm.

"When I came here, I lacked self-confidence and a belief in myself. Dyann, you gave me self-assurance. I realized that people like me for who I am, regardless of the way I look."

People stand up in complete admiration.

"I am pleading for the animals hunted solely for entertainment. Please join me in my cause and sign the petition. Thank you."

***

Chuck is at his seat in the California State Assembly.

"I am introducing a bill to replace the Habitual Offender Law with a Multiple Conviction Law. The objective of the initial law was to keep violent criminals off the streets, so that they wouldn't be a threat to society. The problem was that judges would condemn repeat offenders to the same prison term as first time offenders. Lawmakers passed a drastic law that sentenced three times offender to twenty-five years to life. The bill I'm introducing solves the problem in a different way; repeat offenders will have a mandatory sentence consisting of a multiple of the number of serious offences they've committed. For example if a crime is punishable by a year in prison, a second time offender would have a minimum of two years, a third time offender would have a minimum of three years and so forth. The more the number of crimes, the longer the sentence. This is just and practical."

CHAPTER THIRTY-TWO

Triumph

EVERYONE INVITES CELESTE to talk about her new image, about the Multiple Conviction Bill and the animal trophy ban. She goes in simplicity, as an ordinary woman. Sometimes, Trish accompanies her to attests to Celeste's authentic personality. At other times, she is with Chuck who explains the new California bill. Then again, Sean is happy to praise Celeste for her endeavors. Nick is proud to escort her wherever she goes.

Andy comes to Celeste's apartment where they kiss. They sit in the living room on the sofa where they once made love.

"So Andy, how is it going?"

"Agh I still haven't found work. I think I'll go back in the Midwest near my parents and maybe work in farming. I can always find something there."

"I'm sure that you'll find something here, if you set your mind to it."

"Agh, I can't stay here anymore with all that publicity about me. I'm branded as a dangerous criminal."

"I'm not ashamed of you. I've supported you throughout your stint in prison. I'm willing to do whatever I can to help out."

"It's not that. I don't want to have to face all the comments. It's better if I leave the State altogether. It's not your fault. You did all you could and I'm thankful for that."

"If that's what's in your heart," Celeste replies, not wanting to force the issue by using her spell.

"Well, I guess this is goodbye."

"I'm sad that you can't stay."

"At least I'm a free man and I will cherish that thought forever."

"Goodbye then," she says, as they kiss with heavy hearts. It is a bittersweet victory.

***

Nick invites Celeste to his Spanish style home, located in the Beverly Grove district. She accepts, since Andy is leaving and Nick has been an exemplary friend. It is a spacious house with a generous well-groomed lawn with outdoor living facilities such as a barbecue grill, a vast garden, a swimming pool and a patio. There is a casita in the back for the staff, Maria and Pedro.

Nick confides to Celeste:"I'm glad you talked to me about your ambitions. You told me of the shift of your priorities and that stirred a concern I always had about my legacy. Some wealthy individuals, such as Boldt, build mansions or companies. I've done both, but I prefer to endow humanity with lasting benefits. I looked up the story of Alfred Nobel, of the famed Nobel Prize. Do you know his story?"

"I'm afraid not."

"Well, he was a Swedish chemist. His father was a scientist who invented plywood. The Nobel family owned a factory that made military equipment including explosives, which at that time was much in demand. The explosives consisted of gunpowder, however, Nobel was interested in the much more powerful nitroglycerine just invented, but it could easily detonate because it is unstable. After researching explosives tirelessly, he discovered dynamite and other explosives that were much safer; dynamite was a great commercial success and he became rich after establishing more than ninety factories throughout the world. He invested in his brother's oil business and he because tremendously rich.

Nobel wasn't married and had little family left. When his brother died, the newspapers announced Alfred's death by error and their front page screamed wrongly that the Merchant of Death is dead. Naturally, he had this retracted, but he didn't want people to remember him as the Merchant of Death; he would rather people remember him for the numerous good deeds he did throughout his life. This was very troubling to him, so he decided to create a trust in his name, that each year would reward people in different spheres for their accomplishments. It was the inception of the Nobel prizes.

I'm going to follow his model and attribute prizes to solutions related to our environment and to our humanity. So I called my lawyers to set up this fund and to arrange this announcement with you." Celeste kisses him on the mouth.

Nick issues a press release:

PRESS RELEASE

FOR IMMEDIATE PUBLICATION

FROM: NICK DASH

SUBJECT: ENDANGERED ANIMALS PHOTO TROPHIES

Nick Dash and several wealthy individuals are establishing a running contest of photos and videos of endangered animals in the wild. The photos and videos, rather than be judged on their artistic quality, will be evaluated according to the risk of taking the pictures or videos. Vulnerable and endangered animals will be measured with the same criteria as the current hunting classes. Public records will be kept of all the registered pictures and monetary prizes, the Dash prizes, will be awarded yearly to the riskiest photos of the rarest animals in the most unreachable location.

***

The State of California enacts the Multiple Conviction Law multiplying a convict's felony minimum sentence by the number of his previous felony convictions.

Book of Fairies

IF THERE WERE a book of fairies, it would tell the story of Celeste who was a person of exceptional beauty and a genuine feminine hero.

ABOUT THE AUTHOR

Navy Azure is a pen Name. The author assumes another identity because he wants to protect his private life. He has travelled in many countries and continents. He has befriended people from all occupations, some famous, some infamous and many interesting persons of different sexual tendencies. He speaks a few languages. He tried many sports, from skiing to flying, to scuba diving. He is a man with experience who has children and has had a few female companions, so he is well prepared to write about life and its intricacies.